MINGLING

BLOODS

B.C. Fiola

Page intentionally left blank

Copyright © 2025

B.C. Fiola

All rights reserved

This is a work of memoir. Some names, events, or details have been changed or reconstructed from memory for narrative clarity and to respect the privacy of individuals. The experiences described reflect the author's perspective and are shared with honesty and personal reflection.

First Edition, 2025

Dedication

To my family, for whom every road is walked and every dream pursued. All things, always, are for you.

Acknowledgement

To my sun, my moon, and all my stars--Landon and Isley, you are my universe and I am eternally grateful to be your mom. May your hearts be brave, your spirits fearless and may you always remember your light is destined to shine beyond the horizon.

To my husband and best friend, Glen--Thank you for believing in me long before I believed in myself. Your unwavering faith, tireless support, and steady love made this book possible. You've been my greatest champion, my calm in every storm, and the constant voice that never let me give up.

To my parents, Larry & Nancy--Thank you for not only instilling in me a love of learning and strong work ethic, but for letting me dream and giving me wings to fly.

To my friends--Thank you for demonstrating how joyful life is when shared with good company and for reminding me to cherish every moment of it.

To all my English teachers and Literature professors--Thank you for your instruction, your encouragement, and your confidence in my writing.

Last but certainly not least, to my project manager, Liz, and her team of editors and marketing gurus--Thank you for your expertise, guidance, and patience. None of this is possible without your hard work and all that you do.

In loving memory of my dad, Casey "Doc" Cummings, and Ron Jones.

I am deeply grateful to you all for your love and support. You are woven into the fabric of my essence and the pages of this book.

About The Author

B.C. Fiola has long believed that stories choose us before we ever choose them. Raised beneath the boundless skies and open horizons of the American West, she grew up knowing that wind, mountains, and endless distance shape more than landscapes—they shape people, leaving indelible imprints on their hearts. Those early years continue to echo through her work, giving her writing its sense of space, possibility, and contemplation.

She began her first novel during the swirling chaos of the pandemic, when the world felt untethered and time seemed to collapse in on itself. In search of stillness, she turned to writing. What began as an effort to make sense of uncertainty soon became a source of clarity and grounding.

B.C. Fiola writes from the crossroads of lived experience—family, landscape, loss, wonder, and the small details that reveal what it means to be human. Her work leans into the tender, the wild, and the in-between spaces where identity, connection, and resilience take root.

Away from her desk, she collects the fleeting moments of everyday life—those bright, delicate fragments that linger in memory and later bloom into story. She is guided by a commitment to kindness, a deep faith in love's quiet strength, and the steadfast belief that it is never too late to become the person you were meant to be.

Table of Contents

1

CHAPTER

Her mother's voice faded and was lost in a symphony of chaos as it ricocheted and reverberated in her head, creating a somber cadence each time her heart collided with her ribs. She could feel it wildly writhing and raging within her like a tempest, the aftershocks resonating throughout her body, becoming concentrated and then magnified, like the rhythm of battle drums, ostensibly combating the maddening roar of confusion with exquisitely delicate crescendos and arias.

"Did you hear me, Paige? Your father has gone missing, my love. I… I'm tremendously concerned about him…"

"Wha… what do you mean he's *gone missing*? Why do you keep saying that? I just spoke with him this morning,"

Paige said, almost whimpering now, and although she was nearly forty-five years old, she wished her mother were actually here now to steady her.

"Yes, love," her mother replied with only the slightest hint of an accent. "Are you sitting down? I think maybe you should sit down for a moment. You know how you can get, darling. You said you spoke with him this morning? With your *father*, Paige?"

Paige felt confused and disoriented as her mind raced away from each word her mother spoke with increased speed and compulsion to escape. Lulled into the darkness that swirled between the pinpoints of light floating before her, she could only faintly hear her mother's voice and, although it was calling her name even louder now, it seemed increasingly distorted and far away, like listening under water to the garbled noises beyond the surface. She closed her eyes and exhaled, her body seeming to unravel for a moment, and found herself transfixed within the heavy stillness and dark quiet.

Yet as the calmness settled upon her, she felt like she couldn't open her eyes, like she couldn't breathe, like she had become inert. The panic, seizing the moment, quickly assailed her, and the drums resumed. She tried to inhale, but it felt as though a heavy hand pressed against her chest, attempting to muzzle the heart that now thrashed wildly again. Paige swallowed hard just as the sensation threatened to overwhelm her, and she managed to break through the illusion, gasping for air. Her mother's voice became clear again, and her knees steadied under her.

"Paige! Listen to me, darling," her Dutch accent becoming more apparent now as she was distressed over the reticence of her daughter.

"Mama…," Paige said softly. She hadn't referred to her mother as *Mama* since early childhood. "Can I call you back in a few minutes?"

Her mother asked her sternly, "Paige. You said you spoke with him this morning?"

"Yes," Paige said softly. "Yes. This morning… I… he… Mom, can I just call you back in a little bit? I don't feel so well right now."

"Oh… yes. Of course, my love. Of course. Take all the time you need to gather yourself," she said as the softness returned to her voice.

Paige sighed quietly, knowing too well that the sudden moderation in her mother's voice was less the result of a nurturing temperament and more so Ilse's familiar signal of disapproval at her daughter's *obvious* weaknesses. Too unsettled to argue with her mother, Paige hurriedly told her she loved her and would call her back soon before hanging up abruptly. She closed her eyes and took a long, deep breath before opening her eyes wearily, the bright, pinpoint lights now receding into her periphery. She looked down at the shiny, black screen of her phone for a moment, relieved that the call with her mother was over, and let herself fall back to sit on the hard motel bed. *I cannot believe this is happening,* Paige thought. Her father had suddenly gone missing, and it was only months after she had reunited with him. The initial shock melting away now, and she felt angry at the unfairness of it all; of having lived most of her life not knowing her father, only to finally have the chance to meet him and even work with him, to then lose him all over again. The tears stung her cheeks hotly, and she resolutely wiped them away with the sleeve of her sweater, simultaneously redirecting the focus of her anger on herself, for her self-pity and emotional indulgence, her mother's censure most befitting.

Suddenly, she was startled as her phone rang again, but this time from an unknown number. She swiped the screen and hesitantly answered, "Hello?" in a shaky voice.

The man on the phone told her he was a detective investigating her father's disappearance, but she found herself incapable of immediately responding to him, as shock again incapacitated her, and she grappled with a crushing uncertainty, struggling to understand why a detective would be calling her so soon.

"Misses Jansen," the man recapitulated. There was something intriguing about his voice, something that made him seem oddly familiar, something almost auspicious. She shook off the feeling, cleared her throat, and sat up straight.

"Yes. This is Miss Jansen," Paige replied, starting to feel as though she were coming to her senses again. She shifted her weight against the stiff mattress, which was concealed by an unattractive yellow comforter plastered with enormous brown and orange flowers produced, in a most bastardly attempt, to make it look as though it were hand-painted, and curled one leg under her before settling into a seated position again.

"How may I help you, sir?" Paige continued.

"Miss Jansen, my name is Detective Andrews," he repeated politely. While most people would have shown impatience with her phone etiquette by this point in the conversation, the man remained calm and measured.

Detective Andrews gently continued, "I am investigating your father's disappearance in Ballard. Ballard, *Utah*, Miss Jansen. I understand you are already on your way here?" She smiled as she noted how he had emphasized the word Utah, urging her attention to the matters at hand, rather matter-of-factly.

"Yes, I was coming to meet… well, to join my father in his work. I drove halfway today from San Francisco and had planned on finishing the trip tomorrow. I'm staying the night in Nevada in some small town called Battle Mountain. I believe I'm still about six and a half hours from Ballard."

Paige stood up and walked to the window, pulling back the heavy, musty curtains that hid wispy sheers tinged yellow by the cheerlessness and inattention they had suffered for ages. Beyond the dingy windowpane, her awareness was immediately drawn upwards, and she smiled despite her prevailing distress. She scanned the dramatic augmentation of the tall, snow-covered mountains against the otherwise desolate landscape that surrounded the tiny town, which was quietly and acrimoniously rendered against the otherwise predictably brown and barren Nevada terrain.

She hadn't expected it to be quite as cold as it was and found herself remorseful for not having packed more warm, comfortable clothes. This trip had begun as a professional opportunity, and she had certainly not prepared for the turn of events. But then again, *how could she?*

"Miss Jansen," the detective continued, "I'd like to speak with you once you arrive here. I was thinking we could meet at a small café here in Ballard. *Betty & Barney's*? You can't miss it, ma'am; there's not much out here. Shall we say 9 am on Thursday morning?" She liked listening to his voice; it had a certain confidence and composure that was reassuring to her.

"Yes, I think that should be fine. Thank you," she said, hanging up the phone with a smile. However, the tranquility of the man's voice quickly abandoned her and left her feeling uncertain and frightened again, and her mind quickly returned to the flood of questions she had been gripped by before the call. *What is going on? Why is her mother so concerned? What could she tell the detective tomorrow that would really be helpful anyway? Should she even continue her travels?* Of course, her mother was concerned, but the urgency in her mother's voice lingered. She was certain her mother was desperately trying to work out what had happened, but only just then did it suddenly occur to her how difficult this must be for her mother as well, how childish it was of her to obsess over her own misfortune in a moment that critically affected them both. After all, when her father had called her several months ago to propose a reunion, it was in essence a proposed reunion with her mother, as well. But now, as she envisioned her beautiful mother destroyed by losing the love of her life yet again, she felt her soul ache deeply.

Ilse, her mother, was a physics professor from the Netherlands and a woman of exceptional style, beauty, and grace, all characteristics which Paige painfully knew she had not been fortunate enough to inherit. A tall, slender, statuesque woman with eyes that echoed the essence of evergreens and exuded a delicate, feminine intensity, Ilse maintained her hair in a short, sophisticated bob, even as its golden hues had taken on a silvery quality in her maturity. It added a certain preciseness to her attractiveness, which was further punctuated by the sinewy contour of her jaw line, delineating an intrinsic fierceness, an absolute courage for life impelled by the presence of her Viking DNA.

A melancholy despondence washed over Paige now as she thought about her radiant mother, recalling the story of her parents' love affair as recounted numerous times by Ilse, of how she had met her father, Maxwell, at a summit hosted by the International Science Council at Cambridge University. It was love at first sight for them both. Maxwell was not a conventionally handsome man, creating an outwardly odd match, but his brilliance and charm added so much to his character that Ilse had found him utterly irresistible despite his deep propensity for dissociation, and she was an equal and enviable match to his intellect. For the next several years, while both were working in London, they lived and breathed a fairy tale romance of epic proportions. Entwined bodies and souls, it was a love that was deep and beautiful and profound, a love that brought them to their most authentic selves, where they cherished the smallest whispers of each other's souls.

They gleefully socialized with the other great scientific minds of their generation, frequently traveling for conferences, as well as social gatherings, establishing a community composed of the world's most brilliant minds. As the end neared for Maxwell's work in Great Britain, they discussed their future. Both were dedicated to their work, and while their love affair had been extraordinary, it had also been very distracting. Her father, Maxwell, wished to return to his work in South America, and his mother wanted to immigrate to the United States, where an incredible opportunity awaited her to replace the professor emeritus at Northeastern University in Boston.

In a moment of resolute clarity and deeply measured love, they decided it was in their best interest to pursue their own best interests. Ilse asked nothing of Maxwell moving forward… except *a child*, a part of him to carry within her and of her, a part of him to cherish, as though she somehow understood that physical proximity may forever elude them. She knew it was a haughty request to make of him, but she demanded it for the ultimate culmination of their tremendous love, a love she would not and could not seek elsewhere or from another partner. She wanted only *his* child.

He would always be the love of her life, and, for her, to have had that at all was enough. Maxwell had understandably been hesitant and felt it a cold duty to perform at the behest of his lover. But Ilse, who had always possessed an incredible talent for looking at things in the most simplistic and inherently philosophical manner, was a true apostle of rationalism, gently and lovingly convinced him otherwise. She assured him that his absence would never be considered an act of neglect and that she would welcome his love and his presence in their lives at any time he wished. It was an open-ended invitation of stunning proportions to her one and only love. Go give the world the best you have, *and when you're done, bring your best back to me.*

It was the most beautiful love story, Paige had always thought. Regardless of his absence, she had a happy childhood and grew into a juvenile science prodigy. Ilse never hid who her father was from her or refused to share her memories of him, nor did she speak unkindly of him or express any sort of disappointment at his continued absence. She was also careful not to suggest to her daughter that she was wasting away awaiting his return to their beautiful life and extraordinary love, always reminding her that *"Love connects our souls, and our souls will always be connected"*. For Ilse, the act of loving was enough.

However, it did not save Paige the despair of parental dispensation that began the first time she had been made to feel shame for his absence by children in school. She distinctly remembered that before then, it hadn't seemed to matter much that he wasn't present in their lives, but after that moment, she sensed that she should be keenly concerned at what she might be missing in not having her father there.

Her gentle mother could never remedy this for her, despite her efforts, because he was simply *never* in her life. Paige's only gift from Maxwell, sent shortly after her birth, was packed in a simple brown box and wrapped in brown butcher paper. There was no card or even a note to accompany the package that contained only a well-crafted, antique, golden-hewn kaleidoscope. Her mother had stored it on the very top shelf of her closet, where she had mischievously discovered it when she was about 4. Ilse found her playing quietly in the pool of sunshine that spilled into her room, the beautiful colors flashing on the hardwood floors and dancing across the walls. She explained that it was from her father, a symbol of his love and affection for her. She imagined that he was trying to speak to her through the brilliant dancing colors, convinced that there must be significance to the gift, and it was the driving force behind her pursuit into physics, chasing the light. But his presence only surfaced in memories or stories, like a ghost that refused to let them live their lives quietly, often and awkwardly bumping around and making noises, lest they forget they were being haunted by him.

She had been painfully reminded of this during the trip today with Mika, a Shakespeare scholar and literature professor at Stanford. Although they taught at the same institution, they only vaguely even knew of one another, given their divergent fields of study. And while Paige had only recently read the book, Professor Mika Allensby had written an altruistic and provocative examination of the intersectionality between the literary and artistic expression of civilizations and the correlating success of each culture, all well supported by anthropological evidence and fundamental sociology models she found it was, at the very least, a well-supported analysis, if not an utterly brilliant achievement.

The book had been well-received among both scholars and contemporary readers, an appropriate celebration of the young Prof. Allensby, who had dramatically expounded on the works of American anthropology legends like Hortense Powdermaker and Zora Neale Hurston with seemingly easy brilliance. Paige had been eagerly curious to meet her, as she was often noted to be an energetic and enthusiastic presence who was considered a rising star within intellectual circles and even more so on Instagram.

Paige couldn't help but feel surprised when her father asked her to join him for a research project. Just hearing his voice for the first time in her life was shocking and exciting and full of possibilities. To be invited to work with him was an incredible honor, but he then requested that she consider traveling with Prof. Allensby. It seemed like such an odd request, to ask her to travel with a complete stranger.

However, given what she did know of the young author and the fact that they were both professors at the same university, she nonetheless agreed to the proposal. And after she had taken some time to reflect, Paige even remembered feeling like the travel time would provide her with the unique opportunity to talk with Allensby about her work.

"Oh, well, both my parents were American scientists," Mika had explained. "But, I have a tendency to fail at very practical skills, like those required by science," she said with a generous laugh. "So, I guess I just naturally gravitated towards more creative ventures, like literature. Still, I found it difficult to escape the need to define the world according to the rational disciplines instilled by my parents and their proclivity towards a more *verifiable* order of things. So, the blending of the two areas of study seemed quite natural to me. *To thine own self be true*, you know?"

Mika winked and smiled at her, a gesture Paige often found to be both impertinent and infantile, two of the most unlikable traits among distinguished thinkers, in her opinion. Not to mention the cliché use of a rather mundane Shakespeare quote, from a literature scholar at that. She felt her face scrunching into a detailed delineation of distastefulness, wondering only vaguely who her parents might be.

"How interesting," Paige replied, an obvious tinge of pomposity inflected in her voice. "Both of my parents are academics. Although I'm a *few* years older than you, my parents were very active in the scientific community that often gathered in the Pacific Northwest in the 70s and 80s. Perhaps they all knew one another."

"Yes, perhaps," Mika said. Her reply sounded enthusiastic, but the expression that blanketed her face produced a certain seriousness that betrayed otherwise. Paige felt a twinge in her gut at noticing her response. She harbored a shadowy and elusive shame when she told stories about her parents, something she had done often, implying that they were *all* active in the group together. The truth was, though, that after Paige was born, Ilse moved to New England, where she was no longer afforded the time as a single parent to socialize frequently or actively participate in the community.

As for Paige, she had never had any form of contact with her father, aside from the recent phone calls she had received. There were, however, a few justifiable memories that Paige clung to, a few Christmas parties with her mother where she was introduced to people whose names were in books and scientific journals, and she was elated in the thrill of it all. They were very fond memories for Paige, who, as an intrinsically shy youth, had finally found her people, and there were so many of *her people* to commune with at these events. It was a memory of freedom, of a place where she could finally and fully bloom.

Instantly, Paige's thoughts raced back to the present from her lingering memories when a click at the hotel door shook her back to reality. Mika burst in with a wide smile, excitement boiling over as she squealed, "Oh girl, this town is CRAZY!"

2

CHAPTER

Mika quickly closed the door behind her as the small room began to cool instantly with the rush of outside air. She stood in the ray of sunlight cast into the room where the curtains were still parted, glowing and stunningly beautiful. Mika was tastefully dressed in a blue newsboy hat, a luxurious cashmere sweater layered over a flannel shirt, black jeans torn just above the knee, trendy ankle boots, and an oversized scarf. *She looks like a Pinterest board*, Paige thought to herself, amusingly. While the weather was quite chilly, Mika didn't seem bothered by the cold as she set her small clutch on top of a large cathode-ray tube television.

In the essence of her warm skin tones and soft curls, there was a sustained homage to her mother's ebony lineage, with regal cheekbones and a high, smooth brow. Yet her father's gingerness had managed to surface, here and there, in the tiny freckles sprinkled across her cheeks and where it danced on tiptoes amidst the auburn traces in her hair.

As Paige looked at her, she realized how much she liked Mika's freckles. Although she had often despised her own, they looked so good on Mika. Even her single visible flaw, a tiny scar just above her eyebrow, looked good on her, adding an authenticity to the artifice of perfection. She projected a wistful quality that almost distracted from the impossibly symmetrical contours of her face, from the powerful desire to simply stare at her. Her bright, amber eyes swirled with golden flecks, and her playful, lopsided smile, anchored with the deep crimson of flawlessly applied lipstick, conveyed an innate mischief, an inquisitiveness punctuated and enunciated with a single dimple. Her exquisite beauty made it nearly impossible not to adore her, but she seemed very out of place in this motel, or anywhere less than extraordinary.

"There is people-watching at its finest to be had here! *The people are the city*!" she said with a small giggle, while dramatically unraveling her scarf in grand gestures. She checked her reflection in the mirror, turning her head back and forth, lightly fluffing and twisting her beautiful, tiny curls with her fingers, and she could see Paige sitting behind her in the mirror. Mika thought Paige was comely, but in the most expected and mundane ways. Her alabaster semblance was like that of a Michelangelo subject, in which the master delineated the delicate and gentle defects of the human body, suggesting perfection lies in the imperfections of the subject, a sure sign of divinity, dedicated to and defined by its pallor.

Nonetheless, Mika liked how Paige wore her lengthy, dark hair with long, thick bangs that veiled her brows while accentuating her high cheekbones. Behind the glasses she occasionally wore, large oval eyes shrouded in brown lashes hid the deep blue pools of her irises. Her face was well-proportioned and peppered with freckles, giving her an amiable sort of youthfulness, even at forty-something. Normally, Paige would have opposed her innate attractiveness with her personal style of ambiguously shaped brown, grey, or black slacks fortified with a thin belt and a white, beige or grey collared shirt, often paired with an equally unexciting array of seasonal favorites like corduroy jackets, silk ties or suspenders and then always the final touch a pair of well-worn, black Converse.

Today, with her modest yellow sweater and brown slacks, it seemed to suggest that Paige was attempting to hide in plain sight, to literally disappear into the unsightly flowers of the repugnant comforter. Mika smiled and thought to herself that, under everything she tried to hide herself with, Paige was actually quite eye-catching. She had done her research on Paige Jansen and suspected her manner of dress hinted at something much more altruistic than a lack of self-confidence, appreciating that gender-bending took courage, a courage she imagined had also cultivated Paige's odd mannerisms and unconventionalities.

In a world of intellectuals, Paige wanted to be treated as an equal by her peers, who were usually at least twice her age. Of course, they were also mostly men. Paige did not want or need their attention. She wanted their respect. She wanted to be considered an equal. And she most assuredly deserved it. Not only had she graduated at the top of her class from the world's premier physics program at MIT by age 21, but shortly thereafter, she joined the research faculty of Stanford University, and her current equations for string theory and quantum gravity were now considered among the most elegant to date. Caught up in her musings, Mika scanned Paige's face more closely and suddenly realized that Paige had been crying.

"Oh no, Paige! What's going on?" Her handsome face scrunched up with concern as she turned around to see her more clearly. Mika took a step towards Paige, reaching out her delicately manicured hand to comfort her by cradling Paige's hand in both of hers, gently stroking the knuckles.

"I just received a call from my mother, Ils," Paige said, her voice breaking on the last syllable of her mother's name. "She told me my father, Maxwell, has… gone missing."

Mika's hands dropped at the news, and her countenance, flush with excitement and the cold only moments before, now diminished; the gradations of her mocha inflections receded into paleness, her freckles intensely discernible, and her shoulders dropped under the weight of the news. "Maxwell…?" She whispered questioningly. "Max is… missing?"

Feeling her face flush with the warmth of shame, Paige realized she hadn't even thought to prepare her for the news. And again, the familiar pang of guilt reminded her that Mika must also have known Maxwell professionally, and she should have had the resolve to tell her in a more responsible manner. *She is just a kid, after all.* Shaking her head at her own foolishness, Paige now reached out for her in an awkward and uncomfortable manner, first thinking she should caress her hand as Mika had done, but then deciding to reach for her upper arm, rubbing it clumsily, then patting her arm heavily, her uncertainty rendering the entire performance more absurd than affectionate.

Tears were streaming down Mika's face now as she looked up at Paige. "He's my…" She took a deep breath that broke into a sob as she inhaled, making her lips quiver as she whispered, "...he's my… mentor." The tears poured down her beautiful face and clung to her chin as she exhaled with a profoundly sad moan.

Paige felt the redness of her cheeks expand in all directions as Mika's head rested against her chest. She and Mika had only met this morning when she picked her up for this trip, and she hardly knew her, but it had now become clear that they both shared a rather important connection to him, more than professionally. Paige now realized she had completely failed to consider that Mika *personally* knew her father. *She didn't even personally know him*!

Resentment lurked behind her eyes and lingered for a moment as she gazed glass-eyed downwards and past Mika's hair before quickly shaking herself from the feeling. She felt compelled to remind herself that when her father had called a few months ago, it was in a purely professional capacity that he had asked Paige to join his group of scientific enthusiasts. And while she was initially upset by his manner of reproach and the cold academic quality of it, even her own mother gently reminded her, as she often did, that her father was nothing if not a devout professional and often connected with others best in that capacity alone.

While Paige intrinsically understood that there would be limitations to their relationship and tried to convince herself that she was ok with that, she could not bring herself to abandon the hope that, perhaps on this trip, they could have developed a deep and meaningful bond. The sort of bond she now knew he apparently had with Professor Mika Allensby.

It was a curious invitation Paige did not fully understand, and she had carefully considered what her mother had really meant that her father's devotion to his work was paramount to everything. She had followed her father's scientific career for years and had discovered that her father had grown somewhat eccentric as he had aged. So, when she read that he had formed the Scientific Federation of Science, she thought it was a hobby club of sorts, a strange science fiction club or something. It even sounded ridiculous, *the Scientific Federation of Science?*

While she imagined that her father had an awkwardly charming and nerdy quality, from what she gathered, he was not a pop culture, Star Trek sort of nerd, unfortunately. He was a nerd because he was clumsy, goofy, and at times even funny by some accounts, yet he was a man to be taken quite seriously as an academic in his day. From the stories his colleagues had shared with her, Paige knew he was a man who clearly embraced the understanding that the magnitude of his intellectual abilities was made possible only by the deduction of other qualities like friendliness or the ability to overcome social vexations, a feeling she, too, had known well her entire life. She knew he must be a man who understood that the universe, like all things, has limitations and was certainly not the sort to entertain fanciful *what-ifs* or alternate realities.

Thus, she wasn't even entirely certain what her father was talking about when he first asked her to join the SFS. His greeting was brief and awkward before explaining that SFS was composed of top scientists, engineers, mathematicians, explorers, psychologists, and rationalist philosophers to examine some of the most unexplained phenomena on Earth.

Their participation seeks to lend credence to any existing unknowns, their impeccable standards compelling them only to seek truth (not conspiracies), and their collaborative brainpower would surely be able to finally answer certain questions. His main goal, however, was not to prove or disprove the existence of Big Foot or little green men, but rather to establish a scientific community that was not afraid to ask the questions that may have difficult answers. If an unexplained phenomenon can be experienced but cannot be measured by the best scientists and the most advanced technology, then naturally, they just need to approach it differently and have the courage to examine the experience more honestly.

To find a unifying theory of the universe, he continued to explain to her, they must first come to understand why certain rules do not apply, but only sometimes. He suggested that whatever the explanation, it exists beyond what humankind is capable of perceiving and therefore quantifying. For example, when electrons are wavering in and out of existence, wherever they "go" out of existence cannot be measured or even detected.

He envisaged that *together* they could seek the knowledge that would teach them how to perceive what lies beyond the shadows of the cave wall and instead witness that which is casting the shadow. Of course, the participation of his daughter in this would be the only way to give it the full scientific credence it needed. She was, after all, the leading string theorist of the modern age. Although she felt quite skeptical, she was overwhelmingly eager to get to know her father while exploring his pursuit, even if she had doubts about the actual science of it. When he called again a few weeks later, it was to inform her that he had finalized his team of extraordinary experts for his project, and he wanted her to join them in Ballard, Utah. It was at this time that she learned that Mika would become her travel companion.

Tears welled in Mika's large eyes, and her lip quivered as she lifted her head, the tears silently spilling down her cheeks. *It's ridiculous that she even cries beautifully*, Paige thought, as she considered how much she was beginning to dislike her. It wasn't that she was too young and beautiful, although Paige was willing to admit to herself that Mika's beauty was intimidating; she disliked her for other reasons. Mika seemed perpetually cheerful in a way that was too childish, too contrived for attention: every smile, every head tilt, every action a moment worthy of Instagram. But aside from that, she rambled on about all sorts of things during their road trip, some of which were appealing to Paige, but most of which generally consisted of Mika prattling on about subjects in which she shared no interest.

She couldn't even remember how many times she heard herself say, *"Doesn't this kid ever shut up?"* And when Paige turned up the music for the slightest moment of respite from the idle chatter, Mika had the audacity to reach over to turn it down so she could continue her endless babble. *Besides her beauty, she seemed so... basic,* Paige thought, embarrassed by her deficiency for a better description than cold, colloquial commentary. She seemed so incapable of the greatness Paige had heard about her. So loosely dedicated to her field of study. But as she sat on the bed, crumpling into her arms, Paige felt a momentary pang of resentment towards herself for disliking her. She embraced her, this time without the awkwardness of hesitation, and felt Mika bury her face in her shoulder again, and they relaxed against each other briefly.

"I plan on continuing on to Ballard to see if I can help resolve the matter. I'll make arrangements for you to get back to San Francisco tomorrow," Paige added rather bluntly. She knew she had no tact for these matters and always felt it was best to just get it over with.

"Oh no," Mika replied, looking up at Paige with wide, glassy eyes, sniffling and shaking her head. "I'm coming with you."

Shit! Of course, she is! Paige grumbled to herself. But she forced a half smile and said, "Great. We'll get an early start tomorrow, then."

3

CHAPTER

Paige was lying on the bed with her back facing Mika, trying to sleep, although her mind raced incessantly. In the dim, flickering light of the television, she could *feel* that Mika was staring at her back, just dying to say something about something. She had already grown to dislike her constant chatter, but Paige knew that, if she was being honest with herself, there were things they needed to talk about, and it wasn't just her father's disappearance.

"Do you know much about Sherman Ranch?" she asked as she turned over to face Mika and switch on the lamp between their beds. Mika, who was lying on her side, her beautiful face propped up in one hand that was bent under her, the other draped over her slender waist, a juvenile smile across her face. Paige smiled uneasily.

"Well, from what I've read, it should be an *interesting* adventure!" Mika smiled broadly and sat up a little more, excited that Paige had finally started a conversation. Paige resisted the urge to roll her eyes before sitting up on the bed, both legs folded under her.

"An interesting adventure is an *interesting* way to put it," Paige said with a tinge of arrogance, while Mika nodded and acknowledged the sentiment enthusiastically.

Paige continued as she scrolled through her phone in pursuit of her data, "Formerly Sherman ranch, it is now referred to as Skinwalker Ranch, a name derived from the ancient Navajo myth about a shape-shifting beast that haunts the land. But that isn't the only thing that occurs there; everything from superstitious legends to the paranormal to little green men has been reported there.

According to the records, "*In 2016, the former owner Bigelow sold Skinwalker Ranch for $4.5 million to Adamantium Holdings, a shell corporation of unknown origin. After this purchase, all roads leading to the ranch were blocked, the perimeter secured and guarded by cameras and barbed wire, and surrounded by signs that aimed to prevent people from approaching the ranch. In 2017, the* *name "Skinwalker Ranch" was filed for trademark through Justia Trademarks.*" The property, purchased by a billionaire tycoon in early 2020, has become the subject of numerous studies, including that of a reality TV show and the Defense Intelligence Agency, and, of course, now the SFS. Quite curious, don't you think?"

Mika's face had grown serious but had lost none of its enthusiasm. She sat up and grabbed her laptop, quickly flipping it open and typing rapidly.

"Oh, yes. I remember that now. It happened right at the beginning of the COVID-19 pandemic. Thank god that's over now," she said with an apprehensive laugh, still clicking across her keyboard.

"I know. I still have a drawer full of masks. I'm saving them just in case," Paige said as they both smiled, although a slight uneasiness settled between them, evoked by the memories of madness that manifested during the global pandemic.

"Well, aside from the show that was filmed there," Mika continued, "there really hasn't been much reported since then. But look, the measurable evidence that had been released publicly and prior to that is quite abundant," she said in a serious tone Paige had not heard yet from her as she flipped the screen and shared the open file. Paige blinked and then squinted as she looked at the screen, which displayed a dead cow, its hind quarters completely carved out in a manner that seemed more like a medical procedure than a predatory attack. Paige slipped on her reading glasses and clicked through the file titled "Photo Evidence", which was a compilation of over 50 years of documentation. A large portion of this evidence, produced by Colonel John Alexander, who characterized his work as the "standard scientific approach", was the result of the first organized group of scientists to descend upon the basin. They dramatically built upon the claims that had remained buoyed by prior studies, like that of Professor Frank Salisbury from the University of Utah. The recent discreet interest in the ranch only added to the intrigue, leaving Paige feeling both bewildered by the extensive research on the Sherman Ranch phenomenon and somewhat embarrassed that she had failed to appreciate why her father had been so intrigued with it as a scientist.

While Paige clicked through the pictures, Mika read a quote from Dr. Alexander, a former Army Intelligence officer, "He said in an interview that quote, 'Something else is in control. And if you want to find out, it may allow that, but if it doesn't, this thing keeps morphing and changing'".

Mika reached out and stopped her on a photo that was difficult to make out at first.

"Ok. What am I looking at here?" Paige asked, tilting her head side to side and squinting harder in order to somehow discern the image. It looked like a strangely tropical scene with trees in the shadows until Mika explained further that the photo was taken by Rich Oliver, who claimed the strange shadow is that of an unknown, tentacled entity seen from the inside while it attempted to enter his tent.

With that, they locked eyes and burst into laughter. *It would indeed be an interesting adventure tomorrow*, Paige thought, as they said good night and turned out the lights. That night, she had the first dream.

4

CHAPTER

Grandmother thrusts her hands into the earth with a rigorous motion, twisting her stout fingers back and forth in the soil, before cradling it tenderly in her hands. As I shifted my gaze from her palms to her eyes, I glimpsed the immeasurable fire burning within them, lit by the remnants that spark mighty nebulae into being.

She locks her gaze on me and, in the light of the full moon, gently says, "Dig your hands into the earth, dear. Embrace the sensation of it moving around your hands, try to sense the vibrations of all the things that compose it, recognizing that the same are echoing within you."

Mingling Bloods

I dig my hands into the ground, feeling its hardness at first and then the comforting coolness, taking care to embrace the sensation of it as it moves over and through my fingers. I imagine all its tiny parts shifting and changing, atoms and electrons zooming and bumping around the tiny galaxy of wonder I now hold in my hands.

"Now, wash your hands in the stream. Do you feel the water racing and swirling around your hands, the energy of its movement tickling your palm, and the smoothness of it caressing you? Can you perceive its aqueous transmissions? Here again, you and all your tiny particles appear to remain the same while the water particles change.

The earth particles scatter. But the essence of the earth and water, like yours, does not actually change. It remains perpetual. Water does not change itself because of you; it merely adjusts to your presence and then continues its course. What is the difference between you and the earth? Between the water that races over your hands in the stream and the water that courses in your veins? Are you not all composed of a million tiny things clinging together to be something greater than themselves? Your hands are covered with earth, and yet you feel unchanged.

You wash the earth from your hands, and yet still you think you remain unchanged. Life and death are in constant movement, an endless dance of change and exchange. When you die, your body will return to the earth and the water. But what of your essence, of the earth's, or the water's, what of that remains constant? What will remain of you but the water and earth?

"Your true essence does not change, because consciousness, unlike matter, is not subject to death and decay. When consciousness becomes interlaced with matter, the result is life, in all its many splendid forms and manifestations. Binding the two forces, they pull gently against one another perpetually, creating the circle of life and death. So, you see, you are never truly separated from your spiritual wholeness because it is timeless. Like the water, you must learn to adjust for what your perspective does not allow you to see yet in its entirety. The individual particles of the water do not care if it is your hand or a large boulder in the stream they are slamming into; they only see the chaos that is directly before them. But the essence of water, the greatness of its collective self, is a mighty force that eventually moves the boulder out of its way, one particle at a time."

Mingling Bloods

I sit back on the riverbank, the cool water still clinging to my dirty hands. The dark night is marvelously illuminated by the moon, and the stars are shining so brightly it seems almost simulated. I feel such peace here with her. Quietly, I watch Grandmother with her long, dark grey hair spilling in waves down her back, freed from their braids, and she hums softly while searching a bush for the tiny berries that reveal themselves only in darkness. As her ancient, weathered hands delicately and nimbly pick the moon berries and place them in the small basket attached to her belt, a splash of moonlight illuminates her face. The years have turned her hair from black to a deep, shimmering grey, but it has lost none of its beauty in the transformation. Her tenacious grey eyes reveal an eternal youthfulness and inquisitive nature, commemorated by the soft creases of her face, which adds a transcendental majesty to her entire being. She looks up from her task and smiles at me lovingly, sending a warm sensation through my body as it tingles with the acknowledgement of her love.

"There is an ageless tale of a group of people standing in complete darkness, and they are clustered all around and even on top of a great elephant," she began in her soft, velvety voice. "Each blind person reaches out to feel around and discern what it is that they feel in front of them. The man

standing by a leg imagines this must be a tree, tall and strong!

A woman standing by the elephant's side thinks this must be a wall! The man who stands near the rear will have an entirely different experience," she snickered softly. "But what they all fail to recognize, or perhaps even imagine, is that they are all reacting as though the different parts of the same being are somehow separate, and this separates them. Thus, we must learn to shift our perspective as we learn to experience the whole. This comes from an appreciation that you are not an observer of the universe, but that you are the universe."

Paige opened her eyes, blinking a few times until she realized she was in the hotel room in Nevada. Her breath slowly filled her lungs, and she felt a quiet peace settle over her. The dream had been so vivid, so real. And yet a peculiar impression remained as she considered how it simultaneously felt like she was there experiencing it and yet only watching, merely as an observer, like photos rendered to appear three-dimensional, leaving them with an odd sense that it had simply made the image somehow more rectilinear than before.

Mingling Bloods

She lay there quietly, trying to retain the images and content, trying to commit it to memory. Then something caught her eye against the wall, like a shadow that seemed to move. She blinked a few times rapidly, trying to focus her eyes on the shadow. Fumbling, frantically for her glasses. Hastily, she put them on, straightening them as an apparition began to materialize before her. Once her eyes adjusted to the crooked lenses, she realized it was Mika sitting against the wall, legs crisscrossed under her, her delicate hands resting palm up on her thighs. "Was she… meditating?" Paige asked herself, quietly letting out a small snicker laced with confusion.

Mika's eyes burst open just then, the bright amber swirls of her eyes seemingly collecting the detached particles of light in the room and illuminating them. She looked straight at Paige, her gaze unwavering, her posture frozen. The steadiness of her watchful eyes made Paige feel so uncomfortable that she wanted to look away, but couldn't, so she just stared back at her in silence, slowly adjusting her glasses to their normal position. It was clear Mika was looking directly at her, not simply staring off and lost in thought. It was intentional. It was purposeful. As Mika's gaze intensified, Paige suddenly thought to herself--she had the same dream! As the confusing possibility washed over

Paige, a smile broke across Mika's face, which now seemed to radiate with the same light that had illuminated her eyes.

"Love looks not with the eyes, but with the mind", Mika said in a soft, measured voice before adding a soft laugh. "Want to do yoga with me?" she asked, all the seriousness of her countenance melting away now. Mika adjusted her posture and reached for her phone, which was beyond Paige's field of vision. It was still vibrating from the alarm that had illuminated something set on top of it, something that cast a prism of light across the room and had made Mika's eyes look as though they were glowing. As Paige continued to try to focus her eyes, she realized it was a kaleidoscope. A well-crafted, antique, golden-hewn kaleidoscope. Paige froze.

"I didn't want to wake you too early. I'm always up very early, but I know that's not for everyone. So, I was just getting in some much-needed meditation," she said, smiling energetically.

Paige shook her head with an uneasy laugh. "You scared the shit out of me, Mika. I can't see without my glasses." She sat up on the bed, tossing the covers back, rubbing her eyes, and scratching her head. Her body was achy, and it felt as though she had only just fallen asleep, but she kept her eyes steadily fixed on the prism as she watched Mika slip the small trinket into her pocket and unroll her yoga mat.

"Anyway, I think I'll jump in the shower so we can get going soon. Utah is still six and a half hours away. In missing person cases, it's important not to waste time. My father… Maxwell… may need us," Paige said awkwardly and hesitantly before grabbing her bag and hurrying into the bathroom.

Mika grinned courteously, the little dimple forming on one side. "Of course," she replied melodically. But her smile melted into a much sullener expression as she watched the bathroom door close.

On the other side, Paige hastily opened her bag and unzipped a deep inner pocket where, wrapped in brown butcher paper, her own kaleidoscope gently rested. She unwrapped it for inspection, finding it entirely undisturbed. Her relief instantly turned to dejection, however, and her stomach sank with nausea. She dropped to her knees. Had Mika received the same fucking gift from _her_ father?

5

CHAPTER

As they set out for the remainder of the trip, Paige felt it was best not to mention anything about the prism, just yet. She felt smugly justified in this, as she felt Mika wasn't telling *her* everything either. She had already imagined a dozen or so scenarios to explain the kaleidoscope, but one in particular, she had decided, would be totally unacceptable—if Mika was dating her father. She would throw in the towel and walk away from all of this nonsense forever.

With so much to discuss, including the disappearance of her father, they quickly settled into a professional sort of rapport with one another. Paige, however, soon found herself uncharacteristically open with Mika, even telling her about her fiancé, or rather her ex-fiancé, whom she had only recently broken up with—a secret she hadn't even shared with her mother yet.

"I'm so sorry," Mika said in her expressive, caring manner.

"Thank you. It's been a long few weeks, but I've settled back into my old apartment," Paige replied with a shrug. "It's fine." Paige let out a long sigh, noticing how deeply cathartic it felt to let it out. She continued, "I actually feel quite relieved by the entire unfolding of events. I had love for Chad, and we worked well together in the lab. But, you know, even though I always considered him my equal, I don't think he *ever* considered us equals—especially in domestic and care roles. And I couldn't help but feel perpetually cautioned by the tale of Mileva Maric, Einstein's first wife, who was as brilliant as he was, if not more so. They collaborated together on *his* greatest works, but soon found that she was expected to sacrifice her intellectual promise for their family while he was championed and canonized as a genius. He eventually made the most unreasonable list of demands for her, *like serving me my meals and leaving me be when I say*. It's a devastating end to a brilliant mind. And it's not just hers, of course. Over and over throughout history, men have taken credit for women's intellectual labor while telling us we're not good enough to be in the room. No, thank you. That is not the life for me."

"Preach, sister!" Mika responded cheerily.

"So, when I realized I was pregnant, I knew I couldn't possibly remain in the relationship any longer. I knew the sort of misogynistic expectations he held towards mothers, and even worse, those of society. I wasn't about to give up my career, slowly disappearing into parenthood, while he went on with his life and his career unobstructed."

Mika looked at Paige, her eyes wide, an expression of unlimited happiness bursting forth from her whole being.

"You're pregnant?" Mika exclaimed, practically squealing. "Oh my god, Paige, that's incredible! I'm so happy for you! You are so brave to choose to do this on your own."

Paige couldn't tell if her expression was that of happiness or pity; either way, she found it unbearable. Quickly looking away, staring casually at the road ahead of them as though it were the most interesting thing that had occurred all day, Paige suddenly felt furious at herself. Her face flushed bright red. She certainly hadn't meant to tell her about the pregnancy, and, judging by her excitement or pity, she definitely wasn't going to tell her now that she had chosen to end it before embarking on this trip. Although Paige had been confident in her decision to terminate, it sparked an avalanche of untrustworthy emotions in her, emotions she certainly did not want and wasn't ready to articulate yet, emotions that threatened to overcome her like quicksand—a crushing, suffocating fathomlessness. She knew she was incapable of providing herself the space for healing in this moment, incapable of discussing it further, incapable of the acknowledgment and culpability necessitated by the situation.

"Yes, well, it's very early still. I don't think all the excitement is called for just yet," Paige said, her voice wavering as she forced a smile and swallowed dryly. "I'm not really telling anyone."

"Oh, yeah. Of course. You never know with these things, especially at your age," Mika said with a playful nudge and wink. Paige tried to laugh in response, but she felt tears welling in her eyes and her chest tightening around her lungs, making it hard to breathe. As she glanced over at Mika—the happiness in her expression, the light dancing in her amber eyes—she knew she could not bear the weight of her confession. Paige was certain that Mika's vivaciousness and wonder were the mark of a woman who had not known the pain of forgoing a last chance at motherhood. Or of experiencing the loss of much of anything. She was obviously too privileged, too care-free, and young to be bothered by the more profound complexities of the human experience.

The rest of the trip was filled with small talk about what they should expect in Utah. When they arrived that evening, Paige felt like they should immediately be doing something to find her father. But they had not been granted access to the ranch yet, and the detective had not planned on meeting her until the next morning. Discontented, she engrossed herself in research and tried to put a timeline together. Paige had so few details of her father's disappearance that it rendered the attempt nearly useless.

The next morning, as she waited for Det. Andrews in the tiny cafe, *Betty and Barney's*, she continued to review what she could find on her father's work concerning the paranormal phenomena he had investigated prior to Sherman Ranch, as she had been doing since the evening prior. Her success in her career had hinged on her ability to continually reassess the evidence, her unwavering persistence in seeking truth, leading her to always assume she's missing something. She knew a deep dive into his work would eventually reveal its hidden secrets, if she was persistent enough. The most recent expedition his research team had undertaken was to extensively examine the incident at Dyatlov Pass in the Ural Mountains of Siberia. She had known only casually of the 1959 case, in which, during the night, something had frightened them or forced them from their tent, culminating in the deaths of all nine hikers. While their unfortunate deaths were officially ruled a result of hypothermia, the evidence of brutality and trauma suggested something quite different.

Paige was trying to focus on the testimony and research compiled by his team, but she found herself haunted by the dream from two nights ago. She couldn't shake the feeling of how very real it felt. How much she still felt loved by the grandmother, although she had never known either of her own grandmothers. How it felt like it had been her own experience, like a dream of a memory.

Her thoughts were abruptly interrupted when a cold wind blew over her and the door to the café swung open. A man stepped in with a flurry of snow as he hurriedly closed the door. Small, delicate snowflakes rested gently on his broad shoulders, and he scanned the small restaurant—his eyes quickly resting on her. He was incredibly handsome and well-dressed in a slim-fitted, blue suit and white, heavily starched, collared shirt with small pink patterns on it. His stylish, shiny brown shoes and dark grey, wool pea coat suggested a straightforward confidence as he turned and casually slipped a hand in his pocket. His black hair and beard were mostly grey, and it misconstrued his youthfulness, which, once revealed, created a certain look of distinction that few men acquire—he was most certainly a silver fox. He stepped forward into the room with a quiet coolness and smiled as he walked up to Paige, his bright, blue-flecked hazel eyes seeming to shift in the changing light to a striking bluish green.

"Mrs. Jansen. Thank you for meeting me. This weather is certainly unexpected."

She caught her breath and looked at him as though she should say something, but she could only feel the warmth of blood rushing through her body, her cheeks reddening, and her throat tightening, her voice confused by what its role should be in this moment. He was smiling at her, and all she could think about was how much she liked his smell.

Mingling Bloods

"Mrs. Jansen? Paige Jansen? I'm Detective Andrews. We spoke earlier…" His voice trailed off as he tilted his head slightly and furrowed his brow in a look of concern.

"Yes. I…I'm sorry. It's been a very long couple of days for me. Please, have a seat." She motioned to the empty stool next to her, trying to hold back a girlish smile. When she had googled "coffee shops near me", this was not what she had imagined. The little café in a converted railroad car had a small grill behind the counter where eggs popped in generations of dark-brown bacon grease. The comforting smell of fresh coffee warmed the small space from the frigid winds outside, and the waitress behind the counter seemed in no hurry to attend to any of the few patrons. It had the stylistic look of popular retro diners, but this place had clearly just not changed since the 1950s. A hazy patina of rust and dust dulled the silver legs of the bar seats and red tape-patched tears in the once shiny red cushions of the bar stools, the similarity in hues suggesting only the slightest concern for the overall aesthetic. Another small bar had been erected against the large windows across the room, which looked out towards the mesas. There, a few other patrons had found a stool to sit and drink their coffee while waiting for breakfast.

Detective Andrews smiled at her while still managing a charming show of concern and empathy. He took his coat off and sat down next to her, and she deeply inhaled the warm musk of his cologne, sending a shiver down her spine.

"I am sorry to meet under these circumstances," he began. "As you know, your father disappeared, we believe, along with all his work and research material. Unfortunately, we have very few leads at this point. You said you spoke with him in the morning two days ago, though?"

His eyes had shifted to an emerald tone now, and as he spoke, she felt like she could feel his breath tickling her neck where the fire coursed in her veins again. She couldn't stop looking at his lips, but his eyes were too entrancing not to explore either. She swallowed hard, lowered her eyes, and took a sip of coffee, thinking to herself, *"Get your shit together, Paige!"* She stared into the steaming, black pool, resting her thoughts for a moment at her surprise that it was so good. *The last time she had talked to her father.* It sounded like a reasonable enough question to ask someone if they did not know the unusual nature of her relationship with her father.

"We spoke the morning of the 3rd, on Tuesday. I was finishing packing and preparing to leave for my trip here. We didn't speak of anything out of the ordinary. Just the usual *safe travels* and all that."

He arched an eyebrow before producing a provocative smile just as she looked up from the safety of the coffee and glanced at him, only to feel the electricity pumping through her chest again. *Jesus, Paige, come on! You are one of the leading physicists in the world. Stop acting like a schoolgirl with a crush!*

"I…I do remember that—", she stopped short as the door flung open with a flurry of snow again. In stepped Mika, the snow sprinkled in her full, bouncy hair in the most perfect way, a final shimmering, frozen prism coming to rest on her long eyelashes. She looked over at Paige and smiled while she unwrapped her coat, having only casually been wrapped around her, and flapped it a few times to shake the snow off before removing it and draping it over her arm. Mika sauntered over to the large counter, her heels clicking loudly in the small diner. She was wearing a pair of high-waisted palazzo pants which tied in a bow around her waist, a silk blouse was tucked effortlessly and shimmering with an ethereal quality as her chest heaved slightly underneath. Paige sat there, stunned, and just quietly looked at her for a moment.

"I apologize for my tardiness, Detective Andrews. Isn't this snow just delightful!" she said enthusiastically and slightly out of breath. She thrust her long, slender hand towards him as a smile crept across her pretty face in a way that tends to make men dream of tropical sunsets and passionate love-making. Paige drew her gaze from Mika to Detective Andrews, who had returned the smile with equal charm. Paige suddenly felt a pang of shame wrenching her belly as she rolled her eyes.

"No problem at all… Miss?" he hesitated slightly, "Is it *Miss* Allensby?"

She laughed in a coy, almost childish way, her eyes darting down before peering back up at him through her luscious lashes. Paige felt as though she was now entirely irrelevant to the conversation.

"Miss is correct, but I prefer *Professor*. Professor Mika Allensby," she paused before pointedly adding with a slight nod, "Detective." Paige almost let out a laugh at the ridiculousness of it all while they shook hands.

"Of course, *Professor*." He was still holding her hand that she had offered as a greeting and smiling broadly. But upon his realization of this, he cleared his throat and quickly released her. "Thank you for joining us."

Mingling Bloods

Det. Andrews stood as he motioned for her to sit on the seat to his left, leaving himself standing in the middle of the two women. As he turned back to Paige, he asked, "Now, Miss Jansen, you said you spoke with your father two days ago? On Tuesday morning?"

Paige looked at the man, confused and vexed that he had asked Mika to be here as well. Although Maxwell was her mentor, it seemed odd to grant equal license to her in the matter. She switched her gaze to Mika, trying to figure out why she was still here at all. Mika was smiling at Paige, engaged and eager to hear what she had to say. There was something very authentic about her constant, irritating cheerfulness that irked Paige. She forced a stiff grin and took another sip of the delightful coffee.

"Yes," Paige said, as though she were dreamily musing over a distant memory. "Tuesday morning, about 6 am. I am generally up very early, so he didn't wake me, although I did find it an odd time to call. Anyway, he said he simply wanted to wish me safe travels, so I didn't think much of it after that." She took a sip of coffee before adding dryly, "And it's Miss, but you may call me *Doctor* Paige Jansen."

Her sudden formality made him straighten himself slightly, and she winced at her own choice of words.

Doctor—she never refers to herself as doctor, Paige thought, feeling embarrassed at her own pomposity. Looking at her in an unblinking, observational manner, narrowing his eyes, he said, "The last time your father was seen was Sunday evening as he left to go to his room. You are certain you spoke with him Tuesday morning, *Doctor*?"

Paige felt her heart starting to pulsate with a greater compulsion. *Sunday night? He hadn't been seen since Sunday night!*

"I am *quite* certain it was Tuesday morning, Detective. I had just finished packing the car and was about to go pick up Mika. It wasn't a long conversation, but I do remember him saying that he hoped to meet me here. I didn't really know what he was referring to. I should tell you, though, I have never actually met my father. I know him through his work in science, but I have very little else to delineate our relationship. I thought I had misunderstood his intent. But, honestly, I can't stop thinking about the way he said it. Almost as though he knew the unlikelihood of his being here to meet me." She paused for a moment, mulling over the past few days and the strangeness of it all.

"Here," she said, quickly pulling herself away from the self-reflective trance she had fallen under. "Let me pull it up on my phone. Perhaps that will be of assistance in finding where the call pinged from?"

Paige swiped her cell phone open and looked through her call log, visibly astonished when there was no indication of the call from her father on Tuesday. She showed Det. Andrews, insisting that she had no explanation for the missing call from the log.

"I will call my cell provider and obtain the records for you. I apologize. It just doesn't make sense that it's not here."

"Great," said Detective Andrews, flashing his broad, friendly smile that made her body rush with warmth. "As we await that information, I'd like you both to accompany me to Sherman Ranch. One member of the research team has remained to oversee the closure of their investigation here."

"The closure of the investigation?" Mika retorted. "We were traveling here with the understanding that we would be conducting research upon our arrival. Not concluding the research."

"Yes, Professor, I am aware of the original proposal. But with the disappearance of Maxwell Walsh, the team has determined it is best at this time to return to their homes. I have taken statements from all of them and concluded that it would be unnecessary for them to remain here in limbo." His gaze lingered on her for a few additional seconds before they both smiled and turned their focus back to Paige.

"Shall we head to the ranch, then?" he asked with a smile.

6

CHAPTER

As they drove away from the cafe, Paige sat in the passenger seat of Det. Andrews' black Buick while Mika rode in the back, directly behind the detective. It seemed such a fitting car for him. Cliché almost. She watched the dust swirling behind them in the mirror as they turned and drove down another dirt road. In the distance, a large mesa loomed against the blue sky, boldly claiming its own space against the vastness of the stunning, sapphire atmosphere. Behind that lingered the distant shadows of more mesas. Shaped and carved by ancient seas, the landscape was not only transformed by the grand, aquatic sculptor, but imbued with a certain sense of peace and serenity that lingered still, a soothing amiability that hung in the dry air and curled itself around you like a cat rubbing against your leg. Endless stretches of brown vegetation and red dirt mingled with a light dusting of snow, which was quickly evaporating in the sunlight with an almost mystical methodology, like Ghost Dancers weaving themselves into the morning light. Paige smiled and didn't even try to stop herself from falling in love with the captivating sense of enchantment that revealed itself so pensively and so bravely here.

They turned down another dirt road and crossed over a cattle guard. In the distance, a row of trees stood out against the vast open space of the valley, and just beyond that lay the ranch house. Paige shook herself from the spell of the countryside when she realized that they had begun to slow down. All three of them sat up attentively as the car came to a stop, speechless at what was before them. Standing approximately five feet tall, an enormous wolf-like creature stood still in the middle of the road. Staring at them intently with golden eyes, the beast lowered its head in a manner reminiscent of a watchful predator, unblinking, defensive. They were stunned, and each was so quiet that even the sounds of their breathing were undetectable.

Mingling Bloods

After several moments, the creature simply turned and trotted off the side of the road, turning once to look back before disappearing into the depths of a nearby ravine. The three of them continued to sit silently, afraid to speak into existence what they had just witnessed. While they considered themselves rational people, this was not readily explicable, even with all the knowledge they had combined. Even though they had all read the accounts of the strange occurrences on and around Sherman Ranch, they hadn't expected to so clearly witness the abnormalities themselves. And within moments of entering the property, at that.

"Was that... the dire wolf?" Mika asked somewhat rhetorically, but with a tinge of excitement in her voice as she leaned forward between them. "The reference stems back to the earliest accounts of strange happenings here. Prior to the first European settlers in this area, the Ute Peoples occupied these lands, and myths of a skinwalker have permeated their stories for generations. Legends whisper of a wicked trickster witch who can harness the identity of animals to delight in mischievous behavior. But the evil that compelled the horrors of the Meeker Massacre in 1879 and subsequent mass removal of White River and Uncompahgre Utes has attracted more here. Since then, the sitings have become more frequent, the skinwalkers more emboldened. The ravine where the dire wolf disappeared marks the eastern border of where the modern Uintah and Ouray Reservation begins, doesn't it?"

"Yes, Professor Allensby," Andrews replied, still looking in the direction in which the wolf had vanished. "You are correct."

He took a deep breath, and the car lunged forward again. As they approached the ranch house, they noticed that every window had been shuttered and then bolted shut. It was not what one would consider a "normal" ranch house, where a few dogs greeted you in the drive and livestock occupied the surrounding corrals. The bustle of a living cattle spread was completely absent. Instead of the warm scents of homemade food, the smell of rotting flesh lingered in the air, and brought notice to the corpse of a dead cow near the driveway, its hind quarters missing entirely. They pulled around to the side of the house—which was also shuttered, including a backdoor that was boarded shut, chained and locked. There were thick chains across the second-story windows as well.

Det. Andrews cautiously moved the gear shift into *park* and sat there for a moment as the car idled, a puff of exhaust from the car quietly filling the cold air around them. Looking slowly from one thing to another as though he was deeply considering the safety of continuing this venture, Detective Andrews finally turned the car off. *This whole place is more than just eerie or odd, it's downright serial killer shit*, Paige thought as she felt the hairs on her arms stand on end, her inner gut screaming for them to turn around and head back to town. But Andrews had driven all this way, and he certainly was not the sort to be deterred by what may be nothing more than a grand farce perpetrated by the new, eccentric owner of the ranch. Prior to his purchase of the property, the ranch had operated quietly but successfully for generations, producing some of the finest Limousin cattle in the country. But as Andrews looked around now, he only recognized the scenes from the pseudo-reality, pseudo-science television show—which was now filmed here—and he could not help but feel this was all somehow contrived for entertainment.

He opened his door and casually stepped out of the car. Standing very still for a moment and listening, Andrews then slowly turned side to side, surveying the scene before popping his head in the car and suggesting the ladies wait here while he has a look around. Paige felt instant relief at the suggestion, not knowing where *that thing* could be, and was eased by his demeanor. She watched him standing there for a moment before grabbing his coat, leaving her with the view of his backside, which transitioned from his trim waist to where the seat of his pants was so lusciously stuffed, mocking her wonder and intrigue at what must lie beneath those trousers. She tilted her head as he shifted his weight and suddenly realized that Mika was looking at her and smiling. Mika mouthed *Me-ow* and let out a playful snicker.

"Well, I'm not going to sit here and watch that man and his fine ass walk away and have all the fun!" she exclaimed as she quickly hopped out of the car, leaving only her perfume to linger.

Paige sighed to note her discontent into the emptiness, but turned and got out of the car, nonetheless. Det. Andrews looked over his shoulder at her with a smile. "You ladies don't spend much time listening to what other people tell you to do, do you?"

They both smiled briefly before a seriousness befell them, and they began slowly walking across the yard towards the front of the house. At one time, it must have been beautiful. The raw wood construction had aged beautifully over the decades—becoming a dark, deep ochre. A large open porch stretched across the front of the house, shading the many windows beneath it and opening to steps on each side of the house. As they strode onto the porch, it was hard not to imagine many beautiful moments spent in the rockers, escaping the heat of the afternoon while enjoying the exquisite coolness, eyes closed, listening to the airs and whispers of vanished tides carried on the breeze from atop the ancient plateaus. But whatever remained of that reverie had been locked away now behind the boards and chains. As they neared the front door, they descended from the porch and headed towards the pens and barn, cautiously looking about. Again, what life and warmth had once existed and thrived here had dissolved into the cold, snow-covered ground and then evaporated long ago like the Ghost Dancers.

"Do you know where Dr. Walsh was conducting his research from?" Mika asked as she looked around, certain it was not here.

"Yes," Det. Andrews replied. "They set up a camp about two miles from here, near the base of that plateau over there." He pointed towards the east, where a large bottleneck-shaped mesa was still casting a long shadow from the morning sun.

"I wanted to stop here first, though," he said. "We still do not know the circumstances under which your father disappeared. Given his status within the scientific community and his work involving the Russian hikers from the Dyatlov group, he is considered high risk for kidnapping. However, no evidence exists to suggest that. Yet."

"The Russian hiker research group?" Paige asked, almost naïvely. While she had recently begun to closely examine her father's work in Russia, she had completely failed to consider his work as it might relate to the current political climate of the world, as she dedicated little time to keeping up with such things.

"Yes. Your father overtly revealed evidence in 2018 suggesting that the Russian government played a role in the deaths of the hikers, though the motives of the government remain unclear. Soon after that, a second official investigation was conducted by the Russian government, in which they resolutely determined it could only be explained by hypothermia caused by one of three strange and unusual weather phenomena, one being a purely hypothetical snow hurricane. All this despite that the evidence is straightforward, and the facts of the case do not align with this official outcome."

Paige looked to Mika, surprised to hear that her father's research may have sparked the ire of the Russian government. Mika, however, seemed less surprised and more intrigued by the information. Her full red lips twisted into a bird-like pucker before she asked, "But his report was released well over seven years ago, and the Russian investigation concluded more than 5 years ago in 2019. Why would they have waited all this time to mysteriously kidnap him?"

"Opportunity, Professor Allenby," Andrews replied with a shrug before holding his arms out wide and twisting side to side, looking around at the sizeable expanse of seemingly uninhabited land. "Opportunity!"

7

CHAPTER

By the time they arrived at the camp, the sun had climbed high enough in the sky to bathe the small valley in warm sunlight, melting the remaining snow. Compared to the cold and lifeless feeling near the ranch house, the base camp was nestled in a little dale next to a small, clear stream. Along the banks, greenery sprang to life and mocked the dull brownness that the rest of the landscape had been sentenced to during its wintery slumber.

"I believe you both know the remaining member of the team. Professor Greene?" Det. Andrews said as he turned the car off. Both women knew and revered him as one of the most profound minds of their time. Regardless of their separate fields of study, Prof. Greene was known to both and considered an extraordinary man, capable of explaining not only the most limitless explorations of space and time but also the most intricate ideologies as though they were innately known all along—a rare talent among humanity, let alone brilliant scientists. He was dazzling and warm and exciting to be around. *How perfect to find him in this oasis of life in the desert,* Paige thought to herself.

Prof. Greene walked out and greeted them warmly with generous hugs—even Detective Andrews, who seemed slightly confused by the gesture. Greene invited them into the main tent area, where most of the equipment had already been packed and prepared to be shipped back. They all sat at a large wooden picnic table near a fireplace, where Prof. Greene began to recount the events of the evening when Dr. Walsh had last been seen.

He and Walsh, longtime friends and at one time colleagues, were the first to arrive and start setting up camp. He hadn't noticed anything out of the ordinary concerning Dr. Walsh's behavior or actions. A few other colleagues joined them in the following days, and the excitement had begun to grow for the end of the following week, when the team would be complete. When everyone headed to their tents for bed that evening, nothing was amiss, and Dr. Walsh appeared to be in excellent spirits.

"I'm sorry I can't be of more help to you, Detective Andrews," Greene replied. "You all are welcome to stay here this evening. I'll send for your belongings; my assistants are in town, finalizing a few things anyway. Unfortunately, I will be departing in the morning with the remainder of the equipment. But the folks who set up these camps and take them down won't be here until next Friday. So, in the meantime, you may feel free to stay here instead of the motel in town."

The camp was certainly a welcome comfort over the motel, where Paige was sharing a room with Mika. Each participant was intended to stay in their own tent throughout the duration of the field research; each was furnished with a bed, a writing desk, a small kitchenette area, and even their own private washroom. *It really was quite remarkable how well planned these long-term research camps were,* Paige thought, feeling a sadness for the first time that this event she had planned for and waited for would now not occur. The opportunity just to work and collaborate alongside people like her father, Prof. Percy Greene, and all the others who are considered the best in their fields—it would have been extraordinary. Life-changing even.

Of course, she had had her hesitations. Perhaps like the men and extraordinary women who participated in the making of the atomic bomb, they had no way of knowing that their discoveries would eventually lead them to that horrific ending. Yet, when they were given the opportunity to witness their mathematics projected into a three-dimensional reality, they did not decline the opportunity to see it.

As they viewed the destructive powers of their experiments, they knew it was a cosmic power not intended for something as abject and delicate as humanity. Of course, they were able to recognize that no single man should be able to harness the very spark of existence, that it would be used for nothing but destruction, that such power could now be held only at the behest of a big red button that says "BOOM". Even Oppenheimer—who lacked the morality to be faithful to his wife or to take any sort of accountability for the damage to local populations, particularly the Navajo Nation, caused by the Trinity testing—had ethical concerns about the development of atomic weapons like the H-Bomb. *Perhaps sometimes these things work out for the best*, Paige thought, quietly disclosing to herself the fear of investigating the unknown and discovering that which is not intended for mankind.

After they had all enjoyed dinner together in the tent, they moved out by the fire, relishing the cool night air, the music, the conversation, and the extraordinary view of the stars. Paige eyed Detective Andrews with curiosity and interest while he relaxed in an Adirondack chair, his shoulders beautifully defined in his stiff shirt with the sleeves now rolled up below his elbows, revealing a tattoo sleeve on his left arm.

A rapacious tingle raced across her skin while she admired how the amber light from the fire danced across the contours of his face. He looked at her through the fire, holding her steadily in his gaze before she lost her courage and looked away, trying not to smile and shifting her focus to Mika and Percy chatting away. Mika was staring up at the stars and reciting how it was all *so beautiful that the world would fall in love with the night and forget about the garish sun.* Being near the two of them together was like watching a bonfire—they were warm, inviting, illuminating, mesmerizing. Mika spoke with everyone like she had always known them, and Percy welcomed all those who wandered into his gravity to sit and have a chat about the meaning of it all for a few moments, like an enigmatic celestial traveler dancing with a beautiful star.

The valley's position at the base of the mesa protected it from the fierce bite of the winter winds, infusing the air with a dry coolness typical of high elevations, in which the icy air stings the lungs most unpleasantly. Yet the chill in the air could not lessen from the magnificent views of the Milky Way in the high desert.

Prof. Greene changed the music playing on the tiny Bluetooth speaker to a well-known Jazz artist of the twentieth century. Anyone who came to know him well often found that a good portion of his life could be understood in the music that had filled it. It was a spiritual conduit for him, and he always included his students in his obsession with consuming music in all its lovely forms—*where the mathematics of the universe are expressed within the magnificent confines of the human perspective*, he would tell his students.

Although it was not the basis of their friendship, Paige adored him all the more upon the discovery of this attribute, which had now deeply bound their attachment to one another. She closed her eyes as the Brubeck Quartet wordlessly, flawlessly translated the profundities of existence with the most perfectly placed notes and rhythms, a manner that singularly articulated, described, and envisioned everything—a true masterpiece and revelation of the human soul, of the universe itself—like an eloquent equation.

"Music delivers us," Prof. Greene said quietly as he looked over at Paige, who opened her eyes again and affectionately smiled at him. "It brings us face to face with both the hidden passions and the shadowy depths of the human spirit that lie beyond what words alone can express, that cannot find a way to otherwise express itself."

"Do you think we, humans I mean, will ever be space travelers? *I want to believe* that we will," Paige said, almost more to herself than to him, mesmerized by the stars above her again.

He looked at her quietly.

"Percy, I—" Paige began before Mika abruptly interrupted her.

"Oh my god!" Mika gasped. "Did you guys just see that! That light moving across the sky!"

8

CHAPTER

Paige turned her attention from Prof. Greene to where Mika was pointing. There, along the ridge of a large plateau, a circular light darted in a zig-zag pattern in the sky. The movements were far too exact, too precise, too fast to align with any known technology, and the light itself seemed to throb and pulsate as the colors shifted in fluorescent tones like the Aurora Borealis. It was completely inexplicable, and yet all four of them were now witnesses to it.

"Yes!" everyone simultaneously gasped.

It was shocking and extraordinary to see the lights, knowing that an explanation lay beyond their grasp in this moment. Soon, another light joined, and the two danced in the sky together, twirling around each other, the light of the moon their perfect accessory while frolicking in a well-choreographed ritual.

"Yes," Prof. Greene said slowly, not moving from his relaxed seated position. "They seem to start showing up every night about this time. Sometimes we see up to ten of them, just zooming around up there. And they leave no trace, with the exception of a few residual microwaves. We don't yet understand why microwaves either. Our field studies have been very limited. And after Max disappeared… we just don't really know what we're dealing with here. So, we simply observe." He stopped for a moment, looking across the fire at the three of them, a smile forming across his face. "And yet we find ourselves in this moment, so this is *our moment*, my friends. *Our moment.* To choose to witness the universe as scholars in the pursuit of knowledge or to turn away from the fear of what truths it might show us. Of course, these questions are not easy to answer, and they take time to process, but I'm afraid you all won't have much time."

"What do you mean, we don't have much time? What have you done?!" Detective Andrews' voice boomed with an intensity that was to be expected from a man whose eyes were so profoundly expressive, but was, nonetheless, rather shocking.

Paige heard Prof. Greene trying to ease the detective's concerns, but the words were lost in astonishment as she followed Andrews' gaze. Near the edge of the creek, where the light from the fire dissipated, there appeared to be a shadow that was round and swirling, slowly growing larger and larger. The darkness swirled faster and faster, and they began to feel a breeze before a powerful gust of wind extinguished the campfire completely, leaving them in the cold darkness. In the wake of the wind, a large, dark, swirling portal roared in front of them, the wind whipping their hair. Paige's pulse raced, and she wondered if this was the precipice of a black hole.

"I have not done this, Detective Andrews," Prof. Greene shouted over the wind. "I am no wizard capable of distorting the known laws of nature. This occurs every evening at about this time here. We had not decided collectively if we should go in there. There is no way of knowing the consequences or the ramifications. Yet, I suspect Dr. Walsh may have made that decision for himself." Just then, the wind suddenly began to die down, and the portal quickly shrank, completely disappearing again, leaving them alone in the darkness shrouded by silence.

"Ok, Percy, I think it's time you explain some things to us," Paige said, trying not to convey her impatience, fear, and confusion from everything that had occurred just now and throughout the course of the past few days.

"Of course. Shall we head back inside, my friends?" Prof. Greene said, motioning towards the main tent. Andrews gave him a sideward glance and sneered with abhorrence when he said, "*My friends*", but no one noticed in the darkness as they tried to gather their bearings. Once inside, the warmth of the fire managed to soothe their anxiety for a few moments while they all sat in silence. The things that were happening to them were seemingly impossible. Even a single incident chosen at random from among the many in the past few days was highly improbable, if not impossible. It was as though the universal laws they had all come to understand no longer applied, as though they had all been put to the test and every single one of them proven verifiably incorrect. This meant everything they knew was fraudulent and incomplete. It was deafening to comprehend.

Detective Andrews looked at the professor, seething, and demanded, "Mr. Greene, let me make it very clear to you that

Mingling Bloods

I am not a man who appreciates being bullshitted. You deliberately withheld this information from us, and I need to understand why before I start assuming *the worst* of you. And, believe me, that is something neither of us wants."

"Yes. Let me begin by apologizing to all of you," Prof. Greene said expressively. "I know that was shocking, to say the least. I've experienced it several times now, and I remain certain it is a thing one does not get used to. So please, sir, you must try to understand why I withheld it from you. You needed to see it to believe it, as they say, to believe it. Yet, even after experiencing it, more questions persist. Like, what IS this thing? As I shared moments earlier, we do not entirely know. No one has explored it, with the possible exception of your father."

He nodded and smiled warmly at Paige, holding his hand out for her to come sit by him. She hesitantly stood up and walked over to the table, grasping his hand and sitting next to him on the bench. It was hard for her to feel angry with her friend—he had such a sublime essence, a true sage among the most brilliant men and women—but she was beginning to wonder who she could *really* trust right now. Detective Andrews and Mika both walked over to the table to join them, exchanging a playful smile as they sat next to one another on the bench across from Paige and Prof. Greene.

"If I had tried to explain this to you before you witnessed all of this tonight, we would not be able to move forward quickly, as I would have had to dispel your doubts first or attempt to explain things I do not understand yet. But time is of the essence. We believe this is a wormhole of sorts, a disturbance or a tear in the space-time continuum, perhaps even something like a wrinkle in time and space, if you will. Whatever it is, it is incredibly powerful and beyond our control. The decision to step inside there will prove which theoretical hypothesis is correct, but we cannot know the consequences of obtaining that knowledge, or if we will even survive the experience to understand it anyway. The risks are incredible. It is not something I can ask of you; you must choose for yourselves. But I believe your father has made the choice to accept that risk."

"So, now we are just tasked with awaiting his return", Mika asked with a bit of sassiness Paige had not heard from her before.

"No, dear. It would be iniquitous of me to task any of you with anything. I told you, I am not some grand wizard capable of bending the rules of the universe." He quietly looked around the table at each of them, their faces lit by the light of the fire while his remained cast in shadow. He leaned forward, where his face now caught some light from the fire, resting his one elbow on the table, depicting himself in a very different fashion.

"But I do know where you can find one," he said, his expression like that of a young boy who had just plopped a frog into his mom's hands before she realized what he was doing.

"A wizard? Is he like Gandolf the Grey or Gandolf the White?" Detective Andrews asked, taking little care to disguise his mistrust and dislike of Greene now.

"Ahhhhh… there you go, revealing your boorish dogmatism, Mr. Andrews. *SHE* is *much* better company than Gandolf," Prof. Greene said, flashing a coy grin. Then he quickly made intentional eye contact with Paige and smiled in a most peculiar way. "You'll go to see her tomorrow. I must depart due to untimely circumstances, but I believe she can help guide you to the questions you seek answers for."

"Wait… what?" Paige asked.

"You're still asking the wrong questions, my dear."

9

CHAPTER

After bidding everyone good night, Paige entered her tent feeling utterly exhausted and completely confused. Her mind felt numb and weighed down, and she felt an instant rush of relief and gratitude looking down at the bags that Prof. Greene had arranged to be brought to camp and neatly placed beside the bed. She sat on the bed to test its degree of discomfort and was pleasantly surprised to find it rather incredibly comfortable, like a fine hotel bed draped in fluffy, white bedding and then stuffed with an overabundance of pillows. The sort of bed you sink into and then float back to the top of. The simple luxury was utterly delightful, after all she had been through the past few days—the mere thought of rationalizing it all right now was exhausting. She knew her body was absorbing the shock that would eventually reverberate through her psyche to help make sense of all this, but in the meantime, her body had been operating in survival mode.

She laid back and closed her eyes, quickly thinking over the events of the past few days and trying to ignore the images of Det. Andrews that floated in her mind. Paige was certain the unusual events that had unfolded and her physical exhaustion were what were fueling her emotional responses and attraction to Andrews—it was simply easier to focus her mind on his enjoyably attractive assets rather than deeply considering the chain of events and what that all meant. She shook her head, smiling but disappointed at herself for her daftness—she didn't even know his first name! But she did know that she liked something about him. *Something besides his ass-ets.* Normally, that would have felt like a very peculiar interpretation of her feelings, as *feelings* for much of anything or anyone were not a common occurrence for her. But then nothing had been normal in the past few days. She was just relying on instinct now, and her instincts seemed to like him.

Her instinct was also telling her that Mika may turn out to be more of a kindred spirit than an unnecessary nuisance. Her radiance was impossible to ignore, particularly when wrapped in such a beautiful package and tied with a chic bow. The things which seemed disagreeable about her were things Paige usually assumed were part of a consumer and identity driven population of people incapable of deep thoughts and intellectual pursuits. Perhaps she had misunderstood Mika, but she still didn't feel like Mika was being entirely honest with her, and she couldn't trust her.

Then she smiled as she felt deep reverence for having met up with Percy Greene here, one of her favorite people and a man of such clarity and courage—the courage to pursue the darkness beyond the dark, a rare form of valor that exposes only the greatest minds, like Lovelace, Curie, Goodall, and Doudna. Those who illuminate both with their essential nature and their incredible intellect. She felt certain that Percy would eventually be considered among these titans of the known universe, and she felt honored to be considered his friend.

Her mind then wandered to their plans for tomorrow when they were going to meet the "Grand Wizard", as Percy had called her. It was utterly laughable except that it was suggested at the behest of one of the world's greatest thinkers. *Should she be sure to shower before meeting the wizard? Are there rules to meeting grand wizards, like meeting kings and queens?* Paige felt that a shower, at the very least, was called for. As she turned on the shower in the small washroom, she was relieved to find that the water was exceptionally hot. Knowing that the small water tank wouldn't last long, she hurriedly washed her long, black hair and gave her face a good scrubbing. When she returned to her lovely bed, steam was dissipating off her skin from the shower, as though her own essence was noiselessly disbanding into the air. She felt overwhelmingly drowsy and quickly drifted off to sleep before even putting pajamas on. That was when she had the second dream.

Grandmother holds out her hand and urges me to keep closer to her. We're walking through a thick grove of white pine trees, and their deep, heady aroma fills the air. Grandmother leads the way up the narrow path, through and over the jagged rocks. As I climb ever closer behind her, I can feel the air beginning to change, constricting and becoming more unyielding. Then suddenly, we emerged from the path into a high mountain meadow where dogwoods and red buds sweep across the lower half in a glorious wave. Perfuming the slopes of the mountain, their tiny flower petals flutter about in the wind, indistinguishable at times from the multi-colored butterflies wavering here and there. Along the top, more pines line the grassy expanse and slowly disperse as the top of the mountain is exposed, offering only jagged, lichen-masked rocks. I turn to look behind us, across the meadow to our familiar place, where tall grass and tiny flowers had created a magical setting—a small, wonderful world hidden away, a cloistered reprieve from the mundane.

But today, Grandmother is not here to whisper wishes to the wildflowers and sing with the wind in the trees, as we had done many times before. Her notions will take us much higher this time. Though Grandmother is quite elderly, her precise age seemingly unknowable, she remains nimble, eager still to pursue the wonders of the world. As though she simply decided one day that age had become a needless nuisance, she'd be bothered by no more. She could have been 50 or she could have been 100—it would not have dampened the fire that radiated within her. Although there were many hardships in her ageless life that would have discouraged many, she seemed relentlessly determined to extract everything she could from it while her time remained.

As we climb higher, the trees begin to fall away behind us, and the vista opens to a view from the very top of our world, allowing us to see for countless miles. The air is fresh and clean, bestowing upon us a feeling of lightness. A few peaks of the majestic mountains are still speckled with snow, and I feel my chest swell as we look out over the lands of our kin. Generations of our descendants have lived among these hills and valleys—now cloaked with patches of smoky mist in the early light—respecting the will of Nature to do as it pleased, not as they wished it to. I wondered what primordial blood coursed through their animist veins that helped them understand they were not separate from the world, but that they were an intricate part of it, an expression of nature itself.

"Look, my love," she waved her hand across the line of the horizon, her chest heaving slightly from the climb, a broad, honest smile across her face. "The beauty of the way the light dances across the peaks, see how they gaily cast shadows in return, like a resplendent dancer flaring her skirt. It's magical the way the mist floats through the mountains, like a great spirit watching and guiding us. But what we often choose to believe is that magic is simply something we do not understand or cannot see clearly. That's why it's always important to remember that magic is an illusion, a façade that hides the truth, a masked reflection of the world. We get drunk on magic, drunk on the beautiful

mountain meadows that trick our minds into believing, even if only for a moment, that all the world is so wonderful and magical. However, you know instinctively *that when you look more closely at the beautiful invocation before you, the reality is that destruction—of life, of beauty, of illusions—rages on and on. Magic, religion, the ego—all forms of illusion seek to hide the ordinary from you, to make you believe that only magic can reveal what is extraordinary, and to teach you to surrender your autonomy. We already tiptoe along the precipice of existence as little more than transient personalities, perpetually searching for meaning, for truth, for love, for purpose—and nothing is more precious than the dignity to live life as we choose. To seek the depths of our significance within the expression of this existence, of being human, of being anything, requires courage. So be brave, be honest in your explorations. You must face the illusions, like the clouds that hover above that valley, and shine light upon them until the truth is revealed."*

The clouds had lifted from the dale, and as I witnessed what it had concealed—a rather ordinary valley—I felt the magic beginning to dispel. I felt liberated by the truth and stirred by the semblance of divinity I had begun to recognize within myself.

10

CHAPTER

Paige sat up in the bed, instantly awake and suddenly aware of something pounding nearby. *Holy shit, has my heart begun beating outside myself?* She wondered hastily, trying to clear her head of the dream. Just as she realized it was someone knocking on the door of her tent, the door flung open, and Det. Andrews called out Paige's name. They both succumbed to the instant and irreversible reality that he was standing in her tent, sunlight streaming in through the opening of the door and onto her bed, where she was lying on top of the covers just as she had fallen asleep, only now she was totally naked, having shed her towel during the night.

"Oh!" Andrews exclaimed as he hesitated for a moment, frozen and awkwardly wondering why this was happening right now and yet also not completely hating it. "I…um…god. Paige. I'm… so sorry. You didn't answer. And so… well … I was concerned something may have happened to you."

Paige looked at him, pulling the towel up over her torso, wondering why this was happening right now and also not completely hating it.

"Paige!" Mika burst through the door, pushing past Andrews, seeing Paige on the bed with her buttocks exposed and a towel held against her bosom. She gave Detective Andrews a look up and down with a stern face and said, "Detective, can you please give us a few moments?"

"Oh… yeah… of course. I'll … uh … go get the car packed. Just whenever you two are ready," he said with a nod and a tense smile.

Paige and Mika continued to quietly stare at Det. Andrews until he finally took it as his cue to leave. He nodded again, gave a small wave, and turned, closing the door behind him.

Mingling Bloods

As the door closed, Paige quietly looked at Mika, relieved and embarrassed, and she started laughing out loud. Whatever tension had existed between them seemed to be diminishing now, and Paige was glad to see Mika this morning, particularly after having had another dream.

Mika crossed the small room quickly and hopped onto the inviting bed. She grabbed the edge of the towel near Paige's arm and pulled it upwards in a nurturing and protective gesture to cover her before lightly tracing her hand across Paige's stomach for an instant. Paige tensed at the reminder of her awkward secret, but Mika was looking at her quite intently and seriously now.

"The Grandmother," Mika whispered. Her eyes, aglow like vivid amber flames, were exploring and examining the depths of Paige's soul as casually as though she were reading the Sunday paper.

"You had the same dream, didn't you? About Grandmother. The grandmother in the dream," Paige said before even realizing she was going to. But it just came rushing out, and now she momentarily questioned the sanity of it.

"Yes! I did. And I remembered you being there, being a part of…the me…I guess that Grandmother was speaking to," Mika said before they both fell silent momentarily. "I know it doesn't make sense. But right now, I think we need to suspend our known standards of what is 'real' and have the courage to honestly share what we are experiencing so we can figure this out together. How are you feeling?" she asked, glancing down at her belly again.

"Oh… I'm fine," Paige said hastily, feeling self-conscious and pulling the towel around her more in a habitual attempt to hide herself. "But you're absolutely right, Mika. It's the most logical thing to do at this point. So, tell me about your first dream. Let's see if our accounts are exactly the same or if they differ. We need to be meticulous in our examination and search for the truth, like Jourdain and Moberly."

Mika's face fell placid before she rolled her eyes and then wrinkled her brow, confused by Paige's vague reference. Paige grinned with a certain sort of satisfaction and explained that Eleanor Jourdain and Charlotte Moberly were academics and colleagues who traveled to the Palace of Versailles in the summer prior to becoming colleagues in 1911. It was just a bit of a fun adventure and a chance for the two women to get to know one another. However, while there, they believed they were transported back in time to the moments leading up to the French Revolution. They methodically cataloged and recorded all possible explanations and searched historical records for references to the things they witnessed. In the case of Jourdain and Moberly, the two women experienced events slightly differently, seeing different things and feeling different sensations. But as Paige and Mika shared their experiences, they realized they were utterly identical. The single exception being that they both had experienced the dream through the lens of a single person—whom they assumed was the granddaughter—and yet, only Mika had detected the sensation that they were *both* the observer.

Mika looked at Paige and gently said, "I don't know what lies ahead of us or what this could possibly mean. But I know that we share the same dreams for a purpose, in a design we do not yet see. I want you to know…" Mika took a deep breath, pausing for a moment, "I've got your back as we go through this. I want you to know that… that I'm right here beside you, no matter *what dreams may come*."

Paige felt tears spring to her eyes, and a lump formed in her throat as she tried to process the tidal wave of madness that was threatening to overcome her. Mika reached out to hug her, and her face fell into Mika's chest, tears staining her pink satin night shirt. She hadn't known Mika long, but she suddenly felt very attached to her and very glad that she was in this with her. Just as she felt she was going to melt into a puddle of tears and have a good, old-fashioned ugly cry, Mika said, "Ugh! Listen, girl. I don't mind hugging you, but you have got to cover up that butt first!"

11

CHAPTER

A sudden knock at the door followed by a dazzling stream of sunlight, which was then broken by Prof. Greene standing in the warm brilliance, casting an enormous shadow that looked oddly distorted as he held up two cups of coffee.

"I thought you ladies could use this today," he beamed as he walked into Paige's tent. She had put her pajamas on by now, and they were discussing what the plan should be for today. But they remained hindered with questions.

"So, what should we expect today from the ancient *grand wizard*? How will this help us find my father? Will she guide us through traveling in a wormhole?" Paige was feeling apprehensive about all of this now. She didn't even know her father. She had no idea what he expected to find when entering the wormhole. *And if <u>he</u> hasn't returned, how would <u>she</u> be able to?*

Prof. Greene smiled at her, trying to ease her fears and hesitations. "When you meet the Grand Wizard, you will experience a journey within itself. It's important to remember that embarking on this excursion is essential to your understanding of the wormhole. You must clear your mind of all the chatter about how these things aren't possible. You simply have to entertain the idea that they *are,* because we are observing them. So, *be* a physicist! As a physicist, you know and understand that infinite possibilities exist in an infinite universe. This is your opportunity to discover the possibilities that are most often inaccessible to us, that exist only as theories we may never be able to prove. You both have such brilliant minds, such acute abilities that you are destined to fulfill," he said, looking to both of them, smiling brilliantly. "Now is the moment of your destiny, ladies!"

"*It is not in the stars to hold our destiny but in ourselves*," Mika said with a smile.

Prof. Greene laughed, nodding, and threw his arm around her shoulder affectionately. With that, Mika and Paige both inhaled deeply and looked at one another, locking their eyes for a long moment, both acknowledging that moving forward would mean there was no turning back. Mika smiled broadly and looked at Prof. Greene.

"What time do we leave then, Percy?" Mika's expressive voice often had the effect of listening to a talented vocalist challenging and exploring the possibilities of their gift, leaving the listener with an ethereal experience, a memory of the primitive splendor grounded in the texture and emotions of the human voice.

"You ladies," Prof. Greene replied congenially, "and Detective Andrews will be leaving shortly. It will be a long journey before you reach the Wizard. Unfortunately, I cannot be detained here any longer; there are important matters I must attend to. I have brought you some clothes for today. You'll need to dress comfortably, and you'll be carrying a pack for a bit before you arrive at your destination."

He handed the ladies a stack of clothing that had been designed for the research team's use. Paige looked down at hers, thinking, it was THE most cliché expedition outfit you can imagine—khaki pants, a long-sleeve button-down beige cotton shirt, brown hiking boots, tube socks, and a scarf for field use. Looking over Mika's, she noticed hers was similar but in mossy green tones instead of brown. *At least Mika would look just as ridiculous as her*, Paige thought haughtily.

Prof. Greene hurried to finish packing the large van in which he was transporting equipment. Mika went back to her room, and both women hastily changed. Paige, fully dressed now like she was ready to excavate pyramids and Pharaoh's tombs, walked over to see if Prof. Greene needed any assistance.

"No, dear, but I do believe Det. Andrews may need some help preparing the packs. I'm going to be leaving momentarily. But I want you to know," he said as he reached out to grab her gently by the arm, "that what awaits you out there is *only what you take with you*." He then waved his hand through the air in a movement evocative of a Jedi master.

"Oh God, Percy! You're really quoting *Star Wars* right now?" Paige exclaimed while laughing heartily and smacking him playfully on the arm.

"Universal truths reside within all great adventures," he said with a large smile before hugging her and saying goodbye. Just then, Mika walked out from her own tent and towards them, wearing the green version of Paige's outfit. *Ugh*, Paige thought as she watched her walk over towards them, *of course, she looks fucking amazing in this, too.* Mika smiled and sauntered in a feline-like manner, her hair bouncing beautifully, as if it were already the best day of her life.

"I'll let you two say good-bye," Paige said as Mika walked up and hugged Prof. Greene. "I believe Andrews needs my assistance." She bowed ceremoniously in a goofy manner before walking towards the large main tent, an enthusiastic spring in her step. She must have slept well last night, despite the dream. She felt great today! They finished stocking the packs and loading them in the car before driving off, following a hand-drawn map provided by Prof. Greene.

12

CHAPTER

As they approached the border marking the remaining lands of the Uintah and Ouray nations, they crossed a clear, rocky stream, and Paige allowed her thoughts to wander aimlessly through the captivating landscape. She quietly realized that she was feeling better since she and Mika had their talk with each other and then with Prof. Greene. Yet, none of their questions had been answered, and she couldn't stop thinking about what Percy had said the night before, that they were *asking the wrong questions.*

Looking out the window, she felt so small and purposeless against the vastness of the landscape, where the seemingly limitless sky was held captive only by the horizon in a prison of illusion and where even the plateaus and mesas registered as mere trivial things against this endless canopy. Yet, as they drew near, she discovered how enormous even they were, towering high into the sky and casting massive shadows—a perpetual game the sun methodically, yet blissfully, placated them with daily. It was all utterly enchanting, a place so big that the ego feels free to finally unravel and reveal what lies beneath.

They turned down a small, rough dirt road and drove towards the large plateau with the bottle-neck top, where the lights had been witnessed from basecamp. The Buick rocked back and forth as it bounced in the ruts of the road, slowing them down considerably. With several miles of driving like this ahead of them, they all seemed to accept the discomfort in silence for several moments until Mika reached between the front seats and said, "Hey! I just remembered I made this for you."

It was a shiny, iridescent compact disk, a relic from days gone by when the masses suffered to hear their favorite music in such archaic ways. Paige grabbed it from her, looking at the title scrolled across the front in black Sharpie.

"I made a playlist for you, Mister Andrews," Mika said with a generous and playful smile. "I saw that your car only had a CD player, so I burned some songs from Prof. Greene's playlist last night. I thought it would be fun to have a soundtrack for our Quest!"

"Our *quest*? Plus, this says '*Percy's Songs*', Mika," Paige said, looking at her and squinting her eyes suspiciously.

"Well, I may have burned my soundtrack over his. But can you even buy CDs anymore?"

They all burst out laughing, and Paige slid the CD into the small, oblong aperture—a time capsule of the oddest dimensions—and turned up the volume. The first song was a complete surprise to both Paige and Det. Andrews as the gritty sounds of 311's "Come Original" blared. The old Buick bounced in the dirt, and everyone laughed for a moment before they all joined together, singing along in a mumbling manner so despicable that it would have made Nick Hexum and the guys regret they had ever written it in the first place:

Cause when lightning flashes sweet electricity

All the world then stands revealed with the clarity

Of raw voltage, briefly, we see, and the hope is

You'll be able to tell just what dope is.

Finally, they came to a large thicket of mesquite that had completely invaded the road—which had become little more than a trail at this point anyway—leaving them with no way to get the car around. Detective Andrews put the car in *park* and shut off the engine.

"Well, now we walk," he said matter-of-factly.

"Walk where?" Paige asked as she looked around, nervously noting that there was nothing to be seen for miles.

"There," Detective Andrews answered again patiently.

"To the base of the plateau. I don't see anything there either," Paige said, visibly uneasy now.

"No. Not the base. The top. We'll be going up there."

Andrews was looking up, casually assessing the difficulty of the task at hand now that the obstacle was right in front of them, but wincing slightly. Paige was beginning to panic: *how the hell had she missed that THIS was what they were doing*!? Mika had already enthusiastically hopped out of the car and opened the trunk to take out the backpacks.

"We'll hike to the base tonight, where the stream runs. The same as the one at base camp. We'll camp there and then tomorrow begin our ascent to the summit. We'll lose the warmth of the sun soon as the shadow of the mesa moves our way. So, prepare for a chilly night."

He gave her a reassuring nod and turned to get out of the car before adding, "I have faith in you, Doc."

With that, he got out and shut the door. She heard him talking to Mika as they performed the final checks on the bags. She took a deep breath: *You can fucking do this, Paige.* She grabbed the door handle and looked up at the plateau.

Who the fuck am I kidding? This is madness! I can't climb a god damn mountain!

13

CHAPTER

Paige awoke in the predawn hours—the magical phase of darkness when the stars dance more quietly across the sky like the last of the party guests unwilling to depart just yet, not wanting to break the spell of the music and each other until the very end. She had never in her life slept outside on the ground in a sleeping bag, and she couldn't help but wonder, in this very moment, why not? It wasn't that she had been opposed to the idea; it was more poignant that the thought had never even crossed her mind in the first place. She had always loved the final moments of the night sky and chasing the stars across the fleeting darkness, but she had never seen them like this. As the sky began to hint at its gift of illumination, she noticed Mika near the creek meditating again. *Did she ever sleep?*

"Good morning, Doc," Detective Andrews said. Paige flashed a goofy smile at him, surprised that everyone was awake.

"We should get going once Mika finishes up," Paige said as she sat up and stretched, feeling the cold air tingle along her skin as she emerged from the sleeping bag.

"Sure," Det. Andrews said as he stood up and poked the fire. "Wanna get some coffee in us first?"

"Yes, *please!*" Paige sighed, "That sounds amazing."

Within the hour, they had packed up and set off. There was no clear trail until they reached the clearing where the brush from the creek ended and opened abruptly to the massive red rocks of the mesa. You could see the beginning of the trail winding around to the eastern side, where the light was just breaking over the horizon. It was an incredible sight as the rays of light streamed through the atmosphere, like a great, cosmic lighthouse. Paige remembered feeling the same enchantment during her summer internship at Mauna Kea Observatories in high school. It had been a defining moment for her—thinking that if more people watched the sunrise over a volcano or traced the footsteps of stars, they would be less likely to deny the science that has provided them with all the comforts of their modern lives, they would see that it was the very thing that allowed them the audacity to deny its validity. Paige found it maddening that she should devote her entire life to the understanding and exploration of the natural world and the cosmos—to literally *study the theory of everything*—and yet still people denied the most basic foundations of physics and science in general.

As they began their climb, Paige let her thoughts wander from thoughts like these to the admiration and beauty of the climb itself. Yet they continued to climb for several hours, slowly winding around the large base of the mesa, and Paige found her thoughts becoming focused solely on the effects of the climb on her body. In addition to battling the altitude, she was nearly fifty and completely out of shape. As she climbed over a large boulder, sliding partially down the crevice to leverage herself to reach the other side, she felt she had reached her limit.

"Andrews," she said, bending over to catch her breath, her arms stretched out against the rock in front of her, and reeling from the burning in her legs and lungs. "Can we take a break for a few minutes?"

"You ladies are doing great. We're almost there. We can rest then."

Mika turned back, holding her hand out to help Paige up and over a large rock. "Come on, girl. He said we'd be there soon. It's not so bad when you know it's almost over. Are you sure you're doing ok, though?" she asked, glancing down at Paige's stomach.

Paige grabbed her hand and let her pull her up, welcoming the moment of respite it provided. "Oh god, yeah. I'm fine. Trust me, you don't need to worry about all that," Paige said, her eyes darting downward.

"Well, ok. You better let me know if it's too much or if we need to slow down," Mika said, smiling, then turning to follow Det. Andrews around the turn. Paige took a deep breath and a drink of water, thinking that *it had long since been too much.*

Still, they walked and climbed on for what seemed like an unusually long time to Paige, *especially since they had been assured that they were almost there.* Then they came to a high ledge where they had to scoot around the precipice of the cliff, which then opened to a large, relatively flat area, and beyond that, the entrance of a cave. As they approached the threshold, they could see that it receded deeply into the mesa, and it had been carved intricately, with delicate designs and thoughtful artistry. A man with his back to them faced the entrance of the cave, kneeling, head down, entirely motionless. He was dressed in the red robes of a Buddhist monk, a strikingly odd spectacle for a climber on a mesa in Utah.

The three of them stood there, quietly observing the man, careful not to disturb his tranquility. Paige walked over to some boulders near the edge of the cliff and sat down, taking a long, refreshing drink of water from her pack and staring at the man's back, wondering with amusement if he was a pilgrim on his own journey or a gatekeeper of information vital to their quest. *Great*, she thought jokingly to herself, *now I'm calling it a quest now, too.* Regardless, given the oddity of recent circumstances, she didn't know what they should do. If he ignored them entirely, it would be a pretty good sign that he had no interest in why their paths had crossed here. *But if he speaks—*

"Hello," said the man, although he did not move at all. They all quietly waited for him to say something else, pausing to look at each other with curiosity and hesitation in the reticence. After several silent bland awkward moments, the man placed his hands on the ground and pushed himself up to standing, bowing ceremoniously. He slowly turned around and walked towards them. Stopping at a distance that was awkwardly far away to introduce himself. He bowed again, closing his eyes, pressing his palms together while holding them against his chest, and slowly moving his upper body in a stiff manner, stopping at a 90-degree angle before very slowly straightening himself again.

The man looked up and grinned. "Hey, my dudes. I was just gettin' in my morning meditation before the 'shrooms wear off. Y'all looking for the gateway?" He looked back and forth between them in a very Keanu Reeves sort of way, a smile full of blissful ignorance. Paige looked down instantly, trying not to laugh. *There's no way* this *guy is the gatekeeper for our Quest...*

Mika's voice broke the tension of the moment, singing out with an angelic pitch. "Of course we are," she said with the slightest hint of a giggle.

"Yeah. I was visiting my buddies in Sedona, searching for the meaning of life in the desert and all that shit, ya know, and surfing on their couch. After a few months, one of my bros mentions this place and how spiritual it is. Well, I'm like *whoaaa*, and I was just living on his couch anyway, so I drove up here, sleeping in my car along the way, and living within the mysticism of the desert. It's been a pretty bodacious journey, ya know."

Mika smiled, her eyes flashing brightly, cheeks blushing from the climb, then the emergence of the dimple—a weapon she knew how to wield well among men and women alike. She tilted her head to the side, closing her eyes and returning the bow. "*There is no darkness but ignorance*. Safe journeys and Namaste, friend."

The handsome youngster smiled charitably at her, indifferent to her allure but nonetheless reverent of her vivaciousness. He turned and motioned towards the edge of the cave where the cliff dropped off, holding his palm up and smiling as though he were presenting a letter on *Wheel of Fortune*.

"The questions to the answers you seek lie beyond there. *There is a world everywhere*," he said, smiling again, nodding politely to Mika, and then casually walking past them and down the path in the direction from which they had just come. Bewildered, everyone stared at the emptiness of the sky and wind to which he had just pointed and suggested they follow to continue their journey. Paige stepped backwards and rested her weight against the large boulder again, and rubbed her temples.

"This is known as a place of pilgrimage for the more, shall we say… eccentric, spiritual seekers. There is a series of caves on the way to the summit which were created by the ancient ancestors from the last of the three great eras of the pre-Columbian Pueblo peoples, regularly referred to as the Archaic Age," Detective Andrews said, now examining the carvings at the cave entrance while they stared at him, shocked and wide-eyed. "The remote location of the few remaining *herraduras* is what preserves them. That's the name given to them by the brutal Spanish colonizers, of course, for their customary horseshoe-shaped designs. It's a tragedy that so much of the great civilizations of North America have been lost and destroyed since. Entire nations and cultures and immense cities, enormous pyramids— erased and forgotten." He blew some dust off an engraving and gently brushed it with his hand to reveal the intricate craftsmanship. He sighed and paused, quietly looking at the carvings for a few moments before he continued, "My undergraduate studies at the University of Texas in Austin were an impressive and eclectic exploration of every random class I could possibly take. I now possess an exceptionally diverse Bachelor's degrees in Art History and Anthropology," he said, rolling his eyes and chuckling. "I initially tried a few business majors. But, for me, going to college wasn't easy. I had to do it all on my own. As I bounced from one thing to another that might make me successful or just more money than a working-class life, I found that none of it suited me really. So, I just decided to study what truly interested me," he said.

"So why don't you teach, Mr. Andrews?" Paige asked, somewhat arrogantly, while taking a long drink of water again.

"We weren't all born with a golden diploma in our hands, Doc," he said, pausing for a moment, "I had to make a living. So, I became a private detective, among other things."

"I *knew* it!" Mika cried out. "I knew you weren't a cop! You're much smarter than you look. And I must say, you look quite smart to begin with, Mister Andrews." She turned her head to the side slightly and winked at him, like Bacall winking at Bogart—too smart, too young, and much too beautiful.

"Wait, you're a private detective?" Paige asked, feeling irritated at his deception. "I was under the impression that you were a cop, that you were here to find my father!"

"I *am* here to find your father. But the fact that you *assumed* I was a police detective is on you. You never questioned me or my credentials in any way. And you know what they say about people who assume."

She scowled at him, incensed at his tone and the almost flippant dismissal of his duplicity.

"Prof. Greene hired me to find your father," Andrews continued. "To be clear, he was not entirely open with me about what this investigation truly entailed either. Nor was he honest with you. I am as surprised by much of this as you are. He informed me that I did not have to continue this far with you two, but there are things here I personally don't understand, things I can't walk away from until I've had the chance to understand them better. So, it seems we were all drawn here together in a guise of deception, doesn't it, Doc?"

He looked at Paige intently, as though he knew something about her—like her darkest secrets. She quickly looked away, her resentment melting into shame.

Mika, attempting to defuse the tension, looked at Det. Andrews said, "A P.I. with an art history and anthropology background? How fascinating you are, Mr. Andrews!" She smiled and tilted her head, coyly raising an eyebrow.

Her magnetism held such a communicable quality, a distilled essence of effortlessness that was almost palpable at times and unsettling at others. Andrews smiled, locking his eyes with her briefly, acknowledging his enjoyment with the little game they had begun to play.

"*Anyway*," he said, still holding his gaze with Mika, "the people who built these during the Archaic Era would later become the architects of the famous Mesa Verde." He continued as he smiled now at Paige now. "It was one of the great centers of sacred spirituality throughout the realm. *Herraduras* like this were common markers along the spiritual paths, which extended for hundreds of miles. It's believed all members of society eventually partook in these journeys throughout their lives—seeking to attain a better understanding of the self, a profound search for meaning, a discovery of their own personal truths." Detective Andrews reached into his pack and pulled out some small snacks, passing them to Mika. Paige smiled at him, and despite her discontent and growing suspicions about who exactly Det. Andrews really was, much like her feelings for Mika, she was glad he was there.

Mika passed half the snacks to Paige and said, "You know, on an entirely different subject, not all people are as lucky as we are, my friends. *Fortune brings in some boats that are not steered.* Take the fellow making his way down the mountain. He actively seeks to partake in a fantastic journey that expands the boundaries of what is known about our universe. We're lucky that we don't have to orchestrate our own pilgrimage in order to experience the sublime. It has most certainly presented itself to us," she said as she spread her arms wide before her in a dramatic gesture. Paige and Det. Andrews both shook their heads and laughed at her.

14

CHAPTER

"Ok, ladies," Det. Andrews said, tossing his backpack on again. "Let's see if we can find this trail. This is where the mesa angles back sharply, creating the bottleneck. There must be a way to get to the summit from here."

He walked to the edge of the cave where the cliff dropped off, inching around until he could see a series of foot and hand holes that led up about 5 feet to a small protrusion. From there, the ledge slanted upwards, where a rope was attached to the rock through a sequence of hooks. Paige and Mika were close behind him, looking up at the ledge and the rope hesitantly.

"Once we get to that protrusion," Mika said, pointing, "we just have to hold onto the rope and scoot upwards. I think it just looks harder than it really is," she concluded cheerfully, reaching down to tighten her shoelaces.

Paige stepped backwards, feeling herself bump into the boulder again. She looked up at the side of the cliff, trying to concentrate on what Mika was saying, but her ears started ringing, and an uncomfortably cold sweat had begun to emanate from her brow.

"You'll be ok, Doc," Andrews said. "Mika can go first, and then we'll get you up there. I'll be right behind. We'll go nice and slow, ok?"

She looked at his handsome face, usually so pleasantly adorned with his quiet confidence and easy humor, but now expressing only intensity and resolve. He held his hand out, bringing her to the edge of the cliff where Mika stood. She turned back to look at Paige and smile before reaching around the edge for the first hand-foot cavity. She nimbly moved up the wall onto the ledge, reaching her hand back for Paige as she gripped her wrist around the rope.

"Shit! I can't do this, Andrews…" Paige quickly said as an exhale, feeling completely overcome with fear as stars were beginning to swirl in her peripheral field of vision.

"Come on, Doc," he said softly, "I *know* you can do this. Breathe in for four. Hold for four. Breathe out for four. Hold for four. Keep doing that. Feel the ground beneath you. You can do this."

She took a deep breath, smiled at his exquisiteness, and then focused her eyes on Mika. *Just don't look down*, she thought to herself over and over as she reached for the first indentation. Her legs were shaking so wildly that she was afraid that they might not hold up under her. She closed her eyes tightly, summoned all her strength, and hoisted herself upwards. The first step held. She clung as closely to the rock as she could, trying to breathe out slowly, and inched her trembling hand up to reach for Mika's, her eyes still pressed tightly closed. The warmth and firmness of Mika's hand gripping hers with absolute certainty gave Paige the courage to peek up towards Mika, her smiling face confident, and helped steady her as she reached for the ledge, finding the footing terrifyingly precarious. She clung madly to the rope, her face pressed against the cool rock, legs trembling, tears streaming down her cheeks. Then she felt the warmth of Det. Andrews' hand around her waist as he reached around her and grabbed onto the rope. Slowly, the three of them moved upwards, holding tightly to the rope until at last they made it to an opening that led to a small but much less frightening trail that continued upwards.

Paige took a few weak steps as she crossed onto the landing and stumbled, falling to her knees. Andrews reached out and steadied her, saying, "Let's take a rest, ok?"

After a few moments of quiet respite, they continued climbing again for several more hours, all three of them now feeling the exhaustion. Each additional step Paige took was more and more painful. Her thighs hurt. Her feet hurt. Her back hurt. As she climbed, she went through a checklist in her head, an inventory of sorts to see if there was any remaining part of her body that did not hurt. *Elbows? Yep, that hurts. Pinky toes? Oh yeah, that definitely hurts.*

She also couldn't help but feel like something about this part of the climb was different. Since they surpassed the cliff face, she felt like the air had changed, like the warmth of the sun was more profound, like the ground itself felt almost transcendent. It felt like *they* had changed. The sun was now nearing the western horizon, and it seemed as though the mesa was growing, pressed upward by its expanding shadow, making their journey feel much like that of Sisyphus, perpetually rolling a boulder uphill for eternity. As her concerns began to grow for her ability to continue, they rounded a cliff that opened to another large *herradura*, this one much larger and more intricately carved.

"Ah, we finally made it," Det. Andrews sighed, tossing his pack to the ground with only the slightest sense of defeat. "We'll sleep here tonight. We should be able to find fresh water in the cave from a spring within, according to Greene, and there's plenty of room in there for a fire. I expect we'll be reasonably comfortable." He laughed with a shrug and headed into the cave, slowly exploring the carvings and symbols.

Paige looked to Mika, eager with anticipation for rest, but fighting the frustration at realizing that they were spending the night here, leaving her now to wonder how long they might still be climbing tomorrow. She threw her pack down next to Det. Andrews and followed him into the unexpectedly bright cavern, the afternoon sun illuminating it in warm light. Once inside, they could truly take in the wonder and enormity of the structures, which stretched back further than they could see, and the melodic sound of a small spring somewhere within echoed across the chamber.

"The Archaic desert peoples built their cities within the sides of the mesas throughout this region," Det. Andrews said as he continued to study the reliefs carved into the walls.

"But holy places, such as this, were not occupied full-time. They served as spiritual resting places along the way, often focusing on a certain aspect of the spiritual journey itself. This particular *herradura* focuses on the pain of self-discovery."

"So even the ancients thought this climb was outrageous," Mika asked with a smile.

"Yes," Andrews replied in a slow, trance-like manner, much like a parent responding to their child, having not actually listened to them.

"I'll go look for some wood for a fire," Mika said as she wandered with intention out of the cave.

Paige was gazing at Detective Andrews as he explored the cave, deep in thought, his exquisite lips whispering silently to himself as his kaleidoscope eyes flashed from blue to green under his dark lashes.

"Have you ever seen the Disney cartoon, Mulan?" Paige asked casually, as though they were mid-conversation.

Det. Andrews murmured what sounded like an affirmative response.

"There's this part in the movie," Paige continued, "when she realizes that she can't continue to be controlled by her fear for the circumstances in which she has gotten herself into. So, she starts working twice as hard as the men and twice as long. There's this mountain they all have to climb while carrying water, and they can't spill a single drop, else they must try again tomorrow. So they all try over and over, and they all fail over and over. None can achieve the feat until, eventually, she alone succeeds. It's this beautiful moment when she realizes that only she can walk her path, that the measure of her success in life could and would be determined only by her, and that each painful step up that mountain again and again was necessary to prepare her for what new challenge awaited her at the top. I can't stop thinking about that as we climb this mountain endlessly. *Our Quest*." Paige sighed, looking out the cave entrance, resting her elbow on her knee, chin on top of her fist.

Andrews had stopped staring at the elegance on the wall and looked at her, his brows furrowed with a mixture of confusion and a complete lack of amusement. His eyes locked steadily on her as she turned her head up towards him, not expecting him to be so intently focused on her. Paige blushed, instantly regretful of the senseless babble she had just unleashed on this poor man, and quickly darted her eyes to the wall he had lost himself in moments before, attempting to disguise her embarrassment, which was now streaking across her cheeks. He was talking about serious information that may be necessary for this trip they are on, and she's talking about Disney princesses and *their Quest*. She was so embarrassed. Her face felt like it was on fire, and her eyes were beginning to tear up in response.

Mika's voice broke the peculiar silence of the cave, singing out with a quality that was less vocal and more instrumental, *"That life is better life, past fearing death, Than that which lives to fear."* Her face was illuminated by the light that entered the cave, casting her in an ethereal essence, her hair wild and beautiful, her eyes sparkling as though lit with the fire of stars.

Paige cleared her throat, drawing her eyes back to Andrews, who was still looking at her, but with an odd little smile now. She smiled back and quickly looked at Mika.

"Great, more Shakespeare quotes. Precisely what this moment dictates," Paige said, her sarcastic attempt at a joke falling deafly in the cavern. She stood up uneasily, further humiliated, and walked up to her, laughing lightly and smiling oddly. She reached out and took some of the wood bundled in Mika's arms.

"Here, let me help you," Paige said as Mika looked at her quietly.

In the center of the large horseshoe-shaped cavern was a generously sized fire pit. Having been used by travelers for centuries, it was stained black by a thousand fires and cast in a transcendent enamel. They quietly worked together building the fire, laying out the MREs, and filling their camel packs with water from the spring.

After dinner, as they were sitting around the fire, Mika jumped up and said, "C'mon, you guys. Wanna do some yoga with me? Our muscles need a good stretch after that long climb today."

"I would, but I know you'd just be checking out my ass the whole time," Det. Andrews replied with a smile.

Mika unfurled a mischievous grin for Paige and then playfully provided Det. Andrews with a slow and steady upward look. "Well, of course, Mister Andrews. That's all *any* woman wants. It's our perpetual urge—to adore and worship the male body." She smiled at him expressively before closing her eyes, inhaling deeply, and bringing her hands to her chest, left foot on her right knee in tree pose.

"Yeah, I'm not moving an inch until morning," Paige said, leaning back against her backpack and wiggling her toes against the warmth of the fire. "How in the hell do you even have the energy for this? You are always so… lively. It's disgusting, really," she said caustically.

"When I was ten, my mother and I were in a pretty bad car accident. I was in a coma for several weeks and then medically sedated for a couple more. I suffered a head injury," she said, while running her finger across the scar above her brow. "I also had a few broken bones and a spinal cord injury. When I finally woke up, they told me that I may never walk again, but they were hopeful that therapy could restore at least some movement. It was a long and difficult recovery, but I just kept moving. I feel like if I ever stop for too long now, I may never get going again. Yoga reminds me to take the time to reflect on how incredible our bodies truly are, how many adverse situations it has carried me through, to be kind to it, and most of all, patient and loving." She paused, exhaling loudly, flowing from one movement to the next.

"Mika… I… my god… I'm so sorry," Paige said, looking at Andrews and shaking her head sadly, disconcerted by her careless remarks yet again.

Mingling Bloods

Mika transitioned to warrior pose before continuing, eyes closed, "My grandmother pushed me through the physical therapy. She was tough, her sympathies beginning only at the threshold of her own experiences. But honestly, I needed her to be that tough. Her strength and courage shaped my own and helped me fight through. It made me realize very early that if I was going to walk again, I'd have to fight for it. And yet… there's… there's something else, a more profound aspect, that transpires when you have to endure tremendous infirmities or long illnesses. Something unexpected—a sanctification discovered within the folds of the tragedy. The extraordinary beauty of life becomes more sharply contrasted when you acquaint yourself with the acceptance of your inevitable death and then greet it daily. You don't have to be afraid of it anymore. You've just gotta make every day count."

15

CHAPTER

Dawn was quietly awakening on the eastern horizon as they packed up. What remained of the fire, a few flickering orange embers, cast a dim, umber light in the cave, a final stand against the darkness within. They quickly refilled their water and set off, eager to reach the summit sometime that day. Hope and excitement mingled with their fears and apprehensions while they climbed on quietly for several hours, their muscles burning, hoping to reach the summit soon. A million questions buzzed furiously around Paige's mind as they continued to hike upwards.

In the final stage of the climb, the wind whipped through their hair and tore at their clothes as they clung fiercely to the cold, hard rocks that the path continued over. At last, they reached the summit, which expanded out in a flat, barren stage punctuated only by a tiny shack near the opposite side. As they each scrambled to the top, they stood quietly, motionless, the view hypnotizing them—breathtaking in its vastness, the world below stretched further than the imagination, curving towards the edges where the haziness of the atmosphere blurred the full enormity of it all. Paige was reminded of the dream with Grandmother from the top of the mountain, feeling the same exhilaration as she had felt then, though the view was quite different now.

They walked towards the small adobe house and, as they drew closer, noticed the resplendent gardens surrounding it, as though the little house had sparked life all around it in an otherwise desolate landscape. Flowers bloomed in extraordinary size and variety while bees and butterflies fluttered about. From around the side of the house, they spotted the dire wolf lurking, head down in the same manner as before. *Watching.* They cautiously approached the door, losing sight of the wolf, where the aroma of freshly baked bread hovered in the air.

As they opened the door and stepped in, however, nothing seemed to reflect what was on the outside. Where life was abundant outside, inside, everything was covered in dust, tainted with neglect. The smell of bread was clearly a figment of their imaginations, as there was no light or life to be found in here. And then they all noticed in the furthest corner next to the kiva, a tiny, old woman, slumped over in a chair. Her head hung down, and long, wiry, grey hair cascaded over her face, hiding it. It appeared she had probably been dead for some time now. Det. Andrews stepped towards her in a manner less inquisitive and more compassionate and tilted his head, reaching his hand out as if to touch her. Paige grabbed his arm, slowly and gently pressed it back down, shook her head, and looked into his eyes, expressing her sadness and disappointment at coming all this way for the wizard—only to find her dead. She stepped past him, tears flooding her eyes from anger and disappointment, and headed towards the door. A sudden sensation compelled her to retreat to the quiet refuge of the garden—she wanted so desperately to just sit there as the warm sun hit her face, to pause in its wonder for a moment while the life of the garden whirled away around her. She reached her hand for the door.

"Grandmother?" she heard Mika ask quietly. She turned her head quickly, only to see Mika kneeling next to the tiny silhouette, reaching out to grab her petite hand before quietly repeating her name again.

"Grams…" Mika's hand touched hers as she said it, and the feeble old body suddenly moved, lunging forward and sitting straight up. The eyes that had seemed dead now looked directly at Mika, glowing with the eternal intensity of ancient stars, their light so distant it had long been forgotten. Her entire façade was changing as she apparently bloomed into life, like a flower in her garden. Her face was aglow, then the entire room was bright and radiant, filled again with the scents of a grandmother's house, the dust scattering back from whence it had come.

Paige gasped when she saw that the old woman looked just like the grandmother from her dreams. The dreams that she shared with Mika. *How had Mika recognized her?* Paige felt her whole body paralyzed by fear and confusion. Mouth agape, she stared at the old woman, her hair now salt and pepper and braided down her back, just like in the dreams. Her wide-brimmed hat was next to her on the floor, the same rugged blue blouse tucked under the thick leather belt, the long dark brown skirt, her determined expression, the weathered hands, the walking stick she now noticed by the front door—all exactly as it had been in her dreams. Paige panicked as she tried to determine what sort of sorcery or illusionists could pull off something like this, what sort of trap this was.

Mika began to stand up and take a step back, but the old woman clasped her tiny, weathered hand over Mika's, where it still rested on her other hand. She gently cradled it and looked into her gorgeous face and smiled, like a god smiling upon her angel. The room was so warm now, a fire burned in the hearth, a teapot whistled, as though life here had suddenly been unpause.

"Remember our song, my love?" Grandmother said, slowly caressing her cheek, smiling softly. *"I will wait, I will wait for you,"* she sang softly before whispering something to her that Paige and Andrews could not hear. Mika nodded as tears streamed down her face.

Grandmother moved towards the center of the room, her eyes now on Paige. Once lit, it was a tremendously beautiful home with high ceilings and wood rafters that soared to the center, which was vaulted, and warm sunlight spilled into the room from high windows. Iron-clad candelabras added and even more warmth, but the adobe clay walls were unlike anything she had ever seen—the visible marks of the craftsman's swipes here and there added such a texture and depth, it was like a living work of art. Grandmother seemed to float across the floor like a leaf skimming across the water, swept slightly here and there by the wind.

"Were you planning on leaving so soon, love? You've only just arrived." Grandmother had not yet relinquished her gaze from Paige, but stepped swiftly to the side, coming face to face with Detective Andrews. He stood still and quiet, but with no trace of fear or hesitation. She tilted her head towards his until their foreheads touched, and she clasped her palms around his face, like she was greeting her long-lost child. They paused for a moment in silence before looking up at one another.

"Shea," she said softly, "I see you still have a few *drops of Jupiter* left in your hair?" She gently, lovingly swept her fingers through his hair, and they both smiled at one another, both their eyes glazing over with sentiment.

Shea? Detective Andrew's first name was Shea! Paige couldn't believe she didn't know that yet. He had been absolutely right; she really had made no effort to get to know him, obsessed more with his delightful bum, his overall attractiveness, and his usefulness to her. She watched him closely, smiling in turn at the repose she felt from his gentle nature and good-humored character.

Grandmother then returned her gaze to Paige and motioned towards the door, where Paige was still standing, her arm frozen still just as it had been reaching for the handle, "Would you prefer that we go into the garden?"

The small side garden was partially shaded and bursting with fragrances as the buzz of life, busy at work, hummed around them. They sat in the aloofness of the shade where the honeysuckle grew from a small alcove, a bewitching interval from the confusion that was loitering much too close for comfort. Paige sat on the bench next to Grandmother, looking across the small garden where another bench was bathed in sunlight, and she longed to be there. But beside it, sprawled out in the warmth of the sun, was the dire wolf, its silver coat glistening handsomely in the warm light while it slept.

"*Haw Mushkay*," Grandmother said in a wispy, guttural tongue while the wolf lifted her head lazily at hearing the greeting. She looked at Grandmother unenthusiastically before plopping her head back down, returning to her nap. "She is a guardian, my dear. You need not fear her. Now, I know that you have traveled long to get here, and I know you must be weary. But there are matters at hand that must be attended to first. We only have time for me to tell you what is most important. When you return, you'll be able to enjoy dinner together with your friends. There will be an abundance of food, laughter, and friendship. And may you rest as long as you need to here in the warmth and the light, but you *will* need to continue the course of your destiny."

"Wait, there's no time? No time for what? Do you know anything about a wizard?" Paige suddenly felt very scared and nervous, wondering what all this meant. *Was she dreaming again?* She began to breathe more quickly, sweat beaded on her forehead, and a chill ran down her spine—she felt like she was going to faint.

"I am very old, and it's very tiring for me to expend my energy here. It's much easier for us to meet in another realm, where I can show you and not just tell you things."

"Another… realm?" Paige asked, hesitantly.

"Yes, my love, the realm of dreams."

Grandmother stood up. Although she was a petite woman, she possessed a presence that projected much more confidence than her small frame might suggest. While she was aged, she certainly was not fragile, nor did she suggest the slightest bit of fatigue in her mannerisms. She firmly grabbed Paige's hand, leading her over where the sun spilled across the bench, and the wolf still slept peacefully, and motioned for her to sit.

"Let me make you a cup of tea before we go, dear. Have a rest and soak your bones in the warmth of the light and be blithe." Grandmother placed her hand gently on her shoulder, smiled warmly, and then walked around the corner.

Paige looked at the wolf, feeling less fearful in her state of fatigue and more jealous of its serene tranquility. She closed her eyes and tilted her face upward, catching the full spectrum of light and taking a long, deep breath—remembering a technique her mother had taught her long ago when her anxieties as a child became overwhelming—and she began to imagine the light particles whirling in the air and then, by chance, being inhaled, finding their final resting place, after having traveled for millions of light years, in her lungs, where they continued to glow, sprinkled with star dust.

Grandmother stepped back into the light with a mellow gentleness and reached out to Paige, offering her the steaming cup of hot tea she was holding. Paige opened her eyes and smiled, grabbing the large, earthenware cup with both hands, inhaling the dark, spicy aroma. She had never known either of her grandmothers, but she imagined this must be what it felt like. Safety. Wisdom. Comfort.

"Drink this, dear, then we'll be going soon."

Going where? Paige felt so exhausted, going or doing were two things she had little desire for right now. As she began to sip the tea, she was surprised to find it so deep and black and earthy. The taste and warmth of it seemed to mingle with the minute particles of her body, and she could feel it spread throughout her, passing from her mouth to her throat, to her stomach. Her whole body now warmed by its earthiness, her mind swimming in its luscious tenderness.

She looked up at Grandmother to see her smiling back at her, her hand on her shoulder, resting gently. She wanted to tell her how tired she was, that she wasn't ready for another journey, that her soul just needed some more time in the sunshine. She wanted to bury her face in Grandmother's chest and feel her strength, to listen to her heart beating, to experience the quiet exaltation of a hug. She wanted to rest and sob and laugh while Grandmother held her in the quiet sanctuary of unconditional love. But she found herself unable to articulate any of it, unable to speak or even make a sound. She suddenly felt overwhelmingly hot and nauseous. It felt like the world was spinning, and she just needed to lie down.

"It's time," Grandmother said excitedly.

16

CHAPTER

Paige felt herself drifting off into what she thought was the peaceful respite of sleep. *I just need to rest,* she kept reasoning as she wandered into an aqueous dream. It felt like she was ostensibly witnessing the destruction of the very matter from which she was composed, recognizing some of the bits and pieces of herself as she scattered in every direction. Her mind drifted, anchorless, like a little boat cast away from the shore of a placid pond, coasting alone through the water and transmitting, flawlessly, the reflection of its bright colors against the mirrored surface. As the water ever so gently rippled away from the interference of the boat, it distorted the once perfect reflection, diminishing at once both the art and the artist.

Suddenly, there was another presence. *Grandmother*! She felt her before she could see her or hear her. And then she realized that she herself had sort of materialized again and was sitting with Grandmother in the little boat upon a boundless and introspective sea. It felt like a dream, but one in which she was actively and physically participating. They were surrounded in all directions by blue skies and the soft, lovely light of the afternoon hours, which cast an ethereal essence across the fluffy, white clouds quietly hanging from the astral rafters and then rendered and reimagined exquisitely across the polished surface of the water. Grandmother was divinely beautiful in this light, although she seemed to emanate her own light that shone from within her eyes as they sparkled, each speck seemingly a reflection of a distant galaxy. It felt as though she were truly seeing her for the first time and that she was the most exquisite woman she had ever known.

"Am I... dead? Are you the wizard? Are you... An angel? Are you?" she hesitated, her eyes darting downward. "Are you... god?" she stammered, asking the question with defeat, as though the dreaded proverbial moment had occurred—the moment the televangelist and evangelicals warn about, the warning to all those who might be nonbelievers: If god doesn't exist, what have you wasted in believing? But if god does exist, look at what you have lost in not believing? *Was this… judgement?*

Grandmother's voice broke out into a lovely golden laughter that seemed to fill the entire space, before she looked tenderly in Paige's eyes and said, "No, dear. I am not some ridiculous *god*!" She laughed a bit more before continuing. "But if there were an *all-powerful, all-knowing god*," she said mockingly, "it would most certainly be a female energy. So I'll cut you some slack on that one. You silly humans," she mused and paused to laugh to herself again, "imagining yourselves as gods. You simply lack the complexities necessary for deities! You are not even capable of understanding the full, beautiful majesty that incarnates the mathematics of the universe. Gods would be much more like fungi, my dear. Or hurricanes! But certainly not fleshy little apes. You are a reflection recognizing itself and thinking it is the creative source. Oh, there are so many wonderful versions of life besides *human*." She winked playfully and rubbed her hand softly along Paige's arm before gripping her hand in a tender manner.

Paige couldn't help but feel like this was a misplaced time for humor or playfulness or even sarcasm, but the serenity she sensed from Grandmother radiated throughout her and expanded to form an impression of limpidness, a contentment just to be near her. Grandmother leaned in and whispered into her ear, "Paige. I want you to listen closely." She pulled back and looked deep into Paige's eyes, a very serious look overtaking her gentle face.

"It is important that you understand things, but we cannot linger long here. I know you have many questions, and you must understand that I cannot answer all of those for you. But I can help understand what the right questions are. So, let's not waste any more time, shall we?" Grandmother shifted back on her wooden seat in the boat, reaching up to smoke from her cigar as the sun sparkled and danced on her eyelashes, her head tilted back slightly, eyes closed to further enhance the sensation of the smoke in her mouth, then slowly puffing it out. *When did she start smoking a cigar*, Paige thought, feeling slightly confused. Yet as the warm, ardent sun rays fell on her cheeks, it transported her away from the confusion and incongruities, enveloping her within the sensational warmth of a Mediterranean sun, where the sound of guitars constructed from decomposed melancholy perpetually inspires the poets who weep its absence.

"There are many levels of consciousness," Grandmother began, rapidly enthralling Paige's attention again with the intensity and measure of her voice. "This is where we can meet to speak in the song of dreams, and where you can understand more clearly. When you are not engaged in the original dream, it can be difficult to see it in all its grandness. To see *me*, my child. I am your soul's soul. The Grand Wizard. The Grandmother soul—Yolngu. I am both the original dream and the Dreamer. And *you* are the expression and manifestation of my dreams. The tea I made for you has helped reveal to you the higher level of consciousness necessary to fully appreciate this voyage, so that you may receive information with lucidity, upon which you can then make decisions and act accordingly. To continue the course of your destiny."

Paige wrinkled her eyebrows, feeling hurt and violated. "You… drugged me?"

"I helped you on your journey to return to your essence with the use of ancient human wisdom. Ayahuasca is *not* used lightly." She shifted her chin forward and peered down her nose authoritatively at Paige.

Paige took a death breath and looked around. "Ok. So, we're here in a dream together. You're the grand wizard, the grandmother, the… universe? You're dreaming me, and I'm a dream awakening the idea… that I'm only a dream?"

Paige pinched her eyes shut tightly, trying to think this through. *She had conceptualized these things before, so why was this so hard to grasp? What was making her so resistant to understanding this?* The events unfolding around her were her opportunity to test her scientific theories, to explore fully if her assessments could indeed be laws of the universe, to *be* a physicist—a possibility she had never even entertained, as the odds of probability were so low. But now, a more abundant concept of reality had presented itself, challenging her frail concept of the stalwart reality she had committed to, which she had dedicated her life to, in pursuit of understanding the universe in all its grand complexities. And it occurred to her how futile her attempts had been, how two-dimensionally she had understood things, how much exponentially larger and more complex it all is. How much more intricately connected she is.

"Oh, my darling, your theories *are* brilliant," Grandmother said. "There are many multiverses, as you have extrapolated. I am merely one of possibly infinitely more universes, and there are many levels of consciousness that waft and articulate within the spaces of each, filling the proportions far beyond what you can imagine, even with mathematics. And so, you see, for humankind this is the hardest part. You are often hampered by your innate inability to envision the enormous complexities of both consciousness and existence, given your minuteness and unrefined abilities. Lost in the delight and credulity of your self-professed sagaciousness, the perpetual motion and scientific insight of humanity surrendered valid ancient wisdom for the fulfillment of a more detached knowledge, turning to a quest for the knowledge of what exists within a reflection, not the pursuit of what is casting the reflection. And yet, understanding the complexities of consciousness remains an essential element of human progress, one necessary to continue to propel you onward in your evolution. How do you continue to pursue the knowledge of the universe without ever even considering the limitations of your point of view within that universe, failing to even consider that you are constrained? Humanity must find its way back to the well in which the deep understanding of this is expressed and governed, within which knowledge abounds and expresses the levels of consciousness that once transported and transformed the ancients, bestowing them with a keen awareness of their own existence within the dream, allowing an expansion of reality, allowing for the evolution of the spirit.

"The ancients were not merely observers of the grand dream; they were active participants in it. But the progress of humanity has removed people further from the source, the shamanic structures that had once surrounded the ancient spiritual traditions of consciousness have, at best, been reduced to vague summaries and taught instead as religion to the masses and at its worst, completely destroyed—leaving nothing more than a gospel of superstition and ignorance for those who no longer understand the sophistication of consciousness, lost without the context of the true spiritualist's roadmaps. Thus, in the end, worshipping nothing more than the illusory ruminations of themselves, a fantasy adoring its own inaccurate likeness." Grandmother paused again, puffing her cigar and blowing pillowy ringlets.

"Although… not all is lost for you little meat-sacks. There are still many who understand this essence of spirit that flickers beyond the confines of human structures and the falsity of its hollow religions. It is up to the brilliant scientists like you—those who continue to probe the arrangements of reality and the dimensions of your own existence—to recover this ancient knowledge and use it as an accomplice in your scientific discovery. You can never be lost to your true essence, never removed from the soul, from the source of life that compels you. So, this task is not as difficult as it may seem.

Mingling Bloods

"However, in missing this aspect, man has failed to understand that the multiverses are themselves living entities—they, myself included, *are* the Dreamers. Life is not limited to or delegated differently to an insignificant species on a single tiny planet revolving around an utterly ordinary star within this grand dream, which of course you fundamentally understand. Life is so much more than your little corner. When you see and understand me like this—as a Grandmother or even a comical cosmic Grand Wizard—you instinctively understand that I represent a transfer of the life force across generations of people. But I am not merely a facilitator of mitochondrial DNA, of the elemental knowledge of life, but rather an expression of data passed on from mother to daughter in an endless lineage, an inherited maternal wisdom that encapsulates the essence of life. And yet," she puffed on her cigar, "this is but a small portion of my existence. If you could perceive me in my entirety, you would bear witness to a universe that contains an endless expanse of swirling galaxies, black holes, and nebulae, an unceasingly stunning variety and expression of possibilities. I am all of this simultaneously. You are both of my womb and of my dreams. I am everywhere and everything that you know. I am every part of you, and you are a part of me. You and all that you know and experience are the result of my efforts to manifest in time, substance, and matter. I *am* Life, as it exists within these rules."

Grandmother exhaled dreamy little clouds of smoke, and Paige could suddenly see the horizon begin to change, as though the smoke clouds and the clouds from the sky and the clouds in the reflections were all gathering and forming a curtain of fog on the horizon. Paige could feel the warmth of the sun diminishing as the mist approached them.

17

CHAPTER

"The Dreamers are an expression of infinite possibilities," Grandmother began again, "and the laws that govern me—your universe—do not inevitably govern the others, because their dreams are their own, their laws their own. It is imperative that you understand that multiverses represent infinite possibilities, presenting an elevated likelihood that they may function under different laws of space and time. The possible variations are endless. Additionally, within each world exist many worlds, each with many probabilities, but of course, not all things are possible within each, as there must be laws that govern them accordingly. Occasionally, the dreamers—the multiverses— touch, creating a disturbance in the set realities of both, an opportunity to perceive *their* dreams and *ours*, a sort of cosmic exchange of knowledge, so to speak. The lights you see dancing across the horizon are certainly real, but they are not of *this* reality that you exist within. They are of another Dreamer, complete with its own reality, its own set of rules. Within this disturbance, the laws become distorted in the wake of the disorder, realities mixing and mingling like two great rivers clashing and crashing into one, each carrying its own array of sediment from all the destinations in which the water has passed. Within this blending, the laws and properties that shaped each river get muddled momentarily as the two parts mix and transform the river, creating a new, changed river. Similarly, the result of this mixing and mingling sparks the *birth* of a new Dreamer," she paused and smiled, a sentimental look softening her face. "They are born and then live within the laws that have blended and been rearranged. This happens over decades or sometimes even centuries by your time scale, but on a cosmic scale, this temporary suspension of the laws happens so quickly that some dreamers barely notice.

"The impact of the disturbance nonetheless has consequences because, as you know, *every action has an equal and opposite reaction*, leaving impairments in the fabric of space and time. Eventually, it will heal, and then finally, the exchange between both realities is closed. I guess you could think of these tears like scars left behind on the mother long after giving birth. On a cosmic scale, this process is enabled through the power of dark energy, which leaves behind dark matter (the scar) and distorts time. The dark energy begins to repair the tear by forming what looks like a cobweb, the strands of which slowly expand and grow together until it envelops itself and closes completely. While it remains open, however, the web provides a temporary, maze-like portal between the Dreamers. The wormhole you experienced is the expression of this activity, which, until it heals, provides an open door between the two multiverses. This wormhole just so happened to occur in the high deserts of the Uinta Basin, which is guarded by the dire wolf—a grand virtuoso spirit of nature, and ancient, erudite consciousness, who once lived upon these lands, and now persists within the space to which she is bound, vowing to protect it. But the tear is nearly closed, and what has entered there will soon have three choices: return to their own multiverse, remain in this unknown multiverse once it forms, or travel through to the other multiverse. The latter of the three is the most risky choice because if they cannot make it in time, they will be trapped in the dark matter and consumed by dark energy."

Paige gasped audibly, thinking of her father being trapped. *Consumed. In Darkness.*

"You must not forget, my dear, that the darkness is necessary for the light; they are intrinsically amalgamated, and you cannot extract one from the other. The dark matter you see scattered throughout the universe, my scars, they are the reason that other Dreamers exist, and there is great beauty in that. Dark energy is pure knowledge; it is that which produces dark matter. It only appears so elusive to you because you fail to comprehend knowledge as more than a fleeting thought, still unable to understand that it is a concrete manifestation. Vera Rubin and Alycia Weinberger understood, among others, that *everything is information.* So, to assign arbitrary labels of "good" or "bad" to it only diminishes your insight into the delicate balance upon which all existence teeters. Dark matter and dark energy are responsible for the beauty of what I have become. They are the reason you exist. It fuels my dreams. Dark Energy is necessary for the creative spark of life throughout all dimensions, all worlds, all Dreamers. It is *the* essence, *the* most intrinsic property of continuation, both where the spirit finally rests and where the spirit begins simultaneously. The divine spark, if you must. So, to be consumed by it is merely a return to the beginning."

Mingling Bloods

Paige sat back quietly, trying to think as unfamiliar emotions raged within her that commanded her thoughts to converge on a single point hidden deep within her chest where a swelling pain, borne from her missed chance at motherhood, now rankled.

"You mustn't despair, my dear. We'll get to that." Grandmother sat back and grinned, taking another long drag on her cigar, blowing the smoke into the air, creating an even thicker blanket in the mist. Paige reached out, motioning that she wanted the cigar. Grandmother drew it close to her chest in a protective, yet playful, manner.

"You won't throw it in the water, will you?" Grandmother giggled before she passed it to Paige.

She grabbed it with the tips of her thumb and first finger, holding it like a pencil and drawing it

To her face, inhaling the delightful aroma before slipping her forefinger all the way around it and resting it in the circle of her thumb and finger. *Grandmother certainly dreams in good taste*, she mused as the musky smoke danced around her face like a Spanish bullfighter's cloak—waving brilliantly and fanning a sense of thrill into the crowd, electrifying the matador who smiles when the bull begins to dance sadly, both now fully aware of the death that clings to the dust and floats between them in the arena. Paige smiled at Grandmother with the crude enthusiasm of a spectator and drew slowly on the cigar, content not to be tasked with the weight of emotional sentiments, and puffed out her own smoke ring, filling the mist even more.

"What will happen when you are covered completely in scars and dark matter?" Paige asked, as she stared into the mist swirling around them. She felt as though she could actually *see* the particles floating through the air—not just an imaginary aspect of her mind trying to visualize the profound complexity of a supposed emptiness, like air—she could literally *see* what existed there. As Paige focused more intently to visualize the void, the simple mechanism by which the human brain most readily organizes reality—the convenient, yet clumsy, appeal to define the more general qualities or textures of "air" like warm, humid, or foggy— diminished. By not focusing on the intricate details, which were fundamentally meaningless in a survival context, the interpretation of the imperceptible as simply *empty* permitted a more affable distinction of reality, in which not constantly having to consider how much more lies beyond what is readily perceptible allows for more pressing concerns—such as the likelihood of rain. However, once this awareness has been redeveloped—that air, or the emptiness, is actually filled with billions of particles which are endlessly bumping around—it effectively changes reality itself, at least for the observer. The resulting heightened perception leads to further examinations of that which seems so solid and concrete or empty and vacant, discovering that much of that, too, is quite mutable and intricately complex, partaking in a perpetual dance of energy and motion buzzing around in minute worlds unimaginable to humans. She now understood that this was what Grandmother had tried to tell her in the first dream on the banks of the river.

Grandmother smiled, "I suppose I, too, may someday cease to exist, at least in the manner in which I do now. That is the nature of all things, child. My scars are the testament of my experiences, a collection of knowledge and information, which I pass on every time these events occur. So even if I diminish, my knowledge will continue and perpetuate." Paige looked at her and nodded empathetically. "However, such matters concerning distant futures distract from what you must experience here and now. Your distinct ability to understand the paradox of emptiness, or rather the lack thereof, is essential for the task that lies before you. Where your father has gone is not an easy place to come back from. He is somewhere within the web of the nebula universe, and it is quickly closing in around him. His choices there are the same as all who find themselves there—to return or to stay and risk being consumed. Should you task yourself with his return, you must rely on your knowledge, not your emotions concerning him. This journey will not be easy, and you should know that I will not and cannot directly help you. I am a universe of free will. I cannot interfere in your fate, but I can help you see your life more ostentatiously. I can help you realize which questions you should be asking."

Paige had suspected she would be persuaded to pursue him and had been avoiding it all along. She hardly knew her father—he was little more than a biological contributor to her existence. While she had been obliged to have come this far in seeking the truth behind his disappearance, would she risk everything to go after him and help him get home? Would she risk her own existence to save him from consumption? *And consumption from what? The divine essence of life?* It didn't seem like something he should be afraid of or even pulled away from.

"I can see why you would think that," Grandmother said. "After all, what harm is there if he remains? I am—this universe—a specific articulation of chemistry, beholden to specific laws that govern my matter. Regarding your father's predicament, perhaps it would be easiest to think of it in terms of atomic expression. However, instead of electrons, it is your father who will be held by cosmic superposition. Superposition, with which you are familiar, is the location at which two waves collide, creating a disarticulation—the cessation of expression. Here, within the very nucleus, all cosmic laws are stripped, leaving only two options: To decay or not to decay. *To be or not to be,*" she said with a smile.

"He and his knowledge will be consumed once decay has begun," Grandmother continued, "mingled within the environment of the supermassive black hole that precedes the big bag. Knowledge breaks down to mathematics and enters a state of entanglement, wherein all components of his essence will be inextricably imbued within the new universe and lost to this one. He and all his knowledge will be lost. This is why your unique understanding of the universe is essential to your success.

"However, there is another element that complicates things further, and *that* is why I have brought you here. As you know now, when your father went through the wormhole, so did all his knowledge. Unfortunately, one of his discoveries, known to only himself, was also on his person. It could save humanity and all life on your little planet from the ensuing annihilation that will be caused by global warming. To retrieve him is to retrieve the information that rightfully belongs here and *could* save not only your species, but the entire global ecosystem."

Paige sat there, quietly astonished. This changed everything completely.

"Now… once you are there—should you decide to go, of course," she said, tilting her forehead toward Paige and looking into her eyes intently, "you'll need to keep in mind that there are others who are seeking him and what he holds. Within these disturbances, other beings have also wandered in. They are the dreams of the other Dreamers, and they probe around, exploring the maze, having entered from a similar wormhole on the other side."

The lights!

"Yes, dear, the lights. The lights denote only a single aspect of the many manifestations that can be fashioned by other experts of consciousness from other multiverses, among them are the masters of the dancing lights, the Greys, as they will come to be known to you. It is difficult for you to perceive them as they fully exist, as your eyes lack the developmental configurations necessary. So, they look like little more than greyish, greenish creatures to you in this universe. However, they should *absolutely not* be underestimated. They are experts of exploitation within the effervescent cognizance of the multiverse, awaiting moments like this when the Dreamers collide, where they can manipulate the laws that govern each, stealing wisdom indiscriminately. They wield incredible technologies, far superior to those of mankind, and they are much older and much, much wiser. The dire wolf you met is their equivalent in this universe, devoted to protecting the gateway, the wormhole. However, the Greys no longer serve as protectors but rather as pirates. Their artifices most likely have lured your father there, now lost and wandering aimlessly within the maze of disruption. Upon his decay, the immense knowledge your father possesses concerning the workings of our universe will be released and subsequently consumed by the Greys, fueling their power. So not only does he hold the key to saving all of humanity, but his return would thwart the Grey's in their ceaseless search to consume."

Grandmother sat back, quietly puffing her cigar.

"And so now you see… that is the decision you must make. Will you pursue him to save him? To save humanity? To stop *them*? Or will you even go at all? I cannot guarantee the outcome of this venture, as you must act on your free will alone. You may die either way. And I cannot help you once you enter the dark matter. That is why only you can make this choice, my love."

Paige slumped forward, resting her elbow on her knee, her chin coming to rest on the knuckles of her hand, a comical cosmic expression of "The Thinker" within the dream. *It didn't seem like she had much of a choice,* she thought. The boat was beginning to rock now, and they were completely engulfed in the fog, the waters turning dark beneath them. She peered into the mist, deep in thought and trying to process everything she had just heard. She could see through the fog what looked like trees materializing in the distance, where dark outlines delineated the jagged edges of tall pines against the rocky surface, and the cold, salty water lapped at its shore like an enthusiastic puppy. She could smell the cold, damp air of the ocean, hear the waves beating against the rocks like a warrior beating his chest. Primal. Ancient. Instinctual.

"The time quickly approaches for your resolution, my dear. But first, there are more truths you need to understand."

18

CHAPTER

Through the thickness of the cool fog, the boat bobbed up and down gently in the waves before coming to rest on the rocky shore. Paige looked at Grandmother in a moment of bewilderment. *This was her memory!* Paige suddenly remembered it lucidly—she was about 15 years old when her mother announced that they would be visiting a colleague over the holidays for a Christmas party on Vancouver Island. They traveled to the island and stayed there for a few weeks prior to the party, scheduled to occur just before their departure. The island was a magical place—particularly now that it was shrouded in dreams and the lingering perfume of Ayahuaca—but even then, she had been spellbound by this place. She recalled now distinctly how they had explored with such wonder and contentment through the ancient forests, which were said to be protected by the persistent spirits that resided within the totems around the island, which were perpetually blanketed in fog and moss. It had long been one of her favorite places in the world.

The sea rocked the small boat against the shore, and Grandmother motioned silently for Paige to get out. As she jumped down, the cool rocks below her made a familiar crunching sound. The sea hung in the dark, attractive night air and she breathed it in deeply, letting it slowly fill her lungs—delicately tracing the memories like the bare skin of a long-lost lover, seduced by the mere hint of perfume lingering, abandoning to the urges, inhaling its very essence so that it might mingle with her own, molecules and atoms colliding together in a moment of delightful, hedonistic climax. Her memories here were impregnated with the enchantment and mystery of the island, and she was delighted to find it still whispering in its familiar prose.

Paige could see a path leading into the woods and remembered fondly being here with her mother. Together they had walked down this path, which had been recently cleared and lit by torches, and the air shimmered with the echoes of Paige's "mix" tape from the trip:

Mingling Bloods

Step out the front door like a ghost

Into the fog where no one notices the

Contrast of white on white…

I walk in the air, between the rain,

Through myself and back again

She bathed herself in the melancholy, in the familiar sensations and enchantments of the forest, soaking up its essence as she followed the path, climbing up a steep hill. At the top, the trees burst open to reveal a meadow vivaciously adorned with moonflowers and primordial ferns, elucidated by fireflies pirouetting in the shadows of a large house. The enormous windows were splashed with a radiance reminiscent of an impressionist painting, drenched in the beauty of light—the most delicate and unwavering component of the universe.

Once inside, it was warm and bright and filled with the aromas of food and the laughter and chatter of the guests. They walked through the crowded room, where her mother stopped to talk with a few colleagues here and there. Her mother was not only stunningly beautiful but also a socializer, and people earnestly enjoyed her company. Paige had always been much more reserved, more awkward, less impressed with the social aspects, except for the few times they attended these parties. She loved these occasions and, as they mingled, Paige marveled at the enormous tree in the center of the luxurious cabin. It towered in the large central area, which was sunken, and where the ceiling opened to the second floor. A huge display of windows swept across the whole front of the house, revealing the beautiful trees lining the perimeter, while the central view detailed the magnificent ocean just beyond the cliff on which the house was perched. Even at night, the view was stunning as the moonlight danced across the waves. It was nothing short of a fairy tale.

"You should see the sunsets."

The little voice startled Paige from her dreamy reflections of the ocean.

"But the best part is when you can see the *whales* swimming by!"

Paige looked down at the little girl who was smiling up at her, with a gap in her grin from the recent loss of a baby tooth and the cutest little dimple from her lopsided grin. Paige stared at her, no longer experiencing the memory, but more like a dream of a memory. She tilted her head as she tried to think of what was so familiar about the cherub-like child.

Mingling Bloods

Just then, she glanced up. Across the room, walking towards her on the raised main level was her father! Paige gasped, hands flying up to cover her mouth in a moment of complete surprise. She frantically looked around the room, trying to discern if this was an accurate memory or a fanciful illusion. She watched him, silently, as he smiled and greeted *his* guests, shook hands, and doled out hugs. Then his eyes met her mother's, and he stopped, raptured—as though she had laughed in slow motion and paused in a moment of elysian beauty and elegance—and his expression instantly changed, softening as his eyes welled. Her mother held his stare and smiled with a notably quiet reserve. She nodded to the guest she was speaking with and walked towards him, their eyes still locked. He reached out and grabbed her hand, instantly melting away her stiff pleasantries and bringing a kind and generous smile to her face. They embraced with an affable politeness and started chatting.

Paige was certain she remembered all this. *Had she not realized that she had been to her father's house?* Thinking back, she hadn't really taken any interest in learning much about him until she was about 16, at least 6 months after this trip. She and her mother had a fight, which culminated in her mother accusing her of being "just like your father". She could still feel the ice in her mother's voice when she said it, the somber look in her eyes, how differently she had always said it before then. This time, her mother was not lovingly telling her about their similar qualities; she was accusing her of them. Condemning her for her composition, the 50% of her DNA that was from *him*, which was *like him*. It was no compliment; it was a catalogue of the worst of her.

And yet that was what stung the most—that she had no choice in the matter. *Who would* not *choose to be like her mother?* She needed to know who her father was, who she was, and by proxy what her most terrible qualities must be. He remained elusive and unreachable, and, over the years, she managed to form an idealistic sketch of him, a vague assumption based on his work and his reputation within the scientific community.

The community that was gathered there, that night, at that party. As she scanned the room again, the soft waves of reminiscence washed over her lightly, and she warmly remembered the faces in that room. She looked down again at the little girl, still chattering away, rolled her eyes, and thought, Does *this kid ever shut up?* Returning her attention to her mother and father talking, she imagined now, as she had hundreds of times, how beautifully exquisite their love must have been and how this very moment seemed to verify everything she had constructed.

She saw the little girl dart to the side, where a few steps led to the main level. Paige heard her enthusiastically calling "Daddy!" and was relieved the child had finally left her to return to her parents, wherever they might be. But the room quieted and the air around her stopped moving as her eyes followed the little cherub, her dark curls bouncing, the lights warming her warm mocha skin, the dimples. *Mika! Oh my god, it was Mika. As a child! Surely, she knew her parents! They must have been there that night, too. They must have…*

The wine glass in Paige's hand slipped and thudded softly onto the fur rug at her feet, the red drops splashing across the white fleece, instantly staining it blood red. Her heart stopped beating, her lungs stopped expiring, her entire body suddenly rendered incapable of motion as she watched Mika running, her beautiful, full lips mouthing *"Daddy!"* into the arms of Dr. Maxwell Walsh. Into the arms of *her* father.

19

CHAPTER

Do they have the same father? Paige's head was pounding. She grasped for the wall, for the floor, for anything solid that might bring clarity or solidity to reality. *All this time, this entire journey, she had no idea that Mika was her half sister? That they were both searching for their father! Mika must have known all along. Of course, she knew that fucking bitch! She obviously had been raised by their father here in this magical, damn forest house.* But then she remembered Mika's father had left her mother, had left both of them just like he had left her. Left her mother. Her mother, who had sacrificed their love for his work. She had committed the most remarkable act of love…and he betrayed it! He started another family. Raised another child…rejecting them all in the end.

Paige felt herself falling. The blood red stains of the carpet smeared against her face like a macabre daydream, the cold, hard floor beneath her refusing to offer the comfort she had sought there. She rolled over onto her back, looking up at the soaring ceiling rafters, the enormous wall of windows, the lights flickering in the steely chandeliers—all shaky and unclear to her. In desperation, she closed her eyes, trying to hear the ocean, its ever-persistent motion cultivating a soft hum in her ears. The waves rocked Paige back and forth, and the stars of distant galaxies splashed their light upon the shadowy sea, descending into the dark depths. Paige dove inward and mused casually at the thought of it, *that the star light had traveled so far, for so long, only to end up here, little more than an ornament on the surface of the water on some tiny, insignificant planet. Or even less remarkably, absorbed by the human eye, its beauty diminishing as it slips into the dreams of little fleshy beasts.*

Paige opened her eyes. Soft waves gently caressed her cheek, and the implicit realization emerged that she was now floating aimlessly in the sea. So many things had been revealed to her, but she now felt very uncertain about what that really meant at all. *Was all of this just to save her father? Was any of the risk justifiable to her? Was he even worth saving?*

Then, from within the cool darkness of the water, Paige felt a presence that was small and subtle. She could feel it moving around her, swirling the water and cooing in the quiet, melancholy dialects of lost loves, where dreamers are enchanted by the dreams of their distant reflections. Even without shape or form, Paige knew this essence, what it felt like. Or rather, who. *You are of my womb and of my dreams.* It was her child. Like a breath that had escaped her lungs, no longer a part of her and yet inseparable from her, floating in and out of the air and frolicking in the water, *like a ghost into the fog.* Paige, riddled with guilt and grief, now felt an overwhelming assurance that her child had not diminished into nothingness, that emptiness and nothingness were little more than illusions. Here, within the perpetual consciousness that permeated the multiverse, she could witness what lies beyond the transitions of life and death, where the perception changes. She poignantly felt a sting, a sadness in knowing that she would have to leave here, to leave the sensation of being able to be with *her*, to know *her*. She let herself slip deeper into the water, feeling it wash over her face and embrace her completely, envisioning what her baby would have looked like. She always knew she was a girl, probably with dark curly hair and deep, intensely blue eyes. Paige had seen her in her dreams, and she remembered the way her giggle sounded like a song. Deeper into the water, she could see the curious nature of her daughter's indigo eyes in the darkness and, illuminated by moonlight, watched her tiptoe across the surface of the water above her, her dark hair falling down her back and swaying as she playfully hummed a song. She wanted nothing more than to linger here in the abyss with her…

Then, from within the darkness, a hand reached down towards her face, offering to pull her back to the surface. Paige hesitated, unsure if she wanted to leave, but the warmth and firmness of Mika's hand gripping hers with absolute certainty gave Paige the courage. The cold air stung her face as she burst through the surface, clinging to Mika's hand. *Mika? Her… sister?* She clambered into the small boat, soaked and chilled from the frigid water. Paige looked at Mika, unable to say anything to her, unable to let go of her disappointment in her, unable to see past her betrayal all this time. As Paige turned her back to Mika, she was surprised to see that Andrews was also sitting in the small boat, quietly looking at her rather indifferently. Paige drew her knees into her chest and buried her face in them, shivering.

Grandmother was at the helm, her back to all of them, cloaked by her lengthy, grey hair. With a long paddle, she slowly pushed them onward into the dark mist, humming a tune quietly and lowly.

Paige looked up miserably and noticed the shore, which was now dramatically different from the enchanted wilds of Vancouver Island. These woods were cold and dark, but no less intoxicating and inviting; their very existence suggesting *"an ancient rectitude and vigor of nature"*, as Henry David Thoreau had so elegantly declared. The deciduous varieties had long shed their flamboyant leaves, a process which often enthralled Paige as a child. Upon learning that the leaves actually returned to their true colors with the absence of chlorophyll—embracing, at last, the ostensible beauty which had been hidden within—she liked to imagine that they peacefully accepted their mortality, eagerly plummeting themselves towards the forest floor where they could finally rest tranquilly in their true oneness. She had often wandered these primal lands, obsessed with the paradox of their outward mutability and their inner steadfastness. Looking out at the forest now, she relished in the lingering excitement she once had for spring, how she joyously reveled in the abundance of summer. But her favorite moments with them, with the trees of this forest, were spent in the quiet coldness of wintery afternoons, when the trees stood bare and naked, exposing all the brilliance and magnificence which they no longer cared to hide, an intimacy they willingly shared with neither shame nor conceit.

In the distance, she could hear music as though it were broadcasting through an old-time record player. The same tune Grandmother had been humming. As the music grew louder, she recognized the words of U2:

One love, one blood

One life, you've got to do what you should

One life, with each other

Sisters—

"It's time to return, my loves," Grandmother said softly, as she slowly propelled them into the thick mist again.

20

CHAPTER

Paige could feel the warmth of the sun again as she slowly opened her eyes. She was back in the garden, lying on the bench in the fetal position, the dire wolf still sleeping quietly beside her. She felt momentarily confused. *Did she just have some crazy dream? It all felt so real!* She sat up, rubbed her eyes, and ran her fingers through her hair—realizing it was still wet. Instantly, her mind was flooded with the images Grandmother had shown her and all the things she had told her. It was so much to comprehend, but she found herself struggling less with the scientific aspects and more with the emotional. Mika, whom she had come to like, had betrayed her. Her father had betrayed both her and her mother. And now Paige is tasked with saving *him* while *she* helps her!

She knew she was ill-equipped to deal with the emotions she could feel swelling and rising within her—anger, hurt, deception—and had little desire to continue this expedition at all.

"Paige?" She looked up to see Detective Andrews walking towards her from the house. He looked tired and disheveled, but certainly no less handsome. Paige tried to veil the foulness that was growing within her, threatening both her self-control and basic civility, as she silently glanced over her shoulder at him.

"Paige, would you like to come inside? You should rest. Maybe even eat something. We've all been through a lot," Andrews said, the softness of his voice imbuing the quality of Thoreau's forest—naked, bare, hiding nothing.

But Paige was seething. "I have no desire to dine with Mika. She has betrayed my trust. She has lied to me this entire time!"

"Listen, Paige, I really think maybe you should rest. Like I said, we've all been through a lot. You need to take time to let it all sink in and make sense. You're experiencing shock, which also incorporates denial. You shouldn't make any wild accusations until you've had time to rest and recover," Andrews replied, his voice tinged with genuine concern.

"Wild accusations?" Paige practically screamed. She could feel herself slipping into a chasm of uncontrollable feelings, clawing towards rationalism yet slipping further and further into obscurity.

"Ok, I'm sorry. That came out wrong. Can you just come sit and relax for a bit?" Andrews held out his hand affectionately, his eyes red from fatigue that had failed to still his kaleidoscope eyes.

"No, I think I need to go home. I need to get out of this place. I don't even know what I was thinking coming here. Going on this stupid journey, or Quest, or whatever. I… I just need to leave." Tears welled in her eyes, and her throat felt so dry she could hardly swallow. Andrews gently grabbed her hand, attempting to lead her into the house. She furiously tore her hand away from him and turned away.

"Paige. I know you are hurt and confused right now. But you need to really think about what you're doing. First off, you're just going to leave? It took us two days to climb this mountain and three more days driving just to get here. Where the hell are you going to go right now?"

She looked up at him, his face unusually pale and weary. She had never heard him sound so agitated before, even the night of the wormhole with Prof. Greene.

"And as for Mika… Paige," he continued, "I think you need to give her the opportunity to explain why she was misleading you about her identity. I don't know why she chose to do that, but neither do you. And I think you owe her that."

"I owe her? Are you fucking kidding me? *I owe her*? What the hell do I owe her, the child my father *didn't* abandon?" Paige was sobbing as she spat the words out, hearing them clink on the ground as they fell in the space between them, like a grenade rolling across the floor just before it detonates.

She stared at Andrews, bracing herself for the impact. But the agitation in his voice was not kin to the anger which was erupting from her. Andrews' face softened and his shoulders lowered, conveying his refusal to brace himself in kind, and he let out a long, slow breath.

"Because she saved you, Paige. Mika saved you. You were drowning in your own remorse and guilt, sinking into the dark waters where you would have lingered for eons, sentenced to an existence shackled by your melancholy and contriteness. *She* saved you from that. She chose love despite your desire to rebuke her for her actions," Andrews said softly. He took a long, steady look at Paige before adding, "And let's not forget that you lied to her, too." Then he simply turned and walked back towards the house, leaving her alone in the stench of her rancor.

She thought back to the final moments before their return, when she was floating in the water with the spirit of her child. She remembered feelings of happiness, not despair. She closed her eyes to reimagine the closeness she felt, the oneness, and suddenly found herself becoming overwhelmed at the darkness that lay beneath it. It pulled at her again and again, harder this time, dragging her down in the cold depths. She couldn't breathe.

The pressure of the water became increasingly terrifying. Her heart was beating wildly. She wanted to escape, but she couldn't. She wanted to open her eyes, but she couldn't.

21

CHAPTER

"Paige! Can you hear me? Paige…" Paige slowly opened her eyes, fighting against the weight that bore down upon them. Gasping for breath, she found herself being held in Mika's arms.

"Paige! Are you ok! I thought we lost you. Can you say something, please?" Mika's beautiful face was looking at Paige, her hand gently caressing her cheek, while her head was cradled in her arm and resting on Mika's legs. Paige tried to get up, but her body was so weak she could barely budge.

"No, no. Just rest for a minute. Ok? I've got you. You're not getting rid of us this easily."

Mika grinned, her amber eyes tired but bright, the delicate freckles across her nose gloriously highlighted from where tears had blazed fortuitously across her cheeks. Paige tried to laugh, but she was so weak it sounded more like a pitiful sigh.

"We need to get you inside where you can rest comfortably, ok?" Mika said as she smiled broadly now, her little dimple sashaying and flamboyant.

She and Andrews helped Paige get up and carried her between them into the adobe house. The earthen walls and wooden beams generated such warmth, which was only further invigorated by the bold colors of the southwestern décor, none of which reeked with the extravagance or narcissism of her father's house.

The warmth that emanated here seemed so genuine, so intentional in nature. Near the kiva where they had first found Grandmother, they helped her lie down on a padded bench under a window, opposite Grandmother's rocking chair. From the window, the garden could still be found vibrantly bustling, and beyond that, the bluish-grey outlines of distant mesas stood defiantly against the immensity of the sky, which was now sculpted in an extraordinary array of pinks and purples that were amalgamated with oranges, yellows, and reds. It was breathtaking. Paige turned toward the window and curled her knees up as she sat back against the warm wall near the fireplace and rested her head back. She was utterly and completely exhausted, but she was afraid to even close her eyes now for fear of being pulled into the darkness again. As she watched the atmosphere acquiesce to the nitrogen and oxygen particles that lingered in the solstice sky, Mika walked over to her with a cup of hot tea.

Paige held the cup with both hands close to her chest for warmth, and Mika sat on the bench next to her. "I'm sorry this has all been so upsetting," Mika began, "and I know that I played a part in it." She reached over and placed her hand on Paige's knee affectionately. "I need you to know that I am sorry, Paige. It was never my intention to hurt you. Love all, trust few, do wrong to none. I should have been honest from the beginning." Mika held a blanket out for her and smiled, "Now, get some rest, and we can discuss things in the morning."

Paige smiled back wearily and nodded. She sipped her tea, feeling its warmth permeate her torso, and she returned her gaze to the final moments of the spectacular sunset. As Mika quietly stepped away, Paige felt her eyes grow heavy and her body sink down into the window seat. She watched with childish wonder at the moment of the green sunset flash, and then closed her eyes.

22

CHAPTER

Paige awoke to the afternoon sun flooding through the window and resting tenderly on her face. She sat up dazed and still feeling tired, the heavy weight of exhaustion still pressing on her shoulders. The smell of food slinked towards her from the kitchen, seducing her from her lethargy and beckoning her towards the kitchen area where she could hear Mika and Andrews chatting. She stretched a bit and then wandered over to the table where they were sitting.

"Well, good afternoon, sis!" Mika exclaimed chirpily.

"Afternoon?" Paige asked, rubbing her eyes and feeling disoriented.

"It's ok. We haven't been up that long yet either." Mika smiled at Det. Andrews, in her charming and playful manner, caused Paige to squint her eyes at her, suspicious of the relationship that might be forming between them. Paige felt a slight twinge of jealousy in her gut as she looked her sister up and down. Her Sister. It felt odd to now think of Mika like that.

"Speak for yourself," Detective Andrews interjected, smiling at both of them. "I've been up for a while now. The floor by the fireplace isn't very comfortable. Hard to sleep past noon there," he added with a laugh.

With that, he got up from the table and walked over to the stove, where a pot simmered. As he lifted the lid, the aroma within burst to life and permeated the atmosphere of the small room. Paige watched him attentively, finding it hard not to be beguiled by his bewitching backside every time he brandished it in her presence.

"Why, Andrews, that smells absolutely incredible! What did you make?" Mika asked, her face shining brightly as always, like a soap opera character.

Portuguese soup. My Vovo used to make it for me. It's the ultimate comfort food. Nourishes you to the bone and right through to the soul," he said over his shoulder as he stirred and sipped to taste it, mumbling quietly to himself, "needs more salt."

"Portuguese soup!" Paige exclaimed. "Please tell me it has chouriço."

"Of course," he responded enthusiastically.

"Ugh! My mouth is watering already! My mom and I used to travel south from Boston to Providence, Rhode Island, to see family friends near Newport. We would always stop in this old textile town near there that had been settled by wealthy French merchants and Portuguese immigrants. I can't remember the name now.

But we literally went just for the food. She always says that the food of the working man is the soul of all culture, a quintessential expression of identity." She paused for a moment, smiling to herself and reminiscing about the aroma and satisfying memories of her many escapades with her mother.

Mika arched an eyebrow and looked at Detective Andrews.

"Fall River. Or New Bedford," Andrews said, smiling at Mika before continuing. "Both have a high Portuguese immigrant population. Prior to colonialism and genocide, the area was the home of the Pokanoket Wampanoag nation. Later, members of the Plymouth colony established Freetown there, and eventually it became Fall River. The Irish and French Canadians immigrated there for textile work. But it was whaling that first brought the Portuguese, whose ships would stop in the Azores for supplies and to recruit young men to leave as sailors and whalers."

"Yes, Fall River! So you know it?" she asked.

"Yes, I was born there," he said, laughing.

"Oh my god, I had no idea you were from New England, too! I grew up in Concord, Mass!" Paige exclaimed, wondering sincerely if she should have picked up on this sooner.

"Oh, yes. Concord is beautiful! My family immigrated to the States from the Azores Islands in the 1950s when my mother was just a small child. Fall River is still a hub for the Portuguese from the Azores. But your mother is absolutely right, our food alone is worth a side trip for," he said with a smile, sampling the soup from a spoon.

"How did you have everything to make it?" Paige asked, as she evoked memories of the dark red sausages, the kale, and the potatoes that comprised the pious but divine dish.

"Yeah, I don't know if you noticed, but we're in a magical adobe home on top of an enormous mesa where we tripped on Ayahuasca and met the spirit of the universe," he said with an exaggerated lack of breath and a laugh. "It was all just here for us. Maybe I dreamt about it last night. I don't know, Doc." He shrugged and turned back to his pot.

"I didn't dream at all last night," Mika said. "And I always dream."

"Yeah, I didn't either," Paige said, wondering if it was just the exhaustion.

"Hey, maybe just having Portuguese soup with two lovely ladies is the dream," Andrews suggested in good humor while setting down steaming bowls of goodness in front of them before getting one for himself.

"When I woke, I cried to dream again," Mika quoted theatrically.

"Do you ever stop quoting Shakespeare?" Paige said sarcastically, shaking her head and rolling her eyes, noticing that her foul temper from yesterday hadn't faded much.

"It's my jam," Mika said, as she shrugged it off and laughed before adding, "Shakespeare knows everything there is to know about life."

Following some simple pleasantries, the three enjoyed their dinner quietly before cleaning up. Paige and Mika both sat back down at the table across from each other again, the silence growing more awkward.

"Well, I'm going to give you two ladies some space," Andrews said as he wiped his hands on his apron, which was pleasantly too tight on him. They both smiled and nodded as he walked out the front door to the garden, a book tucked under an arm and a whiskey highball in his hand.

The ladies quietly watched him shut the door before turning to each other in silence. Paige hated these moments, the moments in which she was expected to be emotionally engaged but not too emotional. It never came easily for her.

"Let me begin, please," Mika said softly but firmly. "When our father arranged for us to become travel companions, I did not know we were sisters. Had I known all these years, I would have desperately tried to find you—as an only child, I always wanted a sibling.

So, when he called about a week before our trip to tell me the news, you can imagine my excitement! You'd think that, in revealing this to me, he would have understood that he had some 'splaining to do," Mika said with a wink and a giggle.

Paige continued to look at her with smug indifference.

Mika cleared her throat quietly and continued, "But honestly, I'm not sure he even thought it through much before telling me. I was shocked, confused, excited, and angry. He acted like he hadn't quite expected that." Mika laughed and looked ingenuously at Paige.

"After my reaction and flood of emotions, he hesitated and refused to tell me anymore, insisting that our reunion would be better if we both learned of everything at the same time. So, he asked me not to tell you. Then he disappeared, and I just didn't know how to tell you at that point. Of course, I had no idea that we would end up on some crazy trip like this."

"So, you still don't know the whole story?" Paige said barely louder than a whisper.

"No, but when we can get cell service again, I plan on calling my mom. Hopefully, she can help us put some things together. When dad disappeared, his research did, too. It's imperative that we at least understand the context of his work if we cannot retrieve it. Or him." Mika looked down, her voice and expressions always conveyed such confidence and serenity that when mannerisms like this betrayed her, it seemed out of character.

"Ok. I'll call my mother, too, although I'm not sure how much she can help. My parents have been separated for decades." Paige said.

"I want you to know something about our father, Paige," Mika began. "It's true I knew and lived with him, an opportunity you were denied. But you seem to think that was a benefit to me and a disadvantage to you. I can tell you, he's a difficult man to know. His emotions are elusive, his attention fleeting, his participation nonexistent. We moved to Vancouver when I was about three, and while he lived there with us, his presence was sporadic at best.

Eventually, when I was about 10, he moved out of the house to be with someone else. I later found out that she was just one of many, that my mother had just finally had enough of the infidelities and the prolonged absences. I guess she just finally realized it made no difference whether he was there or not. He would come and go, always stating that it was his work. And it usually was, but it was also his opportunity to do as he pleased without the constraints of marriage and parenthood.

The woman he left my mother for has also long been left behind, but my father is still the same man. Incapable of experiencing true love, incapable of devoting himself to anyone but himself, because no one is ever enough for him. It's difficult to deal with men such as our father. I think your mother protected you from him. And maybe you should be grateful for it."

Paige wrinkled her brow and tilted her head for a snarky side glance.

"Nonetheless, being the biological subject of a narcissistic and careless father," Mika continued, a steady look in her eye, "I found myself faced with two options. The first would be to allow his negligent manners to corrupt my own self-worth, making me one of those girls. You know, the ones with all the daddy issues, constantly searching for approval from men.

Subjecting myself to the same agony and ridiculous expectations that a selfish man had levied on me. Or I could reject the burden and embrace life in a way that he never could. The ultimate revenge, right—still living a happy and fulfilling life despite his efforts otherwise? I could live a life devoted to fully loving, to truly living on my own terms. I refuse to allow that man, or any man, to classify and categorize me. I don't live in anger; I live in love. I can recognize that our father is a deeply flawed man, but I can also love him despite that. And if I can do that, I mean really do that, then I can find a way to love everyone with the same measure of grace. Including and especially myself."

Paige looked at her, unsure of what her response should be. Sometimes listening to Mika was like hearing a favorite song come on the radio, one you shush people over and turn up to hear because it reminds you of something deep and unarticulated within, something that desires expression and needs to be liberated.

"But," Mika continued with a smile, "I think your mother misunderstood that you share this instinctively obtuse characteristic with our father."

Paige shifted her posture and scowled at Mika.

"I'm not saying you're a chronic cheating dog, sis. I'm saying you simply lack access to your emotions, and when you do finally realize that you have some, they become so overwhelming to you that you have no idea how to deal with them. You don't do little cries, do you, Paige?" she said with a playful smile. "It doesn't make you a bad person; it's just how you are. But I think your mother protected you because she thought that was your greatest weakness."

"Mika!" Paige slapped her hand down on the table in a moment of both defeat and anger. She was done listening to Mika if this was going to turn into a lecture from her mother!

"Paige," Mika said with a laugh, "I'm not criticizing you. It's simply an honest evaluation of who both you and Dad are. I'm not saying it's a weakness. It's a tremendous advantage to people who are as smart as you two. To just focus on your work and not be burdened by the entanglements of life."

Paige quietly looked sideways at her, simultaneously furious and also feeling like Mika completely understood who she was. Paige had always felt like she had to construct emotions around things that she should feel, or act upset about, things that just generally never mattered to her. She looked at Mika, slightly perplexed, slightly offended, and slightly impressed. Someone had finally recognized her. Acknowledged her. And said it was ok.

Paige let out a long sigh and said, "I'm sorry I wasn't honest with you about the pregnancy. I know it seems like such a creepy thing to do—to pretend you're pregnant when you're not. I just didn't really mean to tell you about it in the first place. And then you were so excited. Of course, I didn't know then that you were excited to become an aunt. But I mistook your enthusiasm for naivety. I didn't think you'd understand it even if I told you about it. Mika... I... I've been such an asshole to you. And you didn't deserve that. I'm sorry."

"To mingle friendship far is mingling bloods," Mika said, her dazzling amber eyes ablaze. "I was your friend before I was your sister, and I think we should try to keep it that way."

23

CHAPTER

Detective Andrews came through the door carrying their packs. "It's getting late in the day, so I think we should just pack up tonight, and then we'll be ready for an early start tomorrow."

The three spent the rest of the night packing, listening to Mika idly chatting on and on, divulging her bits of Shakespearean wisdom, and resting by the warmth of the fire. Paige felt uneasy, like there was still more to be said with Mika. Additionally, the elephant in the room sat undisturbed while they tiptoed around it; none of them talked about what should be done next. Saving the girls' father was now a pressing issue, one which no one seemed to have committed to yet. However, saving him meant helping to save the planet from global disaster, so saying no seemed like an impossible choice. The weight of not really having a choice fell heavily upon them, even as they set off to embark down the mountain the next morning.

They quietly descended, relieved that they were going downhill this time, and stopped at the large herradura to refill their water and rest.

"What do you guys think?" Detective Andrews asked, "Should we stay here tonight or try to get further down to the first one?"

"I'm fine with staying here," Mika replied, Paige nodding her head in agreement. "It'll be much more comfortable than the smaller one."

"Ok," Andrews said, tossing his pack down. "I'm going to get some wood."

As he walked off, Paige looked at Mika and said, "What are we doing after we get off this mountain?"

"Well, I thought that maybe we needed to talk to our moms, to see if they could help us figure this out. But I'm not sure their involvement will be helpful. I'm not sure what more we can learn about the past that will help us with our present dilemma," Mika replied.

"Yes, I agree. I'm not sure either. But then what are we going to do? I mean… we have to go after him. Right? So, should we… You know, develop a plan or something?"

"Yes, I suppose we should," Mika said with a giggle. "I think perhaps we should speak with Percy again. I'm hoping he can shed some light on things, maybe guide us, or tell us what to expect?"

Paige nodded her head, thinking through their next steps. "I think we should ask Andrews to go home," she said, almost surprising herself.

"Wait, what? Why? He's come all this way with us. Do you not trust him?"

"No"

"You don't trust me, Doc," Andrews said, standing near the entrance of the cave, arms full of firewood, genuinely insulted.

"No! That's not what I was saying at all," Paige said, sounding exasperated. "It's not because I don't trust you, Andrews. It's because… It's because it's a risk you needn't take. Mika and I are his daughters, but there's no reason for you to further endanger your own life for ours."

"Well, that's kind of you, Paige. But I think we all need more information before making any decisions about going into the wormhole," Andrews said in a serious tone, flashing Paige a smoldering look that made her skin tingle. "I want to stay here. And I think I can be quite helpful to you both."

"Yes, I totally agree. I think we should start with Percy," Mika chimed, her cheerful voice sprinkling like raindrops across the cave.

Andrews squinted his eyes at the suggestion, making no effort to hide his obvious mistrust of the professor. It was somewhat uncomfortable for Mika and Paige, who both had a deeply affectionate relationship with him, leaving Paige increasingly questioning Andrew's unveiled mistrust of him.

The following day, they finished the descent and returned to the base camp. They were hoping to be able to get cell phone reception there, but it was too irregular for the calls to go through. Finally, the next day, near the little café in Ballard, they could get a single bar of cell reception. Quickly, they all split up to make separate calls, Paige deciding to call her mother, despite her uncertainties. She had spent most of her descent trying to decide exactly how much she wanted to tell her. While she knew how crazy it would all sound to her, she wanted her mother to have some sort of idea about what was happening—just in case things did not turn out well.

As the phone rang, she still didn't know exactly what she was going to say; she just knew, in that moment, how desperately she needed to hear her mother's voice.

"Hello, darling," Isle said, her accent softened by the gentle nature of her voice.

"Mom!" Paige said, her voice shaking as a lump formed in her throat. "Mom, do you have time to talk?"

"Of course, love. I've been so worried about you. I… I haven't heard anything for days. Have you found out anything about your father's disappearance? How are you holding up?"

Paige took a deep breath, "I'm fine. But mom…there are some things I need to know…"

The line was quiet for a moment. "Ok, Paige. What do you need to know?"

"Mom, you knew about my sister, Mika, didn't you? Why did you hide that from me? I feel like I've been lied to my entire life." Paige said, her voice increasing in volume and trembling on her final words. Lied to my entire life.

She was met with a long silence again before her mother began, "Paige, I'm sorry this is how you learned all this. I've thought about this conversation a million times. I've tried to start it a hundred times. And yet I never know where to begin, I never knew if it… Oh Munchkin. I was always so worried you wouldn't deal with it well. But much of this is my fault. My fault for not trusting that… that you could. Paige…" Ilse whispered. She hadn't called her Munchkin since she was a child, the thought of which brought tears to her eyes.

"Mom," Paige said with a hint of irritation, "I thought you and Dad were…ugh! I thought he was the love of your life! I thought it was this incredibly beautiful love affair that transcended time and distance? I've spent my whole life thinking this. Why would you lie to me about that?"

"Paige, that's not fair!" Isle's voice hardened, her Dutch inflections sharpening. "I thought that, too. For a very long time, in fact. I am not proud of how naive I was to your father's…" she paused, inhaling deeply, "to who he really was. And you should understand that he was and still is the love of my life. Perhaps I am just a hopeless romantic, but what we had was incredibly beautiful. To me, at least. I will never love like that again. However, it took me a long time to see that it was just me who felt the profound depth of our love. I had no idea your father had another lover or another child! Not until the winter we vacationed on Vancouver Island. He invited us there and said that he had something special for us. A house. An opportunity to be together."

"What?" Paige asked, feeling the blood rush to her cheeks.

"It was a complete surprise to me, too, darling. He… he wanted us to live there. On the island. With them. Like a harem or something. My shock, disappointment, and disgust were just overwhelming. I know I should have told you. But he broke my heart. I couldn't let him break yours, too. I… oh Paige… I never want you to feel the sadness and rejection that I felt at that moment. It destroys me still. I loved him more than he could ever love me… I… I am sorry, Paige. I know now that trying to protect you has only made things worse for you."

Paige felt the anger from a few days ago returning to her. This was her mother's explanation and apology?

"Yeah. Ok, mom. I gotta go now. I'll talk to you later, ok?"

"No, Paige!" She hung up the phone.

Still looking at the phone, she saw her mother's face light up the screen. She was calling her back. Paige held down the button to turn her phone off. She stared at the black screen and closed her eyes just as a tear splattered across it. She stepped back against the wall of the diner behind her and slowly slid down it until she sat on the ground, tears quietly streaming down her face.

Looking out at the vast landscape, the red earth stark against the intensely sapphire sky that was as tangible and acute as her mother's heartbreak, she realized then that her mother hadn't lied to her nearly as much as she had lied to herself. She had always thought of her mom as such a strong and determined woman, but now all she could see was weakness and betrayal. Her mother hadn't protected her; she protected herself. Weakness and betrayal.

24

CHAPTER

After Paige ended the call with her mother, she went inside the small café and ordered a cup of coffee, reluctant to imagine that it would be so good again. She had noticed Mika was still on the phone outside when she entered, so she sat at the end of the bar where she had the first time. The server set the coffee in front of her, the aroma commanding her attention. She sipped it, tentatively hopeful, and found herself delighted by the extraordinary excellence of it again, rejoicing in the pleasure of at least having a great cup of coffee.

"Hey," Paige said, glancing up slightly as Mika walked through the door and towards her.

"Hey, girl. Did you talk to your mom?"

Paige nodded. "Did you?"

"Yeah, but I didn't tell her… everything. Ya know?"

"Me neither. I'm just not sure it would have been constructive in any way. They would just worry more about us, even without the destiny of humanity resting on our shoulders," Paige laughed dryly. "Did you get a hold of Percy?"

"No," Mika said, a look of concern coming over her face. "I… I couldn't get a hold of him."

"What's wrong, Mika?"

"I… I don't know. I guess I'm just worried. All this has been so crazy, it feels like I haven't had time to think."

"I know exactly how you feel," Paige said. "It feels… crushing, I guess."

Just then, Detective Andrews walked through the door to join them. Paige could feel the warming sensation of the coffee beginning to feel more like a tingle as she watched him cross the room.

"Well, ladies. Are we ready to return to base camp and jump into a wormhole?" Andrews said with a smile as he held his hand out towards Paige to help her from the barstool. She blushed and looked down at her coffee before gulping the rest of it down.

On the way back to base camp, they noticed another partially dissected cow on the side of the road near the ranch house. Paige couldn't help but feel a twinge in her gut looking at the poor thing, thinking of the entities they would be meeting who engaged in these lurid activities, creatures they knew nothing about except that they were from another universe. Lost in her thoughts, she was startled when she realized they had come to a stop and the dire wolf was standing in front of them at the base camp.

The silence within the car was broken when Mika opened her door and stepped out. Paige gasped as she reached back towards her, but she was already out of the car and walking towards the wolf, its eyes fixed intently on her. Mika walked up to the massive beast, looking up into its golden, watchful eyes, and slowly reached her hand out. It sniffed her hand casually, almost dismissively.

Although they had met the skinwalker before, she remained an intimidating and unpredictable creature to them. Paige felt her heart pounding irrepressibly as Mika reached her hand to the wolf's thick, furry mane and ran her fingers through the stiff hair. Then she slowly tilted her head towards it, touching her forehead to it, and both closed their eyes.

"Holy shit," Paige whispered, looking at Andrews.

"She's the key," he said quietly, not taking his eyes off the two of them.

"Mika?"

"No. The direwolf. She is the key to all this. I can't believe I missed it," Detective Andrews said as the two stood perfectly still before them.

Mika lifted her head, smiling, and the wolf took a few steps back before turning and trotting off towards the creek, where it turned and looked at her again before disappearing into the brush. She turned back towards the car, still smiling broadly, and ran over to them. She pulled open Paige's door and exclaimed, "She's the key!"

"That's what I just said," Andrews said, laughing and throwing his hands up playfully.

"Oh, I'm not surprised at all that you figured that out, Mr. Andrews," Mika said, winking at him. "Now come on! We have work to do before she returns tonight."

"She's coming back? The skinwalker wolf thing?" Paige asked nervously.

"Sunka. They call her Sunka. Yes, she's returning tonight. Now c'mon," she jogged towards the main tent in the center of camp. Once inside, Paige and Detective Andrews found her setting up and turning on several laptops spread out across the tables.

"She's coming back to speak with us, but we need to do our homework in the meantime. Paige, we need your brilliant sciencey mind to research and set up an experiment tonight. I need you to have a clear understanding of how the wormhole affects gravity, space, time, and matter. We know it's possible to get in and … hopefully… out, but not without knowing how to apply the physics."

She rushed back and forth excitedly, twisting her delicate, full lips as she set up the computers. "Mr. Andrews, your anthropology background is necessary in understanding the skwinwalkers, evidence of astral manipulation, and how we can use that to operate it for ourselves. I'm going to use academic sources to cross-reference literary evidence with archeological evidence to see what clues I can discover about our friends, The Greys."

"Oh, so you're just going to binge-watch Ancient Aliens?" Andrews teased while sitting down at one of the computers, arousing a laugh from both ladies as Mika sat down.

"Paige, sit. We have work to do," she said, with only a slight hint of humor this time.

"I think best when I can move. Are you going to be this distracting the entire time?" She glanced over her shoulder at her as she paced towards the back of the tent, arms crossed.

"Ok then," Mika said, making exaggerated eye contact with Det. Andrews, smiling at him coquettishly, then focused on her screen. The three worked quietly throughout the afternoon. Mika broke the silence with music and small exclamations, finding the quiet more disturbing than the silence. As the afternoon sun broke through the door frame, the raucous amber light of afternoon clambered into the room, noisily announcing its arrival, and they all glanced up from their work.

"Is anyone hungry?" Mika asked, stretching her arms and looking over at Paige, holding a pencil in her mouth.

"Ugh, yes!" Paige replied, tossing the pencil on the table. "I definitely need a break right now. What do we have to eat around here?"

"There should still be some MREs in the supply tent. I saw some canned soups and stuff like that, too," Andrews said, stretching his neck side to side and arching his back. The warm light frolicking across the room cast his skin in a beautiful, golden-brown tone, a hint of his Azorean heritage, and Paige couldn't help but feel enticed by it. She watched the colors dancing in his hazel eyes like shimmering prisms, and she felt like she remembered being there, in her dreams, wrapped in a kaleidoscope spectacle of light dancing with color.

"Paige," Mika said, breaking her trance. She shifted her weight to move her head into Paige's gaze, with her back towards Detective Andrews, and made a face that clearly said, "Get your shit together, girl…You look crazy!"

"Let's go see what we can find in the supply tent, Paige," Mika said in her easy and infectiously pleasant way.

"Right. Yes. Let's see what there is," Paige said, tearing her gaze from Andrews and rubbing her eyes, hoping what she had just witnessed was only a mirage.

They rummaged through the pantry, welcoming the canned soups over the MREs.

"Do you know what to expect tonight?" Paige asked, looking sideways at Mika while she piled a few cans in her arms. "From the skinwalker, I mean. Sooka."

"Sunka. Not, no really. Talking to her wasn't like talking to grandmother. It's more like being able to just hear her over a walkie-talkie rather than being immersed in a full technicolor dream with surround sound," Mika said, turning over a can in her hand to read the label. "But I expect it will be quite the visit!" Mika smiled at her with unpretentious enthusiasm. "Did you get much figured out about what you think the wormhole is?"

"Well, yes. And no. I'm going to test some theories tonight when it opens back up. Then I will know more, I can research based on that evidence," Paige said.

"Good! I'm hoping Sunka will shed some light on navigation once we're inside, but I've found what I believe may be a partial fragment of an ancient guide or map. I worry that I may interpret it incorrectly, though. So, I'm really hoping she can answer some of those questions."

"Yes, the more we can verify, the better off we'll be. How long do you think we'll need to prepare for it? A couple of weeks?"

Mika shrugged and turned to look at something on the shelf before saying, "Maybe."

Paige didn't know what an appropriate timeline might be; her entire base of knowledge was purely theoretical until now, and even though she had dedicated her life to the belief in those theories, she worried that in the end, they were only just that—theories.

"But," Mika said, turning to look at Paige now, "I think we need Andrews there."

Paige shook her head, "No, I just…I can't know for certain that he will survive."

"Paige. Paige, look at me," Mika said, smiling. "You two have a connection. Don't tell me you don't see it. Shit, Paige, I can feel it! Can't you?"

"Mika, stop. I know you're attracted to him. I wouldn't be surprised if you're not already sleeping with him. But it's ok…" Paige shrugged and turned, pretending to look at something on the shelf.

Mika laughed softly and grabbed Paige by the hand. "Bold of you to assume I'm hetero cis," she said reflexively. "Girl, of course I find him attractive, who wouldn't?" Her bright eyes scanned Paige's face, looking for the moment she would realize the obvious. "Oh sis, I'm not interested in being with him, although… again, who wouldn't be… I know there's something between you two. Love goes towards love!" She stooped lower to catch Paige's glare and smiled. "Plus, he's like… so old."

Paige forced a laugh, but her mistrust of Mika was growing again.

25

CHAPTER

Paige stepped out of the tent to take in the sunset across the valley, awed by the watercolor tapestry unfolding before her. She still felt so uncertain about everything, but the desert skies pacified her, as though they were whispering in a language she couldn't understand but was compelled to listen to nonetheless. She watched the sky slowly changing as the sun sank below the horizon, waiting again for the green flash, the optical illusion that keeps the sunset hunters contented for days. And then it occurred to her—the illusion! What if the "opening" of the wormhole is only an illusion, a green flash? What if it's been there all along, it just wasn't illuminated?

Paige started to walk towards the wormhole, but felt the weight of a hand on her shoulder unexpectedly. Startled, she turned to see Andrews standing behind her, a perversely serious look on his face.

"Paige," he said softly, "She's here."

Paige felt a pang of uncertainty, but quietly followed Detective Andrews back inside the tent, looking over her shoulder towards the wormhole before entering. There, standing near the fire, she saw Mika and a tall, statuesque Indigenous woman who looked to be in her early-to-mid 40s. Paige was surprised not only to see the woman, having expected the dire wolf, but at her overall countenance. Long, dark hair spilled down her back, much like Grandmother's, but the well-tailored power suit, the 3-inch stilettos, and the briefcase she clutched in front of her certainly conveyed something different entirely. She was poised, confident, and stunningly beautiful.

"I'm so glad you could join us, Dr. Paige Jansen," the woman said. Although she looked like a lawyer about to deliver her closing arguments, her deep, raspy voice conveyed an altruism more like that of a Jazz singer.

"Sun-ka? Am I saying that right?" Paige stood frozen in the doorway, still slightly shocked.

Mingling Bloods

"It's pronounced Shoon-kah. The Algonquin-rooted languages have a very delicate quality, which can be difficult for native speakers of more unsophisticated and guttural languages, like English, to imitate." She smiled vividly and gestured towards the table nearest the fire. "Please, sit."

Paige looked at Andrews, feeling insulted, and desperately needing some small measure of reassurance. His eyes flickered in the transitioning light, and a small grin crept across his face. He pressed his hand against her back, sending shivers along her spine and into her groin, and smiled gently at her as he said, "Come on, Doc."

Paige and Detective Andrews walked over to the table, the woman watching them as intently as the dire wolf had.

"Thank you. Now, let's just get right to it, shall we? As you know, I am The Guardian. In ancient traditions, I am known as a Skin Walker, a shape shifter. To the Navajo peoples of these lands, I am known as yee naaldlooshii (nad lo-she)—by means of it, it goes on all fours. To those who know and understand the ancient ways, who know I stand guard—I am known as Sunka. And long, long ago, I was known as Macha, Daughter of the Evening Star. You may refer to me as you like. I no longer concern myself with the arbitrary and tedious names chosen for me. Long ago, I chose my own name." She looked at Paige as though she was staring through her, more interested in what lay beyond her than within her.

Paige's eyes darted away from the intensity of her glare, which not only made her feel uncomfortable but also deeply frightened. Her research into the legends of skin walkers had not left her with an endearing insight. Nearly all First Peoples in the Americas retain a similar myth paradigm concerning shape shifters, but this ideological tradition encompasses nearly all cultures throughout human time and history—from the berserkers of Europe to the huli jing of Asia to the ilimu of central Africa. In Naabeehó (Navajo) tradition, legends entail stories of great medicine men and priestesses who, in attaining the highest levels of spirituality, had subsequently learned to manipulate reality and rearticulate themselves as the beasts of their choice.

They were cherished guardians, and the ability to embody the characteristics of provincial wildlife more suited to harsh environments made them valuable scouts, chiefs, and members of society. However, while their corporeal deception had once been considered an advantageous attribute of their sacred journey, accounts vary as to why the highly revered shamans had fallen from grace.

Some versions of the lore suggest the naaldlooshii used these powers to avoid capture from European invaders. Or worse, the insinuation was that they were seduced by greed and envy, using their abilities to betray their nations and tribes for their own personal gain or survival. As this became clear to their communities, they were shunned and shamed for their weakness.

The Navajo, in particular, found the behavior so insufferable that they no longer allowed tribal members to practice the spiritual path, to wear the pelts of animals, or even to utter the name yee naaldlooshii among themselves. This compelled the skin walkers to confine their practices to the shadows, where they now lurk on the margins of society, outcast and deemed evil, treacherous beings. The legends pertaining to the skin walker in the Unita basin are infused with the pain and trauma that lingers from the long-standing quarrel between the Navajo and Ute tribes.

The Utes, who had allied themselves with the United States government, sold many Navajo hostages into slavery and executed countless others. As an act of revenge and retribution, the Navajo cursed their wickedness and damned the Ute lands with an evil skin walker to torment and haunt them for all eternity.

Paige shuddered with the thought of a malicious beast-demon haunting the very land on which she found herself, and she looked up to see that Sunka was still looking at her with a burning intensity. She locked eyes with her and, slowly, a mischievous smile crept across Sunka's face.

"You so highly value your education, Dr. Jansen," Sunka began in a steady, almost sweet tone, "and yet you remain so ignorant," she said, lowering her voice. She leaned forward onto the table, folding her hands and tilting her chin downward. "It is true that shape shifters were once highly revered medicine men and high priestesses. That I am one of those priestesses. But your fairy tales that swirl and twist around childish concepts of wickedness and monsters are nothing short of insulting. Not when real monsters lurk all around us." She drew her gaze from Paige and looked at Detective Andrews, the same governed intensity in her eyes. Andrews neither flinched nor retreated, but instead returned the same unyielding look. Paige leaned backwards, feeling Sunka's warm breath hit her face, feeling a sense of both fear and anger rising in her.

"So, it's true then? You've forsaken your people, your humanity for some… wolf superpowers?" Paige looked her up and down with a sassiness that was reminiscent of her adolescence but had remained nothing more than a distant remnant of herself until this moment. Before she had even realized it, the thought had escaped her mind and slipped through her mouth undetected. Mika gasped and looked at Sunka, who slowly straightened up and appeared even larger now, towering over Mika and blocking the light from the fire behind her. Paige clasped her hand over her mouth, shocked even at herself.

"My humanity?" Sunka's voice was growing louder now, more powerful and tangible, her high cheekbones more pontificated and enflamed with defiance. "My Humanity! What humanity do you think I have forsaken? The fictional construct dictated to you by generations of old white men who have butchered my people and called it civilized? Is this the humanity you think I should adhere to? Am I but a savage to you, Doctor? Shape shifters have learned how to manipulate the material aspects of bodily existence, to finesse the manner in which life is expressed upon this plane. We do not seek to manipulate and destroy life itself and while you feign humanity! It is humanity itself that clings to evil. It is the greed and envy of man that corrupts the perception of skin walkers, not skin walkers corrupting some venerated ideal of humanity."

Paige swallowed hard, feeling the sinking sensation of shame settle into her depths, where it rumbled and protested in the prison of her perverse notions. She watched cautiously as Sunka stood up and walked towards the fire, staring into it in an offbeat and somewhat melancholy manner. "I come from the Wičhíyena people. You know us now as the Dakota, a word in our language that means alliance of friends. Before that, the ancient blood of the Hopewell people coursed through my being. I am not a naaldlooshii, per se, because I am not of Navajo blood. Yet my people are all those who are woven into the tapestry upon which the air, water, fire, and earth are woven. Through me, the blood of a hundred plains' medicine men and a thousand mountains' priestesses pulsates—a lineage that, like our great rivers, begins where the waters are born and never die.

Although I have transformed and evolved from my prior configurations, this, the blood of my ancestors, is what remains of my attachment to humanity, my mingling of bloods." She turned and walked back to the table, her voice soft and palpable again. "I am of a tradition where all expressions of life are sacred—women, animals, plants, rivers, stars. What defines the essence of this idealistic humanity you espouse about—charity, compassion, cooperation? You know, at best, it's a dishonest and utterly abstract concept of humanity that you use to mask the fear. The fear that, beneath the grand façade, humans are nothing more than beasts. This is what your definition of humanity seeks. It seeks to hide that which you cannot hide—that you are still just greedy, ignorant, little beasts."

Paige slumped forward, placing her elbows on the table and plopping her chin into her palms. Unsure of what to say, she stammered, "I…I'm sorry…I…"

Sunka rolled her shoulders back, the light shimmering in her dark hair.

"You must learn to be as objective in your daily life as you are in your career. Paige, it is important that you practice this. You will need to rely on it soon. And that is the true purpose of my visit today, not entertaining you with fantastical stories and philosophical debates. As the Guardian, it is my duty to protect the wormhole. However, I am not here to police it or prohibit any entities from coming and going. I am here to protect sacred knowledge and information… from leaving. And that is what makes your father's presence there concerning."

Her face had softened now, as though she had begun, most subtly, to imitate the radiance of the fire behind her. "Speaking on a universal level, the destruction of a planet that is little more than "a mote of dust suspended in a sunbeam" is utterly meaningless. Most of the information that will be lost is so infinitesimal that it is virtually unimportant. Of course, as a guardian, I will have failed. The species of humankind will have failed. And yet, even that is irrelevant among the vastness of existence, where we all become just another footnote in infinity. It is easy to lose yourself like this in the insignificance of your existence until you see that existence itself is the only thing of significance. And then it matters, it matters how you choose to live, how you honor that significance."

Andrews cleared his throat and said, "You said real monsters lurk among us. There's one here, isn't there?"

"Yes, Mister Andrews," Sunka said, tilting her head and looking at him with a sophisticated and seductive smile, her beauty wafting over him like an intoxicating substance. "You certainly are much smarter than you look. And, I must say, you do look quite smart, Mister Andrews," she mimicked.

Sunka drew her eyes slowly along the sharp contours of his chin, slinking her gaze along his neck and across his well-defined, muscular shoulders, lingering a moment longer than was comfortable for him. She angled her head for a better view as her eyes moved downward, slightly arching a satisfied eyebrow at what she observed there. He shifted his posture slightly and smiled cautiously. She then turned her head slowly towards Paige and Mika, keeping her eyes on Andrews.

"Yes. There is a monster among us. A windingo," she whispered, now looking at all of them.

Detective Andrews and Mika both gasped, and Sunka clasped her hand over Mika's hand, as though to steady her.

"What's a…" Paige lowered her voice to a whisper now. "What's a… windingo?"

"The Cannibal," Andrews said, his voice dry and hard. Paige could feel the blood pounding through her body, vibrating in terror.

"Yes," Sunka said, her voice steady but solemn. "The Cannibal. The Insatiable One, devoted to the madness of consumption, the endless pursuit of the most acute and dark proclivities, survival at the cost of anything. The nature of the beast that resides in the depths of all humankind. At once the antithesis of humanity and yet the very definition of it. This is the windingo—more sorcerer than shape shifter, more man than universe. They do not alter their expression as vividly within reality as we do; they alter your perception of reality. They are illusionists, frauds, mercenaries of misrepresentation who claim to reveal an unseen truth. Yet what truth is revealed by illusions, besides the illusionist?"

Paige furrowed her brow, trying to take everything in. It felt like she was in her college philosophy class again, and she had failed to read the assignment for this week. She thought about the visions she had with her grandmother. Was that reality being revealed or the illusion being presented? It felt as though it was becoming increasingly difficult to even discern what was real anymore.

"Ok, so the windingo is an evil sorcerer," Paige started. "And it's among us. So, who is it?"

The three of them looked back and forth at each other. Mika looked knowingly at Detective Andrews, who acknowledged with a nod. Paige looked at both of them, shaking her head slowly, uncertain now of who exactly they both thought it was.

"Paige…" Mika began hesitantly. "Paige, it's…"

"It's not me, you guys!" Paige pushed herself backwards from the table and off the bench, stumbling backwards and standing there, unsure of what exactly they were suggesting.

26

CHAPTER

"It's not me!" Paige said again, stepping away from them before they all started laughing quietly.

"Paige, no one thinks it's you, sis," Mika said, her little dimple snuggled adorably in her cheek.

"Oh. Oh, ok," Paige said, forcing an uncomfortable and unsure laugh.

"But you should sit," Andrews said, patting the bench next to him where she had just been, an uncharacteristically serious look on his face. She looked at the two of them smugly, still suspicious of their suspicions, and sat down.

"The windingo is… Professor Greene," Sunka said, her voice very authoritative. "And we can't seem to locate him… the professor… anywhere."

Paige sat back, utterly shocked, quietly trying to sort out her thoughts about Prof. Greene, one of her only true companions. Had he betrayed her, too? Just like everyone else? Her head was spinning. Reality had finally revealed itself to be tethered only by madness. Like the unpredictable mixing and mingling of dreams, her memories swirled in her mind like delicate, aqueous ballet dancers, twisting and turning around the inner and outer forces of reality, snaking over and around each other until their differences were indiscernible. Paige felt like she couldn't breathe. Reality was questionable, unstable, indiscernible.

She slowly blinked her eyes again several times to focus before realizing both Mika and Andrews were looking down at her, her head in Andrews' lap and her hand in Mika's hand. Everything was blurry, but she could hear Andrew's heart thumping inside his chest, feel his tense muscles pressing against her as he breathed in and out, and she could smell how the soft cotton of his shirt mixed with the delicate tones of his cologne.

"Paige," Mika said. "Paige, just take it easy. You fainted. Here, have a sip of water."

Paige lifted her head, feeling Andrews gently supporting her neck, his fingers brushing through her hair and making her scalp tingle.

"Let's get her some fresh air," Detective Andrews said, helping her to her feet. His arm wrapped around her waist, he helped her outside the tent and sat her at one of the chairs near where she had been standing earlier, before the conversation with Sunka.

Paige took a deep breath and allowed herself to sink into the chair. She looked up at Andrews and grabbed his hand, before asking, almost desperately, if she could just have some time. He smiled, nodded, and headed back to the tent. Paige closed her eyes. She felt angry, confused, and completely exhausted. She rested her head against the back of the chair, her posture slumped and wearied, but oddly comfortable. It felt like as soon as she had closed her eyes and relaxed for a moment, she was interrupted by the sound of Mika's voice and instantly annoyed.

"What are you thinking about?" Mika asked chirpily as she walked towards her. Paige sat up straight in the chair, realizing that it was entirely dark now and rather cool. She looked around, feeling disoriented, but she immediately brought her focus to the area where they had seen the wormhole. She looked at it with a vague sort of remembrance before tracing the shadows of the plateaus beyond and returning to the fire in front of her, which had been started and tended to while she slept. She looked at Mika, trying to hide her suspicions and growing anger towards her, and noticed that a little speaker nearby was gently freeing Mumford and Sons into the cool night air:

It's empty in the valley of your heart...

You cannibal, you-meat eater, you

But I have seen the same

I know the shame in your defeat

"Humanity," said Paige dryly, garnering a small laugh from Mika in response as she sat down beside her.

"Here," Mika said, handing her a highball glass with a generous portion of bourbon neat. Raising her own glass high in the air, she melodramatically recited:

All the world's a stage, and all the men and women merely players; they have their exits and their entrances; and one man in his time plays many parts.

Mingling Bloods

She did a little curtsey and bow before sitting next to Paige, giggling.

"You know Mumford is inspired by Shakespeare, too," she said, taking a seat in the chair next to Paige.

"What is this?" Paige asked as she inhaled deeply the substance within the glass, wrinkling her nose with obvious disdain. "Whiskey?"

"Small batch, single barrel bourbon from a little distillery in Appalachia country," Mika said, taking a long, enjoyable sip.

"Are you a bourbon connoisseur?" Paige asked with disdain as she took a small sip of hers. The earthy aromas and slight sweetness were much more palatable and pleasant than she had anticipated, the warmth of it spreading across her chest as she swallowed, hoping it might temper her foul mood.

"I like booze in general. But I do love acquiring the art of a master craftsman in their industry. There are so many talented creators in microbreweries and small distilleries, people who are just crafting extraordinary expressions in food and alcohol; they are nothing short of virtuosos. It's an exciting time for people who like art, like to eat, and like to drink. And like to talk about the meaning of humanity." Mika smiled and looked at Paige, her crooked smile almost betraying her slight inebriation.

"Yeah, it's alright. Did you bring this with you?" Paige asked, turning the glass to see the prism of light dancing within the amber liquor.

"No," she said, leaning back. "Our father did."

"Oh," Paige said tersely, unable to disguise her derision. "Is it, like, something you guys both enjoyed? Together?" Still looking into her glass and avoiding eye contact with Mika—feeling a qualm and antagonistic sentiment swell in her chest, impelled by the warmth of the bourbon—she wondered why it even bothered her.

"No," Mika said quietly, but with a tinge of contempt. "I told you. He was rarely present in our lives, and when I was ten, he abandoned us entirely. My grandmother helped raise me after he left. His mother. He and I haven't shared anything or made precious memories of anything since I was a very young child. I try not to be sentimental about it. But I guess there are some itches you've just gotta keep scratching, eh sis?"

Paige sat there quietly, her disagreeable mood now devolving into outright anger. But before she could think of anything to say, Mika continued.

"Dad was from Appalachia, you know. He grew up in a way that would be considered very impoverished, very… uncivilized, some might say. But for him, it was never that. His mother, Grams, raised him in a manner that was… it was very unique, I guess, if not just outright avant-garde for her times. She was this hardy mountain woman, a feminist by nature, raising her son alone in the wilds. But she was not a simple woman by any means. It was a seemingly unforgiving environment, but she lived vibrantly within it. And she was quite respected for it. It's also what made him, at one time, a brilliant ambassador of science into the remote forests of the world, which is why he can translate so easily between the broad spectrum of human life that shares an appreciation of wonders and mysteries within the natural world.

This ideology she taught him, it's like his inner language. The way he appreciates and understands the natural world is both exasperating and enchanting. So, I guess I can understand why you can't help dreaming about it, wishing to dance on tiptoes with him like some childish little girl. But believe me when I say this, Paige—It would have never been that, and you certainly didn't miss anything."

The small speaker filled the space their silence had solicited with the long, instrumental refrain of Tash Sultana's Blackbird. Paige wanted to let it take her away, to let them delineate the geometric contours that defined her soul, to rest in the comfort of connection and the reprieve of music. But instead, she couldn't help but focus on her discontent, fuming and quietly thinking about her mother, about how ethereal she thought the love affair with her father was. How foolish she was to even believe in such things! Had Mika's mother felt the same? There was something cold and cruel about it she refused to dismiss, something that seemed intentionally ignorant. The way Mika explained it away as his nature, almost as though he were merely a victim of his character and not instead a man too cowardly to glance backwards and see what was destroyed in the wake of his nature, his work, his whims.

"Have you ever watched Shakespeare's *As You Like It?*" Mika asked, pouring them both another couple of ounces.

"Maybe once, in college, I think?" Paige said, shrugging, knowing she hadn't.

"If you had seen it, you would remember. Fun sister fact—it just so happens to be my personal favorite! Such a brilliant and beautiful paradigm on how all of the most extraordinary events in life are better when bestowed with a dose of laughter, good old-fashioned fun, and a vivacious enthusiasm for life. Not every aspect of humanity is told through the tragedies, ya know. I always tell my students— you may not get to choose which part you play, but you do get to choose which plays you watch."

Mika reached over and clinked her glass against Paige's, but Paige pulled her glass back and scowled at Mika.

"How clever," Paige said callously, making an acrimonious face at her.

"What's your problem tonight, Paige?" Mika asked, leaning forward and forcing eye contact.

"My problem? Mika, my problem is all of this," she said while sweeping her hand with the drink in it across the horizon. "My problem is this damn wormhole. My problem is going after that asshole so he can save the world. My problem is Percy and Suka, or whatever their names are, and the grandmother. And my problem is you and Detective Andrews fucking and having a good ol' time while all of this is happening!"

"Whoa, Paige! I told you, it's nothing like that! I just flirted with him. It's just a bit of fun." Mika stood up, genuinely shocked and hurt by the accusation.

Paige stood up to face her and tossed her drink into the fire, sending hissing, billowy black smoke into the space between them. She then threw the glass on the ground, where it clanked and rolled in the dust. As the smoke cleared, Mika stared at her in utter disbelief.

"Stop calling me sis. You may refer to me by earned title—Doctor Jansen," Paige jeered.

"Paige, please don't do this…" Mika said softly, holding her hand out towards her.

Paige turned her back to Mika and crossed her arms, fighting back tears she didn't want her to see. Mika shook her head, let out an exasperated breath, and started to walk away. She stopped suddenly and swung around, somewhat drunkenly, and lost her balance slightly. Walking over to Paige, she pulled an old black and white photo from her back pocket, unfolded it, and tossed it at her, saying spitefully, "Here! I'm so sorry you never got to meet her."

Then she pivoted dramatically, again walked away angrily, calling out, *"Oh, how bitter a thing it is to look into happiness through another man's eyes!"* Then, turning to walk backwards for a few steps, she shouted, "I'm not at all tired, so I think I'll just go fuck Andrews!"

Paige turned, incensed, and scowled in her direction before looking down at the photo. She picked it up and gasped, her hands began to tremble, and she dropped the photo again. She stood there frozen, just looking at it for a moment, before finally picking it up again and turning the photo over to read what had been scrolled across the back in faded black ink: Grams Walsh. It was her father's mother, their grandmother. And the grandmother from her dreams.

27

CHAPTER

Paige stormed to Mika's tent to demand answers, only to find that she was not there. She could feel the blood pulsating through her jugular and finding its way to her temple, where it throbbed and festered. She swung around quickly, knowing full well what was happening now. As she pushed open the door to Detective Andrews' tent, she expected to catch Mika in the act of ultimate betrayal of a sister. She slowly, quietly pushed the door open.

The lights were on, a half-full glass of bourbon sitting on the desk, Andrews' deep, spicy cologne still wafting through the night air, but there was no one in the tent. She apprehensively peered around the room, unsure if she should go in. But at that very moment, she heard a scream and jerked her head around as she listened, the sound seemingly originating from the center of camp—where the wormhole was.

Paige began to jog across the yard until she realized she was neither in the best shape nor wearing the best undergarments for such activities. So, she instead briskly walked through the darkness in the pale moonlight until reaching the central area, looking back and forth, searching for either Mika or Detective Andrews, but finding neither. Uneasiness instantly evolved into panic, knowing that there weren't many other places they could be. And she knew she had heard a scream. Panic now quickly turned to terror. She started calling for Mika and Andrews, desperately hoping now that they were just seeking privacy for their filthy acts elsewhere. But no answer came, only the minute murmur of the stars swirling on the horizon.

She went from tent to tent, calling into the darkness, trying to understand what could have happened—only moments had passed between the last time she saw Mika and when she heard the scream. She frantically searched all the tents in the camp numerous times, tears now streaming profusely down her face. She felt like she couldn't catch her breath. She felt like she couldn't make sense of anything. The rational rules that regulated her life relented and retreated. In a brief instant, she knew and understood that this was the precise moment that her fragile hold on reality had finally given way—an erudition that was, unfortunately, lost to her entirely in the next moment.

For hours, she paced from one tent to another, sobbing, mumbling, and repeating the things that she had said to Mika; at once mocking herself for her childish outbursts and foolish complaints while simultaneously solidifying her conspiracies about Mika, Andrews, and their betrayal. Don't call me sis… so clever… I know what you've been doing… I knew from the beginning she was a whore. She then began to yell their names over and over again, mumbling in the intermission, her voice becoming raspy and frail from the shrieking, the tightness in her chest restricting her ability to project her voice much louder than a whisper, the cool air mocking her efforts in the effervescent particles that shimmered in the high desert air.

"Paige!" a voice called from the darkness. "Paige, is that you?"

She looked up and stumbled towards the voice, weak and hysterical from her long search. Squinting, she peered into the darkness. The voice sounded familiar, but she couldn't place it.

"Percy…?" Paige whispered. Then slightly louder, "Percy!"

She stopped and looked into the darkness, where the professor emerged with an exhausted but relieved smile on his face.

"Paige, my dear, thank god you're here! My truck broke down, and I thought it was a good idea to just walk here. I very much regretted that idea several hours ago." He chuckled light-heartedly, and Paige found it difficult to resist the familiarity of his charm.

"I am very surprised to see you, Professor," Paige said barely louder than a whisper.

"My god, Paige, what's happened?" Percy stepped closer and wrapped his arms around her. Despite everything she had been told earlier today by the woman of beastly transformation, she melted into his arms.

"I… I… Percy, I'm so glad to see you." She closed her eyes and buried her face in his chest, listening as his heart thumped, melodical and composed. He pulled her closer and kissed the top of her head, stroking her hair down her back.

He always was one of the best huggers, she thought as she let him lead her back to her tent. Once inside, he helped her over to the bed and pulled the blanket over her gently.

"Let me get you some water, dear. You rest here, and I'll be right back. Ok?"

Paige smiled and nodded her head, gazing after him affectionately as he turned and walked out the door. She had always adored Percy. How could she possibly believe the things that were said about him? She had never, in any way, felt afraid of him. Closing her eyes, she pulled the soft blanket under her chin, inhaling the delicate fragrance that lingered from laundering. She felt safe now.

When she opened her eyes, she saw Percy sitting at her desk, slumped over and snoring loudly. His glasses were still in his hand, and a glass of water with a pitcher was on her bedside table. She tilted her head and smiled at him, adoring the ingenuous manner in which he was sleeping. Taking a long drink of water, she noticed that the sky was just beginning to brighten. She gulped down the remainder and threw on her shoes and jacket, tying her hair behind her loosely.

Quietly, she tiptoed out of the tent, determined to find out where Mika and Andrews were last night and where they were going, eager to search the tents again in the light. But there was still no sign of them. As she began to feel panicked again, she turned to go towards the supply tent and was abruptly met by Percy, holding out a coffee.

"Good morning, dear! I thought you could use this," he said in his familiar manner. Paige smiled and took the coffee from him, inhaling the aroma and finding herself pleasantly surprised.

"Percy!" She exclaimed, looking up after her first sip, "This tastes just like the coffee at the café in Ballard! What's your secret, dear man!" Paige laughed and took another sip, feeling her mood much improved by his presence and a great cup of coffee.

"Well, I could tell you, but I'd have to kill you," Percy said with a cheesy grin. Paige laughed and threw her arm around him, adoring his endearing talent for movie quotes and dad jokes. But her laughter quickly quieted as they began to walk back towards the supply tent together. She stopped and looked at him.

"Percy, do you have any idea what is going on here?"

"Well, I told you. We tried to study the wormhole, but your father disappeared before we could gather much evidence. I wish I had answers or that I could explain things, but I don't. I left to speak with some colleagues of mine, whom I had hoped could shed some light on it, but no one can really say one way or the other until we can find ways to measure and study it. Our knowledge of such things is entirely theoretical."

"Detective Andrews and Mika have disappeared. I am increasingly concerned that they may have fallen into the wormhole."

"My god, Paige! Why didn't you say anything before this?" he said as he looked down, stroking his beard and thinking. "No, no. I'm sorry. You practically collapsed last night. And we couldn't have done much then anyway," he said more to himself than her. "But we need to get to work right away," he said, looking up and turning to walk to the main tent.

"We met her," Paige said, her voice trembling. He stopped, his back to her; he stood rigidly, almost defensively. "We met Sunka. She had some interesting things to say about you, Percy."

"Who is Sunka?" Percy asked, turning towards her with a genuinely puzzled face.

"Don't fuck with me, Percy. Everyone has lied to me and betrayed me. But you, my oldest and dearest friend… Please, Percy… I need to know the truth!"

"Paige, my dear, calm down. Please! Of course, I'll always tell you the truth. I don't know who this Sunka is. And I haven't the slightest idea what I'm being accused of. Please, let's go sit and talk. Then we'll make a plan to find out what's going on here and how we can find Mika and Detective Andrews, if they indeed did fall into the wormhole. Ok?"

She stared at him, glassy-eyed from fatigue and stress. She felt like having her feet planted there may have given her the strength to resist her fondness for him, but she smothered the thought and followed him. Inside the tent, they sat across from each other at the table near the fireplace again. He smiled warmly and reached out to grab her hands. She tensed her shoulders and inhaled deeply, but did not pull away.

"When you're ready… tell me about the last few days. Did you find the Wizard?" he asked gently.

Paige looked at him quietly, still unsure of his intentions but certain that he could not be this windingo that the she-wolf spoke of. He was goofy, lovable, and adorably always out of the loop. But he was also brilliant and had such a warm magnificence about him. In all their years as friends, he has always been sincere and cheerful, and he made her feel safe. She smiled at him and squeezed his hands back.

"I wouldn't say Wizard is the best classification. But yes. Yes, we did," Paige said with a laugh. She went on to recount their adventures and mishaps leading up to the conversation with Sunka yesterday afternoon.

"That was the last time I remember seeing Detective Andrews. Later that evening, though, someone lit a fire while I was sleeping. I assumed it was Andrews. Mika doesn't do things for other people," she said contritely, producing a brief silence. "She's not the person you think she is, Percy."

"Paige... I've known Mika for some time. That's not fair."

"You haven't seen them, Percy, what they've done. It's really quite... well... it's disgusting really at a time like this."

"What have they done, Paige? What did you see?"

"Well, I... I didn't really see them do anything. But I'm certainly not stupid."

"Paige, I don't know what you're referring to, but—" Percy stopped mid-sentence and stared at the door in shock. "Macha…"

Paige could feel the blood draining from her face and could feel the icy stare of Sunka as she turned. Looking over at Percy, she noticed an absence of fear or guilt. She saw admiration in his eyes. And lust. He clearly has no idea who this woman or she-wolf is or what she's capable of, Paige thought, as he was standing up, smiling broadly and charismatically, walked over to hug her.

28

CHAPTER

As Percy hugged Sunka graciously, she simply stiffened and sneered. She looked straight at Paige as she stood there awkwardly, unbending. There was something notably different about her this time. She looked at Paige, not through her, and her steely dark eyes betrayed an element Paige had not expected. Fear.

As Percy pulled away, Sunka looked at him with a firm and uncomfortable grin before turning to Paige with a more solemn expression again. Percy walked back towards her casually, smiling and acting as though none of this were out of the ordinary. Paige and Sunka both stood still, looking at each other quietly.

"Come, ladies. Come sit so we can have a chat." He smiled, looking at both of them.

Paige glanced at Percy and then quickly back to Sunka, now feeling the fear she had seen reflected in her eyes. Her heart began to thump harder and faster, her breath quickening, palms sweating.

"Paige," Percy said, less kindly now. "Sit."

"Professor, I'd like to speak with you in private, please," Sunka said, her poise and presence returning to the mannerisms of a woman who knows her power. With a close-mouthed smile, she coolly straightened her suit, which he had slightly wrinkled from the hug, and ran her fingers through her long black hair as she pushed it to her back. She was polished, intimidating, intense, and aggressive. And Paige couldn't help but find her utterly spectacular in this moment.

"Oh, but my dear friend Paige says you've had plenty to say about me already, Macha," Prof. Greene said, his voice calm and level.

"Yeah, I'm going to go get dressed. You guys feel free to talk amongst yourselves. I'm feeling a little verklempt, and it's way too early for this shit," Paige said as she turned to walk out of the tent.

"Don't forget your coffee, Dr. Jansen," Sunka said, nodding in the direction of her cup on the table. "It sounds like you need it."

Paige grabbed her coffee and hurried out of the tent, avoiding eye contact. She didn't know what to do now, but she felt like getting the hell out of there was certainly the best idea she had had in a while. As she entered her tent, she took another large gulp of coffee and quickly dressed, throwing her clothes in her suitcase and gathering her personal items. She glanced in the mirror, found herself as unimpressed as usual, and turned to walk out of the tent when something caught her attention in the corner of the room.

She froze and slowly looked over to see what she thought looked like an armadillo tail moving behind a small bookshelf. Paige turned and slowly walked near it, curious to see what an armadillo would be rummaging for in her tent. Instead, she was shocked and surprised to find a small creature that resembled one of the photos from Mika's files, its shadow captured from inside a tent. Only slightly larger than a house cat, it was covered in dark, indigo feathers that shimmered with an eerie iridescence and stood up like peacock feathers, but in a manner that resembled a mountain range with numerous peaks rather than a fan. It was sniffing around in the dirt and scratching lightly here and there. Paige smiled to herself at the thought of this cute little guy looking so scary in that picture.

Just then, she heard something outside of her tent and immediately crouched down, listening for voices. One of the other tent doors banged shut loudly, and the little creature skittered off. Paige closed her eyes, took a long, deep breath, trying to calm the noise in her head long enough to concentrate, and listened closely to see if she could determine what was happening. As she released a long exhalation into the cool morning, a large plume of vapour filled the air and crept out the door, its little fingers creeping here and there like a cloud of death seeking all firstborn.

Everything fell silent again, and she began to tremble as she held her breath, afraid of giving herself away. She looked around quickly and found a shirt to wrap around her mouth. She then grabbed her nearby backpack, taking only a few things from the suitcase as necessities, and tossed it on her back.

She crept to her door, the silence broken with every deafening movement she made, her body popping and cracking with age. Peeking out the door, her legs were trembling so much she wasn't sure if she was even going to be able to walk. She closed her eyes, took another deep breath, checked to make sure she put a sports bra on, opened her eyes, and exhaled as she sprinted to the next tent. Kneeling down, she listened again. Still, absolute silence.

Paige bowed her head, seeking her courage and strength, and finding herself wanting. Thwarted and disillusioned, she simply remained quietly huddled there—her head hanging down in defeat, trembling in the cold morning air.

"Paige!" She heard Sunka whisper. "What are you doing?"

She was standing over her, tall and magnificent, and looking down at her with utter disgust. Paige looked up and started crying.

"I… I can't do this. I can't do any of this!" She dropped her head again and started sobbing rather loudly.

"Ugh, will you shut the fuck up?" Sunka whispered loudly as she grabbed her arm and pulled her to her feet. "Yes, you can do this, Paige. You think you don't have an option in any of this? You think you're the victim of unfortunate affairs? You think you are cursed to be your father's daughter and just like him?" She pulled Paige close to her face, her flawless skin glowing with morning dew. "What you don't consider is that it is precisely all of those things that make you the best person to do this. You are the absolute, most brilliant mind of your time, Paige. And you know it. You are a splendid human. Your work is thought-provoking, unprecedented, and meaningful. You are a generational icon. And you are the only person capable of doing this."

Paige blinked and looked at her, unsure of what to say, but feeling as though her eyes had suddenly come into focus. Just then, Sunka reached out and smacked her across the face—more theatrically than cruelly—and Paige gasped in shock, recoiling from her.

"Sorry, I thought maybe slapping you back to reality was what you needed," Sunka said, wiping the hand she had slapped with her hand on her pants before adding under her breath, "Ugh, humans are so gross."

"No, I got it just before that. But I probably deserved being slapped, anyway," Paige said, shrugging but still rubbing her cheek.

"Ok, listen. You need to go," Sunka said.

"Yes! That's exactly what I was thinking!" Paige said, adjusting her backpack, uncaring that she was following Sunka if it meant she could get out of here somehow.

She nodded to Sunka as she quietly turned and walked stealthily along the side of one of the tents, motioning for Paige. How does she walk silently in stilettos, Paige thought as she tried to be quiet, but nonetheless received a judgey look from Sunka as she began trailing noisily behind. They stopped briefly between tents before hurriedly crossing the expanse of the next.

"Do you always make this much noise?" Sunka scolded.

"Sorry," Paige said, panting slightly.

"We're almost there anyway," Sunka said, looking back and forth with a watchful, wolf-like intensity.

"Where? Where are we going?" Paige asked, looking behind them and listening closely.

"The Ayahuasca in your coffee should be kicking in soon. I'm sorry it had to be this way, but you have been very perverse at times."

"What! You fucking drugged me, too?"

"Yes, because you're going to need it. Now, listen. Rely on your knowledge. On the things you know to be true. You must look deeply enough into your own reflection to see what lies beyond."

From behind Sunka, she could see Percy walking slowly towards them in his usual, casual manner, one hand in his pocket, the other swinging carelessly at his side, a charming smile beaming at them both. Paige began to breathe more heavily as she shifted her focus back to Sunka.

"I know he's coming. Do not forget that I am the Guardian. I will protect you here. But I need you to retrieve your father's work so that I can help protect all life here, not just yours. Let your courage be as magnificent as your knowledge!"

The wind caught Paige's hair, and she looked behind her, realizing suddenly that the wormhole was opening right behind her. She could feel the gravity of it pulling on her, and she looked back to Sunka, panicked and afraid. Sunka smiled at her warmly, raising her arms towards her. Paige reached out, relieved that Sunka was going to pull her back. But instead, she felt Sunka's hands push her shoulders, and Paige felt the wormhole pulling her in. As she felt herself falling, she yelled back, "You bitch!"

"Macha, why do you always want to pick fights with me? Not all siblings fight like this, you know." Percy said, his voice calm and charming, smiling at her affectionately, both hands in his pockets.

Sunka turned around and fixed her hair where the wind had slightly disheveled it, a haughty smile on her face.

"Next time, I will have to chase you further away. But I must say, I am impressed to see you here so soon. I really thought you had become much slower in your old age."

"Sis, no matter how far away, I'll always come running back to you," Percy said, shrugging charismatically and taking his hands out of his pockets, holding them up and offering a hug. "We shared a womb, and we will always share this life. Come on, bring it in."

"Bleh," Sunka said as she sauntered past him, looking him up and down before walking up the hill, smiling. She turned back, looked at him affectionately, and waved just before she disappeared over the top.

He smiled and waved in return. But as she faded from his sight, so too did his smile.

29

CHAPTER

Darkness. Cold darkness. The wind was screaming around her pitilessly. The echo of her last words resonated unceasingly throughout a cavernous space: You Bitch

You Bitch

You Bitch

You Bitch

Over and over it echoed, like a personalized circle of hell—her own voice repeating it boundlessly, obstinately chastising herself. Over and over. Again and again.

This is it, she thought, this is how I disappear into oblivion?

"No, silly," she heard a gentle voice say. "You can stop it any time you choose!"

Paige wasn't even sure she was still a physical being; everything felt disconnected. But as she hastily tried to calm herself by taking a deep breath, she could feel the minute particles of air moving through her lungs. Slowly, she realized she not only still had a physical presence but that she could even see a little now, the darkness slowly dissipating, although the overall visual was still blurry. She blinked a few times and reached up to rub her eyes, appreciating that everything seemed to be intact. When she opened them, a grey and dimly lit, foggy landscape expanded before her, crisscrossed with lighter grey paths that created an immense three-dimensional web-like boardwalk in every direction. In the distance, a single, dim, amber light pulsated.

"See," she heard the voice say again, "you can stop it. Easy peasy, lemon squeezy."

The echo instantaneously dissolved. Paige turned around, looking for the voice, surprised to see the little creature from her tent again. Only now it was nearly as tall as she was, the color of its flashy plumage even more vivacious and enlivened—like turquoise waters reflected against white sands—and it exuded a sparkling radiance that flickered against the faint fog that hung around them. She could now see what she assumed was its face and was instantly struck by the pleasant, affable cuteness of it. With large, gentle eyes surrounded by extraordinarily long lashes, its face resembled something like a giraffe or equine.

"Oh! Hello," Paige said, instantly captivated by the creature, "you've grown!"

It grinned widely like a Cheshire cat and spoke slowly with flamboyant inflections, "Yeeesss. The guardian told me I should await your arrival. But I had expected you much sooner. I do appreciate timeliness, you know. With this wormhole becoming unstable, I just went ahead and found you!"

"The Guardian? You mean Sunka? Or Macha? Or whatever name you know her as," Paige said.

"Yes, that is who I mean. Names and labels are often quite arbitrary, aren't they, Doctor Paige Jansen?" the creature responded.

Paige looked around again, still feeling confused and confounded. "Yes, I suppose they are. And, um, please… You can just call me Paige. What should I call you?"

"What would you like to 'call me'? Bitch?"

"No," Paige said, shaking her head and looking down, disappointed in herself. "I mean, what is your name?"

"Oh! My name. How fun! Well, my name isn't really expressed in words; it's more of a representation of geometry, an equation of sorts, I suppose," it said, grinning again. "But perhaps for simplicity, you can call me Fred. I do like that name—Fred. Do you know there was a most extraordinary human expression named Fred? Fred Rogers. Do you know him?"

Paige laughed a little, "Yes, I do know of him. Mister Rogers?"

"There, you see? There are often many names attached to ethereal, eternal essences. So, for now, I shall be Fred and you shall be Paige," he said, rather triumphantly.

"Ok. Nice to meet you, Fred," Paige said, tilting her head and smiling. "And what shall we call the Guardian? I know her as Sunka, is that agreeable?"

"It is my absolute pleasure to meet you, Paige," Fred said, his blue radiance shifting to a more ultraviolet spectrum now with hints of bright pink, twinkling luminously in the dim setting. "Yes, let's call her Sunka. I do love how fun that is to say. Sunka!"

Paige laughed, wondering what this delightful creature was or where he had come from.

"The Guardian," he began spectacularly, declining to hide his delight in myths and intrigue, "an ancient and immense life-spirit perpetually bound to her tiny, little corner of earth," he waved his feathers dismissively. "And yet, she is of the very earth. She is that which both permeates and protects life. The link between consciousness and life. You see, long, long ago, in an ancient ceremony from the top of the great pyramid in an impressive metropolis now known as Cahokia, she and her twin were bequeathed perpetual life beyond the confines of their human bodies, blessed with the ability to transcend the corporeal and animate instead within the metaphysical.

She not only represents the feminine aspects of life, she manifests them. She is a spirit of nature, her twin a spirit of humanity. It's a very Yin and Yang sort of thing, you know. The intention was to unite the two essences, held in harmony by their identical biology. But, girl, we all know family ain't ever easy!" He paused and laughed in a high-pitched voice before continuing.

"Anyway, as her strength grew, her ability to manifest physically and manipulate that physical presence as she wished grew. While there are many of these ancient spirits on your little planet, few are as fierce as her. The intrepidness of a thousand generations pulses through her veins, but the carnage of genocide and unchecked free enterprise weakens even the most valiant spirits of nature. Modern life exasperates and diminishes her capabilities. Yet even as she withers, she remains one of my favorite consciousnesses. My Earth bestie, in your peopley terms."

"And what about Percy? Professor Greene? Is he... is he a..." Paige stopped short. She couldn't even bring herself to say it.

"Windingo?" Fred asked nonchalantly.

Paige flinched at the sound of the word, feeling the ire that seeped from it every time it was said aloud. "Yes..." she muttered.

"Well, yeeees, girl!" Fred said with a flair of sass. "But you already know that, don't you?" He paused and studied her for a moment. "Well, let me tell you: it's not as bad as you think, ok. The Windingo, The Cannibal. You know the legend," he said dramatically, "that's why it terrifies you. Oh, honey, but you really don't know, do you?" Fred hesitated again before continuing, "Percy is Sunka's brother! He's unbound to the earth and free, as a manifestation of humanity; thus, the whole cannibalism thing. The greed. The destruction. The… oh, you know what your weaknesses are as a species. It is not only your nature to destroy yourselves and everything around you, but it seems to be your whole damned purpose of existence. But, nonetheless, he is quite charming, don't you think? I do greatly adore his quintessence. It's almost inescapable, you know? That's why your father ran. To try to escape him. Haven't you figured this out yet, baby girl?" Fred paused and looked at her as he witnessed the confusion churning around her countenance.

"You know, most of these boundless human spirits roaming the earth are not nearly as charming or as vigorous as he is. His magnetism draws him to more powerful, higher levels of consciousness. So, you're really quite lucky that he has attached himself to you," Fred laughed, his feathers shaking and casting tiny, shimmering sparkles across the grey path.

"So… is he… my friend," Paige paused and turned away, afraid that she might start crying. "Is he a bad guy?"

"Oh, honey! No! No. He's not a 'bad guy'. However, I'm not really sure what that's supposed to mean. Nothing is simply good or bad. Yet what's good is good and what's bad is bad. You really do struggle with the whole equanimity and awareness thing, don't you, girl?" he said with a sassy laugh.

Paige snorted as she let out a little laugh, still trying to hold back tears.

"Daaa-ling," Fred said with wonderfully theatrical intonations, "nothing is all good or all bad. There are neither angels nor demons. Nothing is simply black or white. Yin-yang represents finding balance. Finding in the middle. The ebb and flow?" He shook his head at her puzzlement. "These grand virtuosos of consciousness, like Sunka and Percy, they are a universal expression, they are where these things meet. It is the balance itself that propagates and sustains their existence."

Paige turned back and looked at Fred, in all his beautiful magnificence, and he wiped a tear from her face with a soft feather. She smiled and sat down cross-legged on the grey path as another tear slowly slipped down her other cheek. He knelt down beside her.

"What you know and understand about him is true, Paige. He is your friend. You have been a prodigy throughout this entire human expression of yours. And he has carefully made sure that you are protected. Challenged. Given the room to grow. He has been there watching you and protecting you for a very long time. His affections are sincere. I believe it is his intentions you do not fully understand, his desperate desire to maintain balance often requires that he drip white paint into the blackness."

Paige wiped another tear. "So…ugh. What does that even mean? Why am I here?" She asked, burying her face in her hands anxiously before running her hands through her hair.

"Well, you're here for your father, Paige. He knows he must explain certain things to you. Then perhaps you'll understand why Percy has acted the way he has. And you'll understand why Sunka forced you to come here. When you understand, when you seek prajñā, you will find truth. As your most incredible Mae Jemison once said: The future never just happened. It was created."

"How am I even supposed to find him? Just wander around this maze until I stumble upon him?" Paige asked, rubbing her temples.

"Well, there's no need to be sassy," Fred said, feigning indignation. "It wouldn't take a child prodigy and now renowned physicist to just do that, now would it?"

"So…" Paige said, looking around. Then she looked at Fred and noticed that he was focused on the dim, amber light. "That? What is that?"

"Come on, Paige. You are in the in-between. The grey. That which is but does not exist yet. An in vitro universe."

"It's… It's the nebula. The spark before the big bang…" she said quietly.

"Yaaaaaas, girl! And isn't it gorgeous!" Fred shimmied his feathery plume, and his illumination increased, bringing detail to the infant star thundering in upon itself. "The Yin Yang—cohesiveness, correlation, balance. When two universes collide, the result can cause a supernova-type event of pure, extremely dense, conscious energy. Surrounded by a cocoon of dark matter that forms in response to the damage of the event, this becomes the womb of a new universe! But the unchecked intensity immediately causes imbalance and instability, and almost instantly it disintegrates into a black hole.

As the black hole begins to consume, the singularity at its core pulls and eventually devours all the matter, causing an imbalance that then tilts it in the opposite direction. Sparking a 'Big Bang', as you say."

Paige clasped her hands to her face and wiped the tears streaming down. She had never witnessed anything more beautiful in all her life. The spark. An infant universe— absolute fragility and devastating beauty compressed into an infinitesimal drop of dark matter, before: BOOM. The beginning. Consciousness. Life. It was breathtaking.

"Ugh," she said softly. "Amazing." She sniffled and wiped her nose, not quite expecting as many boogers as there were, and laughed to herself. "So, I have to go there to find him?"

"Yes, you delightful little physicist, you," Fred said with glee. "The Greys are there!" He paused, seeing her reaction. "Oh shit. I suppose no one's told you about the Grey's, either? Huh!"

"Well, sort of," Paige said, knowing that she should feel apprehensive of them, although not entirely sure why. "But yeah, not really."

"Oh. Oooohhhh. Okay," Fred responded with obvious agitation. "I told her. I told her she needed to prepare you for this. I cannot believe this bitch sometimes!"

Fred looked away dramatically and sauntered colorfully for a few steps. Paige watched him, trying not to smile at his dramatics. He turned back and said, "Ugh, ok. I'm sorry. You called her a bitch. And then that just really felt right. And… I got caught up in the moment. I'm sorry! So, where were we?"

Paige laughed, "The Greys."

"Yes. Ok, buckle up, buttercup. So, this is the in between, the grey. That which is but does not exist yet. As you now know, it's possible to pass through this space while it teeters on existence. But, as it does not exist yet, there are very few definitive 'rules' that govern this space. It inherits maternal qualities like gravity, mass composition, and density distribution. But aside from that, it's the wild, wild west, baby!" Fred smiled and chuckled gaily before continuing. "They were first called the Greys because they had mastered these spaces. Information exists within this space as cosmic energy—the celestial knowledge of each contributing universe—and it swirls around freely before the precise combination of information is compiled and combined within the density of the black hole, sort of like the process of DNA, but on a grander scale.

The Greys were once just scavengers, collecting random bits of information and knowledge and escaping before the moment of the big bang, when all possible exits close and the new universe breaks away from its origins to emerge with autonomy. As they acquired more and more information, they became more powerful. Their technology is wildly impressive now, and you've glimpsed only a small portion of it."

Paige nodded, thinking about the lights in the night sky.

"When you first found yourself here, I told you that you could stop the echo if you wanted to. And the reason you did is because here, where no rules exist, you can kind of create your own. You just have to stay inside the guidelines of the maternal universe."

"Grandmother…" Paige whispered.

"Yes," Fred nodded and grinned. "Exactly. So, you automatically have the upper hand. A superb understanding of the natural laws of the maternal universe. Understanding that is crucial to time and space travel through here, which is much more pleasant than more… traditional methods."

"More traditional methods?" Paige asked.

"Oh yes. There are many ancient Earth cites, places where the portals are protected and were once revered. Dozens of sites across your planet harbour this forgotten wisdom, protected and kept secret for eons. Places like Cahokia, where the twins transmuted into ethereal spirits. Hampi, Thebes, the Katmandu Valley, Machu Picchu, Petra, Angkor Wat, Bagan. Chavín, obviously. Many others have been destroyed and forgotten, particularly across the continents of North and South America. But the few that are known to remain are fiercely protected for their portals, for the gateways that open the labyrinth of time and space. Your father has rediscovered these ancient portals, or rather, more precisely, a primordial map of the portals.

It was his intention to travel back in time and influence certain key events so that the Industrial Revolution would not lead to the devastating and irreversible result of global warming. While it's a charming little human thought, it's nonetheless unacceptable. The ancient wisdom strictly prohibits such nonsense. And for good reasons, as you know! The chain of global events and history will be irrevocably altered in ways that cannot possibly be predicted. It's reckless, and he must be stopped. That's why you're here. To retrieve the sacred manuscript and maintain the proper timeline."

Paige looked at Fred silently, unable to respond.

"Of course, none of this even takes into account how difficult the journey is for humans through the ancient ways.

Taking a shortcut through here is much easier. Believe me," said Fred with a self-delighting laugh. "You must know the ways to make it through, and any changes in the timeline, accidental or otherwise, could alter that completely—leaving him stranded within the maze of the space-time gateways. Worst case scenario, he alters event after event, wrecking all sorts of unknown havoc."

"My father is… a time traveller? I thought I was here to rescue him, not stop him? None of this is making sense," Paige said, feeling exasperated.

"Well, I wouldn't say he's a space-time traveller. Not yet, anyway. He simply possesses the map needed to travel the ways. That's what you're here for—to rescue the archaic wisdom. The dreams about your grandmother were projected by Sunka but composed by the universe—she can contrive consciousness, as she does a physical presence. It's why you and your sister had the same dream. She's very powerful and very capable. She wanted you to end up here. If, and I suspect when, you try to return, you should be aware of this."

"How do I find my way back?" Paige asked.

"Back? There is no going back. Only forward. The three of you—you, your sister, and your future husband—will need to meet me here in 48 hours, before the wormhole becomes unstable. Check your watch now. That's plenty of time for you to find the key and map, procure them, and be back here. It'll be easy peasy, lemon squeezy!" Fred said, laughing again.

30

CHAPTER

"Whoa, ok. My future husband?" Paige laughed, shaking her head. "And who might that be?"

"Detective Shea Andrews, of course! Listen, girl, I'm not even from the same galaxy, and that man turns me on! You're at least of the same species. Why wouldn't you be trying to make him your mate?" He looked her up and down with a whimsical playfulness, and she burst out laughing.

"Ok, fair enough," Paige said, still laughing. "But before that can happen—before the whole escape and marriage bit—how am I going to save any of them? Procure anything? I would need an electrically charged spaceship to protect me from the heat and radiation—technology which doesn't even exist. Yet it would also need to possess highly advanced technologies for speed and be somehow intuitive enough to account for and offset the distortion of space and time that would be demanding and disorienting. Do I just imagine such a thing, and it happens? This seems too easy."

"Well, no, dear," Fred said with a giggle. "It would literally and mathematically take you, like, forever with that little brain of yours to accomplish such a feat. So, that's why you just need to get captured. Well, we need to get captured!" His feathers shimmied and fanned out while he wiggled back and forth in a little dance. "Daaaa—ling," he paused dramatically, "I've been in serious need of a good trip around a black hole anyway!"

The illuminations from his plumes grew dramatically and shimmered against the fog. At first, the light shimmered as it passed through the surrounding mist, but in the twirling particles of air, vapours seemed to materialize and solidify, and soon the mesmerizing and swirling spectacle of the nebula appeared closer and more dramatically detailed.

Her heart paused in wonder as she watched with unreserved euphoria, rapt by the scene, before quickly turning to look at Fred again. "What do you mean, get captured? Now I have to escape being captured and a collapsing portal? For fuck's sake… Do they already know I'm here?"

Paige quickly felt the joy and ease that had comforted her since meeting Fred turn to a cold and chilling panic. Was this a trap all along?

From a distance, where the nebula pulsated, a dim stream of light, like that from a flashlight, zig-zagged back and forth and slowly grew larger. Through the fog, it was difficult for Paige to tell how quickly it was moving until it was nearly instantaneously upon them, hovering in near silence above them now. A slight breeze blew through Paige's hair, and she looked, terrified, at Fred, who was smiling.

"Freeed! What the fuck is happening, Fred?" Paige screamed, feeling total and complete panic now as her weight shifted backwards and she began to levitate.

"Oh my god! Ahhhh! Freeeeed?" Paige watched him continue to smile at her as she floated upwards towards the enormous craft that soared above her. The searchlight was now shining downward and directly in the path of her ascent, blinding her from being able to see where or what she was going into. Oh my fucking god, she thought as her vacillating heart succumbed with terror, I'm being abducted by aliens!

The light grew closer and closer, and Paige could feel the warmth that radiated from the craft. She felt the familiar solidity of matter beneath her feet again and realized it had only taken seconds for her to be transported. Before she knew it, Fred was standing next to her.

"Greetings, friends, and welcome to Victor One!"

Paige was startled and jumped slightly at the sound of the voice. She quickly spun around to find a woman behind them, smiling in an overtly friendly manner. She was tall and slender with lustrous, wavy red hair and stunning green eyes.

"Please, step this way and remove your clothing. You'll feel a brief breeze around you, then you'll be provided with fresh, sanitized garments. Do be timely about it, though. There is a lot to see, and we are all excited to have you here. Especially the Commander." The woman smiled again with manufactured affection.

However, Paige couldn't help but feel instantly comfortable and even safe, in a sense. The woman continued to grin kindly as Paige quietly smiled back for a moment. The woman nodded her head and waved her hand towards the door to her right.

"Please, Doctor Paige Jansen," she said as the door slid open. Inside, a bright, well-lit room awaited her. Paige looked at Fred, who smiled and nodded enthusiastically, cautiously stepping over the threshold. "Place your soiled clothing in the black canister. Enjoy your stay, Doctor Paige Jansen."

"Oh, you can call me Paige. And thank you," Paige said, smiling hesitantly and waving awkwardly as the doors slid closed. She looked around the room, sure that they must be watching her and feeling uneasy at being forced to strip nude. She took a deep breath in exasperation and accidentally smelled herself. She definitely needed clean clothes. Closing her eyes, she pulled her shirt over her head. Once she was done undressing, she was met with a brief and brisk breeze. Then a small door opened on the wall near the entry door, and a golden jumpsuit was folded neatly on the shelf within.

Once she was dressed and smelled much better, she stepped out of the door opposite the one she had entered. On the other side, she found Fred waiting for her. Her hair was still a wild mess from the wind, and the jumpsuit, which must have been designed for the aliens on this ship who were apparently all very tall and slender, was ill-fitted. On Paige, the legs bunched at the bottom around her ankles and dragged on the floor as she walked, making a wisp-wisp-wisp sound with each step. She also had to roll up the sleeves three times. However, the midsection was incredibly tight and uncomfortable for her, as her breasts and belly stretched the material to its maximum. Fred looked her up and down with a deserved degree of sassiness.

"Girl, this is not a good look for you," he said, laughing, his cheeks flushing a deep purple.

"Jesus, Fred. You think I don't know that? I could use a little emotional support right now, you know," Paige said, laughing at herself and pulling furiously at the tight material around her belly.

"Oh, they aren't here today, but maybe you'll get to meet them if you stay a while," a soft, inviting voice said from behind them again. This time, a blonde woman stood before them, no less beautiful than the first woman they met. She was predictably tall and slender, well-fitted in her golden jumpsuit, and she had a kind and loving countenance displayed within the mystic realms of her red-lipped smile.

"Who are they?" Paige asked slowly, somewhat mesmerized by the woman.

"Jesus… you mentioned them? They are one of ours, of course. We've been trying to help you little creatures for centuries." The woman smiled again, her hands politely folded in front of her. "Oh my, where are my manners? You must be so overwhelmed right now! Come, dear, let's sit," she said, waving her hand towards another door down the hallway. "My name is Gillian, Doctor Paige Jansen, and it is my pleasure to finally meet you."

Paige reached out to shake the hand she had presented, feeling uncertain and confused.

"I know, dear," Gillian said, this time without actually speaking out loud to Paige.

Oh shit, they can hear what I think? Paige thought in a panic.

"Oh yes, Doctor. You humans have a lot of chatter in your little minds, so we tend to ignore most of it. Does that make you feel more at ease?"

"Um, sure," Paige said, forcing a smile.

"Shall we then?" Gillian said, pointing towards the door again.

Paige and Fred followed her into a room that had several large windows, but they revealed nothing more than the foggy, endless greyness beyond. Inside the dimly lit lounge-type area, a few round couches, some hammocks, and bean bags were scattered about, and there was a large foam-ball pit off to the side. Reggae music played quietly in the background, and a friendly-looking, handsome young man behind the bar was meticulously polishing a glass and smiling at them.

"Is it martini-thirty aboard the Victor One?" Fred said, sashaying across the room towards the bar, his enthusiasm and excitement nothing less than charming.

"It always is for you, Fred! You know that. So, what'll it be, ol' chap?" the bartender said, flaunting his Cockney accent.

"Ooooohh, Honey! You know that accent gets me every time," Fred said, laughing flirtatiously. "Make it a Cosmo for me, love. What will the esteemed doctor be having?" he asked Paige.

She smiled slightly and then furrowed her brow. "Oh… um. Whatever you're having, Fred, is fine with me. But we really shouldn't dilly-dally. I have so many questions."

"Yes, there are many things we must address," Gillian said from directly behind her. "I will take you to see your father soon enough. But before we do, the Commander would like to meet you."

"Oh wow, ok!" Paige jumped, surprised to find her standing so close behind her. "I don't think I need to see a commander or anything like that. You and I can just go over a few things really quickly, then you can take me to my dad, sister, and companion, and we'll be on our way."

Gillian looked at her and laughed as politely as one can laugh at another. Fred salaciously stepped closer to them, a martini glass snuggled securely in one of his feathers.

"You are a funny little human," Gillian said as she slipped her arm around Paige's shoulder, nudging her towards another door. "Come. He's waiting," she said firmly.

31

CHAPTER

Gillian led them through the door and then through a series of hallways, followed by a bewildering network of elevators, making Paige feel disoriented and confused. Finally, they passed through a door that opened into an expansive, impressively opulent room with high ceilings, its magnificence magnified by white walls and white marbled floors. There were several beings in the room, milling about and chatting casually, but the mood shifted instantly when the room fell silent. As they entered, everyone quietly watched Gillian lead Paige across the room, her *wisp-wisp-wisp* echoing into the silence. They stop in front of a tall, handsome man with dark hair and dark eyes. Everyone wore the same jumpsuit they had provided for Paige, but they all looked divinely beautiful in them. The man in front of them, in particular, filled out his silvery gold jumpsuit quite well, with precise attention paid to the unique contour of his muscles, which, when flexed, triggered an erotic shimmer that rippled across the suit. He smiled candidly at Paige, and she felt a warm, sultry sensation creep across her cheeks.

"Hello, Doctor Paige Jansen! Welcome to the Victor One," the man said, still cheerful and friendly as he held out his hand to greet her.

"Oh, uh… hi," Paige said clumsily, embarrassed by her reaction to his charm and good looks. "I… um… wow. It's nice to meet you, as well. Please, just call me Paige, though," she stammered, her cheeks flame red now. She wiped her sweaty palms on her pant leg and quickly shook his hand, unsure if that's even what he wanted.

He looked at his palm, slightly repulsed that it was now sweaty from hers, and wiped it on his pant leg. "Ok, *Paige*. Thank you for meeting with me. I'm sure my old friend, Fred, has been a wonderful guide, but I know he never stops gossiping about me. Tell me, what did he say? By the look of your bewilderment, he must have made a terrible first impression of me! Always being catty like that, Fred is," the man said, laughing and grinning coyly at Fred. "Come, you should rest. Let's step into my cabin, shall we, and speak more candidly? Privately."

Paige followed him, alone, through to a smaller, more dimly lit room where he motioned for her to sit in a large, comfortable-looking leather chair. He walked over to a small cabinet by his desk, behind which a signed and framed *X-Files* poster stated, 'I *want to believe,* ' and poured two glasses of bourbon neat. He walked over and handed one to her.

"An old friend of mine introduced me to small-batch Kentucky bourbon, and now I offer it to all my new human friends," the man said. "It is a true delight of the human senses, no?" he asked charmingly, deeply inhaling the aroma before taking a long, slow sip.

Are we friends? Paige wondered. *I don't even know his name.*

"Ah, yes," the man said, this time telepathically as the woman had done before. "How rude of me! I am Valiant Thor, Commander of this ship, and a delegate of The High Council—or THC, if you prefer. I've been sent to thwart and redirect the violent, self-destructive evolution of humans before they destroy themselves and their planet."

"Yeah, how's that working out for ya, Val?" Fred said sassily, joining them extemporaneously. "I'll certainly take one of those whiskeys while we watch them burn it down, though," he chuckled affably. Valiant walked towards Fred while Paige stared hard at him, appalled by his somewhat dismissive indifference to humanity. Valiant chuckled and clinked his glass to Fred's.

"I do miss you when you're gone, old friend," he said, smiling adoringly at him. "Speaking of burning one down," said Val as he reached over and grabbed a tall, glass bong, beautifully crafted with swirls of red, orange, and yellow sparkling throughout. "Care to join us, Doctor Paige Jansen?" Val asked, smiling broadly.

Paige simply stared at him for a moment in utter shock and confusion before replying timidly, "Just Paige is fine. And is that… um… marijuana?"

"I would think a scientist would have the decency to not use outdated, racist terminology and call it cannabis—but yes," Val said as he motioned for her to join him.

"Ugh, no thanks," Paige replied self-righteously.

"You silly little humans. Really… always so uptight! That's why we spend so much time trying to loosen up those sphincters for you before you blow up yourselves and the planet," Val said, winking at Fred before taking a generous hit.

He exhaled and passed it to Fred, who took an impressively larger hit, held it for more than a minute, and then exhaled loudly, just a wee cough at the end to clear his throat. He sat back and sipped his whiskey, settling into the chair in a cat-like manner.

"Ok, Val," Fred said, lacking his usual sass while he smiled at Paige, "You really should explain things to this poor child. She has no idea what you're talking about. Also, let's be honest, honey, since you already brought up sphincters—you know you just *like* the butt stuff. But of course, you know I'm not one to yuck your yum. You do you, baby!"

Valiant Thor and Fred both laughed while Paige just sat there, stunned, feeling as though *there was a joke between them and she was the butt of it*. The beauty of the pun transmuted by her thoughts was not lost on them, and it spawned another raucous round of juvenile laughter from the two. As they finally calmed themselves, they each took another generous hit, and Fred cleared his throat.

"Paige, daaaaling," he began in his joyous manner, "Mr. Valiant Thor is kind of a big deal, though he humbly tries to play it off. But, I mean, just look at him! Isn't he spectacular?"

Paige was certainly struck by the majestic human nature of the alien man, especially because her idea of "The Greys" was something very different. She kept trying to remember what Grandmother had told her about them, but she didn't know what to believe anymore. Having now met the Greys, in all their exquisite glory, in all their flawlessness… *maybe it was the ayahuasca?* But as she took in the entirety of man before her—his eyes sparkling with vigour and wanting, his dark features and olive skin invoking a Mediterranean essence that obliged his entire exceptionally well-developed, muscular frame with great confidence—they seemed quite fantastic. His smile was inviting, entrancing, and dangerous. She felt both provoked and aroused by it, and she enjoyed the pleasure she experienced while examining his golden jumpsuit, no detail left untouched, every delightful delineation of his stunning physique revealed.

"Yes, Paige," Val said, breaking her trance, "the Ayahuasca does help you perceive us more clearly."

Paige felt her face flush with impiety and embarrassment as she reminded herself that he could *read her fucking thoughts*. All of them. *Good god*, she thought in a panic as she tried to wipe the images from her brain she had just been visualizing.

Val smiled and laughed lightly, "Don't worry, we get pretty used to that. We just tune it out most of the time. Now, shall we get down to business?" he asked before taking another hit from the bong.

"Um, yes," Paige said, though she was increasingly confused.

Val passed the bong to Fred again, exhaled, and said, "Well, it's difficult to know where to begin, so I'll just start with myself and my time spent on Earth among humankind. I was appointed by The High Council, an intergalactic collaboration of what you would consider scientists, who are devoted to monitoring life in your galaxy and ensuring its survival. We have observed your planet, specifically, for some time now. Rarely have we felt the need to obstruct the course of evolution or human events on your planet. However, that being said, in the current age, Earth year of nineteen-hundred and fifty-seven, I was sent by the Council to meet with President Eisenhower. My mission was quite simple—to stop a nuclear war from occurring on Earth, an event that would not only devastate and destroy your own planet, but one that would reverberate throughout the entire galaxy. So, I lived with the American government for several years, as did three of my officers. One of whom was Gillian, whom you met earlier. In our time spent there, we attempted to convince all nations to disarm their nuclear weapons. A task we clearly failed at. However, I do not consider our entire mission a failure. Nuclear war has become, at the very least, a reduced threat. Plus, our partnership with humans across the globe has led to our understanding of advanced Earth biology and the acquisition of greater knowledge. Our long-term goal remains helping humanity hurdle their horrifying propensity for violence and destruction."

"Wow, ok… I have so many questions. First of all, I thought you all were from another universe? Why are you concerned with protecting our galaxy?" Paige said, trying not to let him know that she had been warned about them.

"Ah, yes… Sunka, she never lets anything go," Val sighed and smiled at her knowingly. "No, I am not an invader of your universe, just your galaxy. I was born a short hop past Venus, in Andromeda. And, yes, in my past, I was, well… as *some* might say, a pirate. I find that to be much too harsh a term, though. Don't you, Fred?"

Fred smiled and winked at Paige. "I suppose so. That was ages ago, anyway. Sunka *never* forgets anything. *Literally*," Fred said. "Since those days, Val has done good work with The High Council. He's even almost respectable now." Fred looked at Val playfully and shimmied his feathers in a flirtatious manner.

"Good work? Mutilating cows? Abducting scientists? I don't even want to get into the butt stuff you guys keep talking about. *This* is your good work?" Paige asked skeptically.

"You humans, always getting hung up on the best parts," he said, laughing and reaching over to refill her whiskey. "Let me explain. Please?"

Paige looked up from the glass and into his sultry, enigmatic eyes, which imprudently and immediately obliged her to surrender her anger and suspicions towards him. Her skin tingled as he smiled at her gently. She nodded and acquiesced, knowing full well that she was being manipulated by his magnificence, but nonetheless satiated with his noteworthy form of persuasion. Val sat down in the chair next to her, crowding the small, intimate space between them. She could feel his body heat, as though it were bulging outward, distending and thronging itself against her. She swallowed dryly, trying desperately to mask the thoughts that were traipsing promiscuously through her mind. Grabbing her glass, she downed the entire drink hastily. Her hands trembled as she turned slightly away from him, placing the glass on a small table and taking a moment to steady herself. She turned back to the commander, who was smiling at her patiently.

"When we approached President Eisenhower about the nuclear weapons," he continued, "this was not our first contact with humans. Among those whom we had interacted with prior, our main focus was always on the scientists, on those who sought the pure pursuit of truth and knowledge, those who have propelled human evolution. Politicians, businessmen, religious leaders, military men—they are seldom concerned with truth, so we placated them in hopes of getting what we wanted. Denuclearization. They wanted to test us, our clothes, our IQs, our abilities. But it was not understanding these men sought; it was technology. Exploitation. Power. It is no coincidence that American technology excelled at this time, particularly in space technology. In exchange for what they learned from us, they offered abductions of any Earth life forms we wanted for study. As long as we kept it quiet and the numbers reasonably small."

Paige inhaled and trembled on the exhale as she looked at him wide-eyed, tears brimming in her eyes.

"I don't know why they thought we would want such a thing, to be honest. Perhaps they thought we'd like to conduct similar, grotesque experiments on sentient beings? Regardless, we accepted this proposal, but for our own, very different purposes. Not long after that, the SFS was founded by your father, Maxwell, and we officially met with the group in 1969 to address the many questions and concerns they had about the trajectory of human civilization. And rightly so. Even then, the indicators of global warming were bluntly evident and repeatedly ignored, allowing avarice and unchecked power to consume not only your species, but your entire planet."

32

CHAPTER

"We could see then that humans had sealed their fate, even if they had averted a nuclear holocaust of galactic proportions," Val continued in his deep, steady cadence. "And so could the SFS scientists. Now, some 50 years later, the measures that *must* be taken to save your planet would have to be executed expeditiously and immediately on a global scale, with all governments and peoples cooperating and working together. This," he paused and exhaled, woefully shaking his head, "this is your species' greatest challenge—and you are failing miserably. Looking at this situation rationally, we've concluded that the probability of human survival is statistically zero. The effects of global warming are now irreversible, and after a mere 300,000 years of existence, it seems your species is doomed, along with many others on your planet. Although life will recover, evolve again, and continue on Earth, saving humankind will require a creative solution. Your father, Max, with the full support of the SFS, suggested an exodus to another planet and sought our assistance in doing so. Another world. Another chance. The genius of his proposal was that *this* time, the most brilliant minds in all of humanity could design their civilization, their destiny. Thus, the search began—with our help. Or shall I say, our guidance? Understanding how to travel through time and space has been our greatest contribution to humankind, though very few of you even know of it. Exposing the gateways, like the one you came through, makes space-time travel much easier than the older methods. Getting here wasn't so bad, now was it?" he said, smiling and offering Paige more whiskey.

She shrugged, already feeling the previous two in the warmth of her cheeks.

"Ok, hold on, there's a lot there," Paige said, biting her lip as she looked at him, holding her glass out for a refill, "what about the abductions? You just sort of glossed over that part."

"Ah, yes! This is the best part," he said, smiling at her alluringly. "When the greater scientific community voted affirmatively for evacuation, it sparked genetic research inquiries. They were interested in editing human DNA—fixing the typos and such, as well as preparing it for life on a different planet. But human technology had a lot of catching up to do in these fields, and we were in a unique position to help them get there. So, the abductions are purely for the purpose of research. To help mankind survive on the new planet that is being cultivated just for you. And you, my dear sweet genius, are the alpha creation of all that research. Congratulations!"

"Yaaaas girl! Cheers," Fred called out merrily, holding his empty glass out and smiling coyly at Valiant, who graciously poured him another drink.

"I'm sorry… what?"

"Yes," Valiant said again patiently, nodding his head enthusiastically, "Once we managed to work out all the kinks through our own research, we felt confident that we could alter human DNA shortly after conception, thus eradicating the disease and constant degeneration typical of your species. The recolonization will include all of you selected by the SFS. And now that you, your sister and Mister Andrews are here, we can proceed!"

"Proceed with… what exactly?" Paige said, feeling a terror begin to grow deep within, her head spinning with the revelation that she has alien-altered DNA.

"Transport to the new colony. You can get there through several portals on earth, but this way is much more relaxing. Now, please, let me show you to your room. We'll be here in Orbit for the span of several more Earth days. You'll need some rest for the journey."

"Wait! What do you mean? I haven't agreed to this! How was this decided? Does my mother know *any* of this?" Paige stood up, terrified and exasperated. She took a step backwards and bumped into the small table, knocking it over and breaking the glass as it fell to the floor.

"Paige," Fred said calmly, "calm down, girl. We're trying to help you. Let us help you, dear." He smiled, his sweet face trusting and friendly.

A thousand thoughts raced through Paige's mind. She wanted to fight back, to escape, to get out of here. But how could she possibly do that? And where was she going to go? She had no idea how to get back, if there was a way back.

Then she remembered that Mika and Andrews were here. If she could just calm down and go with this, she thought. *Suppose she could just get to them.* Together, they could find a way out. She inhaled deeply and exhaled, turning to face Valiant.

"Ok, I'm sorry. This has just been a lot to take in. Maybe you're right. I think I really need to rest for a little while," Paige said wearily.

"Yes! Gooooood! Good. I will have Gillian show you both to your rooms. Once you are rested, I'll bring your father to you. You can finally meet him, and he'll tell you all about all the things!" Valiant smiled and waved towards the door, which slid open to reveal a middle-aged man with a friendly smile on his face.

Paige forced a smile and turned to follow the handsome, athletically built man. Fred smiled and waved coquettishly to Valent before hopping up and prancing happily alongside her.

"Girl, you don't know what a treat it is to stay here. The rooms are plush, the amenities endless—I'd highly recommend a massage while you're here, happy ending and all—these guys really go all out."

"You've been here before, I take it," Paige said, trying to hide her fear but sounding arrogant instead. Shaking her head at her distasteful tone, she caught herself wondering, *did he just say happy endings?*

Fred chuckled. "Oh, yes. Val and I go way back. We've had a lot of fun together."

"Oh," Paige said uneasily, trying to smile and pretend she wasn't freaking out about a million things at this point: *So, she was just supposed to go to her room, relax, get a happy-ending massage, get a good night's sleep, then meet her father for the first time the next day on an alien spaceship headed to a new human colony, let him casually explain to her why her DNA is altered and why they are absconding en masse? No big fucking deal, right?*

"Oh, of course, it's a big fucking deal," the fetching gentleman said telepathically. "We've all worked very hard for this to happen. You should feel privileged and excited at the opportunity before you, not only to save your species but to better it. Fred, here's your room, love," he said, arching his eyebrows seductively.

"Shall I see you later tonight?" Fred asked.

"I should hope so," he said, giggling.

Paige looked back and forth between them, confused and disturbed by what was transpiring.

"Paige, I'm sure I'll see you before we leave. Ciao, babe!" Fred exclaimed as he entered his room excitedly.

The man blushed and snickered to himself again and waved playfully to Fred. "This way, doctor."

"You can call me Paige," she said, waving to Fred as the door slid close.

"I know," he replied plainly, continuing down the hall. "Please follow me, doctor."

Paige looked at him and scowled, assuming and hoping that he could see it telepathically.

"Your attitude isn't helping matters, doctor. The commander has been very patient with you. I shouldn't think that you'd expect such partiality from all of us."

"I'm sorry. This is just a lot to take in," Paige said, sighing and turning to walk after him. "It's *all* been a lot, honestly."

"Here's your room, doctor," he said, stopping just as the door slid open. Inside the dim, amber-lit room, Paige could see that it opened to a small living area, with perhaps a kitchenette to one side and possibly a sleeping area off to the other side. Vivaldi's violin concerto played quietly and, somewhere unseen, a water feature mirrored a sparkling cadence and cast it across the room.

"Looks just like the Holiday Inn," Paige joked.

He unenthusiastically replied, "I will return later, once you've rested, eaten and bathed. The precise time of my return awaits the commander's orders. Until then, goodbye, doctor."

Paige smiled at him, despite being both confused and afraid. She stepped into the room, and the lights automatically brightened to a more comfortable level. The room was beautiful, like something out of a Tolkien novel, with ample foliage cascading down beautifully chiselled granite, with grand arches and lovely alcoves. It was striking, splendid, spellbinding. As she spun through the room in complete awe, she didn't even notice the attendant standing near the water fountain until she backed into her.

"Oh my god! I'm so sorry. I didn't know anyone was in here," Paige said.

"That's quite all right, Doctor Paige Jansen. My name is Aaina. I'm here for anything you might need during your stay," the young woman smiled and bowed. Her deep brown skin tones glowed against the jewel-toned jumpsuit she wore, and her exquisite features resembled those of women from the Indian subcontinent. And like all the other aliens, she was remarkably beautiful.

"Please, this way. I've drawn you a bath. Prepared to be treated like a princess, Doctor Paige Jansen. We are all excited to have you here!" the young woman said, seemingly wholeheartedly.

"Oh, please—just call me Paige. And I can just take a shower. There's no need for all this," Paige said as they walked over to a large, sunken pool scattered with fresh flowers. The steam was rolling off the water, and candles filled the air with delightful runs of lavender, beautiful notes of honeysuckle and lovely crescendos of rose.

"Oh my," Paige whispered. "Is this for me?"

"Yes, of course," Aaina said with a giggle. "Take your time, I'll be back to check on you in a bit."

Paige watched her as she walked away and couldn't help but feel an aching attraction to her—her warm skin, her luscious hair, her voluptuous hips, the way she swayed at the waist when she walked—she was stunning. Paige shook her head and turned to take in the exquisiteness of the room again. She reached down and felt the water, which was warm and soothing, and she knew she couldn't possibly resist the temptation to bathe in it. She undressed and tiptoed into the water, feeling its sincerity envelope her. Wading gently into the pool, she found a seat to relax into. She rested her head back and closed her eyes, reclining in a moment of silence before a thousand intrusive thoughts marched across her mind. She had been through the most incredible, unbelievable events in the past few days—and now this. Altered DNA? A new human colony? She couldn't help but wonder if her mother knew about any of this. *Was her entire life a lie?*

Aaina returned, ambling gracefully towards Paige. She was now nude, with the exception of her bikini bottom, and held a small jar from which she was extracting an unknown substance before dripping it into the water. As she walked around the pool, Paige felt embarrassed and uncomfortable, now unable to look at her.

"I am under strict instructions that you should rest deeply. This constant thought chatter simply won't do. I'm adding some aromatics to help relax you before your massage," Aaina said.

"Oh no," Paige said, feeling tremendously uneasy, "I don't need a massage."

"Nonsense," Aaina said, smiling. She set the small jar down and gently entered the warm waters, moving closer to Paige.

"Oh… ok. Yeah, I really don't—" Paige stopped short as Aaina placed her hand on her shoulder.

"There's no need to be afraid," she whispered softly, her hot breath seductively stroking her neck. She maneuvered Paige to sit in front of her on the step, her hands still on her shoulders, and pressed her body closer. Paige could feel the hardness of her nipples as her bare breasts softly pressed against her back, her firm legs now gripping around hers. Her hands trembled with fear, but her thighs quivered with excitement. Paige closed her eyes, the warm water and the vapours quickly relaxing her, and she let her shoulders drop while she exhaled, though it sounded like more of a moan.

"There, you see. You *can* relax," Aaina said, delicately tracing her finger along Paige's ear before massaging her scalp.

33

CHAPTER

Paige opened her eyes and looked around the room, confused for a moment until she remembered where she was. Except she was in bed now and dressed in pyjamas. *Did she…?*

"The healing powers of the bath finally lulled your mind into a slumber, Doctor Paige," said Aaina politely, stepping forward towards the bed. "I then massaged you and dressed you. You have been sleeping for 11 hours and 17 minutes now."

"Um," Paige said, lifting the covers to look at her pyjamas. "You dressed me? And… massaged me?" Paige asked.

"Yes, Doctor Paige, We—"

"Please, Aaina, just Paige is fine."

"Of course, Just Paige," she said with an innocent smile, stepping closer to the bed and sitting on the edge. She grabbed Paige's hand and held it in between hers. "I am a healer," she whispered, smiling confidently now. Suddenly, a warm flush rushed through Paige's hand, up her arm and into her chest, where she felt it pulsate.

"I massaged you because I am a healer, Just Paige. And no, there were no *happy endings*," she said with a giggle. "Not without consent, anyway. We may look like humans, but we don't behave like such beasts. So don't worry. Fred is always playing around, making jokes about anal probes and such. You never can tell when he's serious." She smiled and stood up. "You should feel quite well now. There are some fresh clothes for you over there, and there's a little something for breakfast, as well. Your father should be here in about an hour." She made a clicking noise, and the lighting changed from the dim amber light to sunlight pouring in through the top of the arches. Paige could feel the warmth instantly, even though she knew the sunlight itself was artificial.

"Oh, ok," Paige said, feeling anxiety beginning to trouble her appetite. "You know, your fabrication of sunlight is a little off; daylight hues are never quite this pink."

"Oh, how nice. But it's not intended to fabricate the light from your Earth star," Aaina said before turning to leave.

Paige furrowed her brow as she continued to look at the door where Aaina had been. *Then what sun's light is it intended to fabricate*, she wondered. Flipping the covers back, she noticed that she really did feel good physically. Her normal pops and creaks silenced, she energetically hopped out of bed, landing on the cool floor where a pile of fabric quickly pooled around her feet—like everything else she had worn here, the lovely silk pjs were designed for someone much taller. *And thinner*, she thought sullenly as she pulled at the uncomfortable waistline of the pants, trying to pull them up higher. Walking over to the fresh clothes, she found yet again an ill-fitting golden jumpsuit. Reluctantly, she dressed and enjoyed the breakfast waiting for her at a table near the fountain in the warm, pink sunshine. Across the table, a beautiful display of fruits, pastries, yogurts, cheeses, meats and breads was offered. But the unpleasantness of the jumpsuit adequately suppressed her hunger, so she poured herself a cup of black coffee and sat in the warm light. She took a sip and recognized the distinctive loveliness of the coffee from *Betty & Barney's* café in Ballard, her last memories of *home*, as it were.

She knew she had to talk to her father in order to understand everything more clearly. Although she had imagined this moment over and over in her mind hundreds of times, it had never looked quite like this. She didn't even know where to begin. *Should she call him Dad? Maxwell?*

A knock at the door startled her, and she spilled coffee on her leg.

"Ah, shit!" Paige jumped up and set her cup down, noticing that the hot coffee simply rolled off the suit and on to the ground without absorbing any of the heat or liquid through the suit. "Hold on," Paige said, reaching to clean up the coffee before noticing that it was now completely gone.

Perplexed, she walked over to the door and realized she had no idea how to open it. There were no handles or even seams in the door, and no apparent control panel. She waved her hands around the door, trying to find some sort of sensor, but nothing worked.

"Who… who is it?" She asked hesitantly.

Silence.

She cleared her throat, "Um, hello?" she said a little louder.

She leaned in closer to the door to hear, and suddenly it slid open. Paige stood there, staring into an empty hallway. Confused, she took a step forward to peer into the hallway when she was startled by Mika's face.

"Ah!" Paige exclaimed, stumbling backwards awkwardly.

"Shhh," Mika said, holding her hand out to steady Paige. "Do you always make this much noise?"

"Mika!" Paige said loudly before catching herself and whispering again, quietly, "Mika! What are you doing here?"

Paige was relieved to see her, even though she had been furious with her when she disappeared. She hoped her madness had been her own experience and not something she would have to explain now.

"Come on, get inside before anyone sees us," Mika said, grabbing her arm. "And what do you mean, what am I doing here? Do you mean here in a nebulous universe on an alien spaceship? Or here in your room? Or just here, existing, at all?"

"Yeah, that's fair," Paige said, laughing quietly. "But why did you come to my door?"

"Because I heard you were going to hold an audience with our father. And I intend not to miss what he has to say to you. Now, where can I hide before he gets here?" Mika asked, looking around.

"So, *you* haven't talked to him yet?"

"Oh, this is perfect," Mika said, climbing under a small bench, hidden behind a half wall of the arched gazebo area where the breakfast table was.

"What? You're hiding? There?" Paige looked around and noticed that all the breakfast items had now been removed. The table was now set with only two coffee cups and a very old-fashioned and well-patinated silver coffee carafe. Looking around to see if Aaina had returned or was nearby, the hairs raised on the back of her neck—although she didn't see her or anyone else in the room, she instinctively felt that they were not alone.

At that moment, the door slid open again. There, standing in the doorway, was her father—Maxwell Walsh. He stood there casually for a moment, both hands in his pockets, his expression neutral but leaning more towards boredom than anticipation, and stepped into the room. He walked up to Paige rather matter-of-factly and, stopping to stand about three feet away from her, his hands still in his pockets.

"Hello, Paige," he said with a polite southern accent, yet without conveying any emotion.

She looked at him silently for a moment. There was no doubt in her mind that it was her father; they practically looked like twins. He was short in stature with a sturdy build and wore his dark hair indifferently long and wispy, with the front cut just below his eyebrows. Dark glasses obscured his deep blue eyes, but wonder and excitement playfully articulated his bushy brows.

"Hi," Paige said uneasily.

"Well, shall we sit?" Maxwell asked her, motioning his hand towards the small table.

Paige sat down, unsure of what to say or do. She nervously crossed her legs and smiled at him across the table.

"Do you know," he began nonchalantly, "what the most frequently requested item is by Earth time-travellers upon their return? Coffee. *Good* coffee. Hopefully, *great* coffee. But nonetheless, coffee. 8 out of 10 times." He poured them each a cup as he spoke, avoiding eye contact and focusing on his task. Finally, he set the server down and looked up, a small, satisfied smile masking his intentions.

"I know you have a lot of questions, and I hope that I can answer them all, in due time, of course. But first, I think it's best that we get two more cups sent down and some of those delicious pastries brought back."

"Two more coffee cups?" Paige asked, confused.

"Yes, one for your sister over there," he said, pointing to the wall where Mika was, "and one for Detective Andrews."

Surprised and unexpectedly excited, Paige looked around, trying to find Andrews. He stepped out of a shadowy alcove and into the lovely pink light. He walked up to her father and held his hand out to shake his, clasping his upper arm affectionately with his other hand.

"Max," Andrews said, "Good to see you. Mika," he said, raising his hand to wave. "Hi Paige. It's great to see you, too." He smiled genuinely at her, giving her a half-body hug, and she couldn't help but feel soothed by him.

"Ladies," Maxwell said, gesturing to the table as a tall, handsome young man entered with more coffee cups and a platter of fruits and cheeses. "Don't forget those pastries, kid."

"Well, I'm glad we can all be here together like this. It makes things much easier. I trust that you've all been treated well since you've been here?" he asked as he picked a few grapes off the platter. They all nodded quietly in return as the young man set down the pastry platter.

"Oh—thank you, young sir," he said. Speaking to them now, he said, "These cheese Danishes are nothing short of perfection!"

They all sat quietly and watched while he took a bite, thoroughly enjoying himself. He looked up to see that they were all impatiently looking at him.

"Ah... Yes," he said as he set the pastry down, regrettably. "I suppose I should begin with you, Paige. When I first began my relationship with Valiant Thor, it was in the early 1960s, and I wasn't involved with your mother yet. A decade or so later, talk had begun to circulate about the possibility of a human exodus and relocation. Ilse and I were romantically involved then, and it was she who suggested that Val and his companions may be able to help us. The reality is, they have not only helped us—they have saved us. We could never have developed the technology to make this a reality this quickly without their help. We could never have even hoped to recolonize on the other side of the galaxy without their help."

"Saved us? Our planet and its many species are still doomed. While… what? The boys' science club and their offspring all run away? What part did my mother *really* play in this?" Paige asked her father bluntly.

"Ah, your lovely mother. How is she?"

Paige tilted her head to the side, confused by his attempt, only now, at polite conversation.

"When we began discussing the possibility of altering human DNA for our ultimate survival, your mother was the biggest champion of the idea and was eager to be the first to offer a child of her womb for genetic alterations and repairs. But as our ability to achieve that reality grew near, Ilse and I realized that our relationship was not destined for long-term success. She still supported the idea of our child being the first and, thankfully, she agreed to raise you on her own. In fact, by the time it was all said and done, I think she was glad to be rid of me. Besides, she did a much better job raising you than I ever could have. My presence wasn't necessary." He shrugged indifferently and sipped his coffee.

"That's not true," Paige said quietly while looking down at the table.

"Oh?" Maxwell asked with amusement.

"That's not how she tells the story at all. You broke her heart. And mine. Skipping out on us was not a gift, no matter what you tell yourself."

He quietly looked at her, stunned and surprised that she had said such a thing to him. She held his gaze coldly, shrugged indifferently, and sipped her coffee. "Don't worry," she said calmly, "I'm not going to ask you to explain yourself. You know, I've waited years to ask you why you abandoned me, anticipating what you would say, wondering how I might respond. But just now, I finally realized that there's no explanation you could ever provide that would justify your actions. All your messiness and excuses. Your weaknesses. Your cowardly desertion. Your entitlement to the idea that you owe your children nothing more than your genetic material as a parent. I don't even care anymore what your explanation might be; it'll never be good enough to justify the anguish you have caused."

He shifted in his seat and cleared his throat. Mika looked at Paige, unable to hold back a small, contented smile.

Mingling Bloods

"But—I would like you to explain what makes you think you can fuck with our DNA, then lure us here, abduct us and take us off to some new colony without even so much as an explanation, let alone, 'Hi, I'm your father'. How many of us are there? Have we all been misled and kidnapped?"

"Such strong words, child," Max said, sipping his coffee, refusing to acknowledge her scowl, and nonchalantly having another bite of his pastry. "So emotional, just like your mother. Let's at least *try* to show some restraint from the hysterical language, shall we? Now, when she and I agreed to proceed with altering you on a genetic level, our goal was to eradicate anything that might prematurely damage your body, like cancer or autoimmune diseases. Once we were capable of isolating these abnormalities, we could repair or remove them entirely. Thus, helping with the long-term survivability of our species. The next year, in 1979, Andrews was the first of twelve more born. In time, our increasing knowledge of the genome led us to the inevitable selection of certain, more… shall we say, *desirable* genes over *survival* genes. Val led the way with this, demonstrating the true power of their technology. We began simply selecting certain features, like eye colour, and discarding others, like idiopathic short stature. As a sort of playful joke—or maybe just narcissism—he altered Andrews' DNA to have what he called '*kaleidoscope eyes*', a trait common among Val's own kind." Max chuckled softly, sipping his coffee again.

The three of them stared blankly at each other—incensed, shocked and speechless.

"Of course, by the time we got to Mika, we were experts at selecting beauty traits," Max said, smiling and raising his cup towards her, a bizarre gesture of merriment in the moment.

"Why would you keep this information from us until now?" Mika said, her face wrinkled with revulsion.

"Oh, it wasn't necessary for you to know. You have all been closely watched and guided for many years. Each accomplished in specific areas of human greatness, which you can now contribute to the colony. Paige, with your advanced human understanding of Physics. Andrews, your expertise in ancient American civilizations. Mika, Shakespearean literature, the most beloved of the dead poets. Of course, there are so many others, all equipped with aspects of deep human knowledge. The list includes not only scientists, but also the brightest artists and some of the most magnificent humanitarians. I'm sure you've noticed them. They come from across the globe and are ready to begin our civilization anew. A new chance for humanity to escape its destiny, and its inevitable penchant for destruction."

"But…" Paige said, hesitating, "We are *abandoning* Earth! You propose that we just leave the rest of humanity, and probably all other lifeforms, to global destruction?"

"Unfortunately, yes. After the American election of 2016, the political turmoil that grew across the globe with the pandemic, and finally the unchecked gluttony and widespread chaos of the second Trump presidency—these events distinguished all hope for climate reversal action on an international scale and will ultimately herald the final stage of the planet's demise. We are beyond the threshold of retrogression; global warming is inevitable and irreversible now. Val and the Council have already decided to secretly dismantle the atomic components of the nuclear weapons of all countries. They can still destroy each other, for sure, but it won't cause a planetary collapse and the ensuing tidal wave of devastation across the galaxy. Best to abandon ship now, before it's too late."

Paige sat back against her chair, feeling its cold stiffness against her back.

"And really, Paige. You must be fair. *We* did not *abandon mankind.* The scientific community has been issuing warnings for well over a century about the inescapability of global warming, since Arrhenius published his prediction in 1896. We have fought tirelessly against political pressures, against the greed of the fossil fuel industries. Against endless power and corruption. Against ignorance and capitalism. But it was all for naught. So, we had to be realistic. We had to find another way to save our children. And our species."

"So, you plan on just moving us all to a new planet and then what? *You* rule over us, redesigning the patriarchy to fit you and yours? Redesigning humanity as *you* see fit?" Andrews said, his voice steady and stern, his lips making the most exquisite movements as he spoke—sending shivers down Paige's spine.

Max looked from Andrews to Paige and smiled. "Oh no! Not me," he said, laughing to himself. "I have long been in favour of a socialist matriarchy, as have most of my colleagues. But yes, this *is* our chance to redesign humanity. To escape the forces that hinder us and bind us to our less affable qualities. Forces like your *friend* Professor Greene."

"Percy?" Paige said, feeling protective of her connection with him.

"Yes, Percy. The Windingo. Sun of the Morning Star. Whatever you'd like to call him. He has shadowed you for years. Protected you, even, in his way. The last thing he wanted was to lose you here, to this space he cannot enter. He is, after all, a spirit of humanity and firmly bound to Earth."

At that moment, the door slid open again.

"Mom?" Paige cried.

34

CHAPTER

Ilse stood in the doorway—statuesque, fierce, warrior-like.

"Mom!" Paige yelled and ran to greet her, throwing her arms around her.

"*Vertrouw hem niet*," Ilse whispered in Paige's ear as they embraced. She pulled back to look into her mother's face, which showed no signs of the fear in her warning. "It's wonderful to see you again. I've been so worried!" Ilse said, deeply emphasizing her accent and embracing her again.

"My god, mom… what? Have they captured you, too?" Paige asked, both shocked and elated to see her mother and confused by how she was behaving.

"Come on, Munchkin," Ilse said calmly, "Let's sit, shall ve?"

They walked over to the table as the young man from before rushed past them with a silver serving tray containing one martini glass, with one olive, and one silver shaker.

"Ah, Ilse! You are as divine and radiant as ever!" Max said, pulling out a chair for her to sit.

"Oh, shut up, Maxvell," she said, her exaggerated accent brilliantly on point now, and pulled the chair from his grip to move it closer to the others. "This has gone on for long enough. They deserve the truth."

"Well, by all means, Sugar," Max said, smiling despite her grimace.

"Don't call me Sugar, you old pig," she said with an odd playfulness this time, looking him up and down.

"*As you wish*," he retorted, smiling bashfully.

"Hello, everyone. I'm Ilse Jansen, Paige's mother, as I'm sure you've worked out by now," she said, smiling at them charismatically. "Mika, you've grown into a stunning young woman. I'm sorry we've not had the opportunity to meet formally yet. I've heard such wonderful things about you.

Andrews, hello again. You do seem to show up everywhere, don't you?" She leaned over and embraced him, placing a peck on his cheek, causing Paige and Mika to exchange baffled glances.

"Um…" Paige began, still confused at the interaction between her mother and Andrews, now holding hands in a friendly manner. "Mom, what… what are you doing here? Do you have any idea what's going on?"

She smiled for a moment longer at Andrews, squeezing his hand tighter before letting it go, and then turned back to Paige. "Well, yes, Munchkin. I've pieced together most of what happened over the past few days. That's why I followed you here."

"Mom… please stop calling me that," Paige said quietly. Grasping her mother's arm, firming as she leaned closer and said even more hushed, "You shouldn't be here! I have no idea what these… people, I guess? These aliens… I have no idea what they are capable of."

Ilse looked at her and smiled sweetly, tilting her head before whispering back, "Ah, but I *do,* dear."

Paige stumbled backwards, as though the soft breath of her mother's words had unleashed a sudden and unexpected power, a power Paige had not known from her mother. Her eyes widened, as though seeing her mother clearly, at last, for the fierce, powerful woman she truly was.

"Oh, Munch, you are always sooo dramatic," Ilse said as she steadied Paige and sat her back down. "Let me explain," Ilse said sweetly to Paige, then looking at the rest of them. "What Max and Val have told you is *mostly* true. Your DNA has been altered, your talents rigorously embraced, your destiny kept from you. All true, but this was not my choice," Ilse said with a sassiness delightfully reminiscent of Lili Von Shtupp. "The council voted and ve decided, collectively, to keep the truth hidden, to protect you all in case ve couldn't pull this off. It has been a monumental feat on our behalf," Ilse said, looking at them all with a compassionate disdain. "But I do apologize for the deception."

"What *council* voted on this?" Mika asked.

"The Scientific Federation of Science," Max replied.

"The SFS?" Paige asked.

"Yes," Max said, resting his feet on the table.

"Put your feet down, you filthy pig," Ilse said, this time without the lightheartedness.

"Yes, of course. My apologies," Max said, seemingly embarrassed at his actions for the first time in his life. He cleared his throat and continued, "Your mother and I are both delegates of the council. We, the scientific community of Earth, formed our own council in response to first contact with Valiant Thor and The High Council, hoping to find the most diplomatic and democratic way to interact with them. Your mother, Ilse, is one of our most respected and venerated voices on the SFS delegation, and soon, we hope, she will be a sitting member of The High Council."

"So, are… are you two together?" Paige asked.

Ilse poured the martini from the shaker into her glass and took a sip before replying, "Ugh. Hell no," making a contemptuous face. "We are most definitely *not* together."

She sipped the martini and smiled, seemingly contented now. "You know what 8 out of 10 humans returning from time travel *really* ask for? Booze," she said haughtily, raising her glass towards them. "Just ask, Chrissy, at *Betty & Barney's* cafe next time you're there," Ilse said, looking at Mika and winking.

Mika smiled back at her. She found her very likable, but she always liked powerful women.

"Anyway, thank you, Maxvell, for your support of my nomination. However, The High Council is something we can discuss at a later time. Right now, I think it's best to discuss the colony and what to expect there."

"Wait, so you're in on this?" Paige said vehemently about her mother's audacity.

"In on it? Munch, I helped design it!" Ilse said, sipping her martini again, picking the olive spear out and then setting the glass down. "I've never been a fan of lying to you about it, but this is how we save humanity. *You all* are how we save humanity! Ve can be a model across the galaxy."

"Mom, I said stop with this Munchkin shit! You're not even listening to me, are you? Stop talking *to* me, like usual."

"Stop being an impetuous little brat, Paige! Try to have some gratitude for all the sacrifices made by thousands of us for you to have this singular opportunity." Ilse straightened her spine and gave Paige a steely look, a look she had never seen from her mother before, a look that sent a chill down her spine.

"Ilse," Andrews said steadily, "perhaps you can give us a better idea of what it is exactly you are offering us." He smiled politely at her and then shifted his gaze to Paige, locking eyes with her intrepidly. Regardless of what obstacles were spinning around in the storm of madness that surrounded her lately, when she looked into Andrew's eyes, none of it mattered. He made her feel all sorts of *something*, something she couldn't quite articulate yet, something she had never felt before.

"Yes! Yes, of course. It really is quite marvellous, isn't it, Max?" Ilse said happily.

"Imagine it—a blank slate, a whole new world to—"

"Ugh, for fuck's sake, Max. Please shut up!" Ilse looked at him, peevishly crossing her arms and pursing her lips tightly. She wasn't about to let him take credit for all her hard work.

"Alright. Fine. You tell them then," he said, shrugging and reaching for another Danish.

"So, imagine it," she started, sarcastically, "a blank slate, a whole new world…" She cast an additional, disapproving sideways glance towards Maxwell just as pastry crumbs tumbled down his chin and rested on his rotund belly.

"Of course," she continued, looking back at them, "we've had to be careful not to mess it up this time. Not to let politics and greed destroy our chance at a new model of human society. That is why the council remains so important. We *had* to do things better this time. Like renewable energy, eco-friendly habitations, and for fuck's sake—no patriarchy, no religion, no capitalism! We did away with a lot of things. Thanks to the incredible research of people like Ruth Benedict and Sherry Ortner, your mum," she said, nodding at Andrews, "we have a much more accurate and clear assessment of our human origins—both our failings and our achievements—and thus we built a roadmap from that. We *can* learn from our mistakes as a species. I believe we've managed to create something really quite extraordinary—a self-sustaining, egalitarian community on a foreign planet. We have numerous proposals for societal organization, all thoroughly researched and explored, and, oddly enough," she said peering over her shoulder smugly at Maxwell, "our research found that matriarchal socialist societies *are* more successful and therefore a more desirable choice for our colony."

"Just as I was saying," Maxwell stated, waving his hands in a self-congratulatory way before plopping his feet on the table again, rather triumphantly.

"Get your *fucking* feet off the table," Ilse said slowly, her eyes like a steel blade upon him now.

"Yes. Sorry," Maxwell apologized, avoiding eye contact again.

Mika looked at him sadly and shook her head in disappointment, then asked Ilse, "Will we be the first ones there? The first of '*us*', I guess?"

"Yes. We, the council members of the SFS, have a meeting with Val later today. Once everything is finalized, we can proceed to the colony."

"And what if I don't *want* to proceed?" Paige asked, defiantly.

"Oh, you'd rather die a miserable death, witnessing the horrific end of days and fiery death of Earth? Rather than perpetuating our species?"

"I'd rather I have a choice in the matter, mother!" Paige could feel the blood rushing to her cheeks.

"The choice is obvious, Paige," Max said.

"Shut up, Maxwell!" Paige and her mother both yelled at him.

Silence fell across the room. And then Mika began to laugh. First, it was just a little snicker that slipped out. Then everyone looked at her, and she couldn't hold it in. Most theatrically, she declared:

"Behold, our human actions, as they do, I doubt not then but innocence shall make false accusations blush and tyranny tremble at patience."

"Mika, what the fuck does that even *meeeean*? You know Shakespeare was a woman—Emilia Bassano—right? Stop venerating some dead English aristocrat who doesn't deserve the credit. No one fucking cares, Mika!" Paige yelled, losing her patience with everything that was happening in this moment.

"I think," Andrews said softly, looking at Paige, "that a break is in order. While Maxwell and Ilse attend the meeting, it gives us some time to process, prepare, and discuss this further. I found that the ship readily supplies information when requested and is impressively intuitive."

Silence fell across the room for an awkward moment.

"Yes. Well then," Maxwell said, breaking the silence. "We really should be going. Val doesn't like to be kept late."

"Oh, Val doesn't give a shit, Max. He'll just take a few extra bong hits before we get there." She rolled her eyes and turned to hug Paige. She stroked her face lovingly, brushing her hair behind her ear, and acknowledging the gravity and difficulty of the situation with a singular look, perhaps the most mystical superpower of motherhood. Grabbing her tightly by the arm as she embraced her and whispered, in Dutch again, "Listen to Andrews. You can trust him. Mika, too."

Paige tried not to react, but hoped the tears offered their own penance for their treachery as they coursed inaudibly down her cheeks. She still didn't completely understand what was happening, what her mother's involvement was, or why it seemed that everyone she loved had either betrayed or abandoned her. But she instinctively knew, in that moment, that her mother's love had not and would not falter.

35

CHAPTER

The doors slid closed behind Ilse and Maxwell as they left the three of them—Paige, Mika and Andrews—alone in the room.

"What are we going to do now!" Paige asked them, finally releasing her panic.

"We're getting the hell out of here. That's what we're doing," Andrews said, smiling at them both.

"Sure, but *how*? And before *we* go anywhere, I need some questions answered. How do you know my mother, Detective?" Paige said, trying not to let her voice break.

"Well, it's a bit compli—" Andrews stopped short, as Paige interrupted.

"No! How. Do you. Know. My mother?" Paige said, gesturing pointedly with her hands to emphasize her demand.

"I work for her. Like I was saying, it's complicated. I make a living as a private detective, and work for your mother in a similar capacity, as a history detective. I swear that I will explain all this in due time, but right now we really need to get out of here. This may be our only opportunity."

Paige looked at him steadily, wondering how she could possibly continue to trust him when he had kept so much from her. But she knew he was right. "Ok, how do we get out of here, then?"

He smiled at her and walked over to grab the martini shaker from the table. "Here," he said, pouring it into the glass. "You both finish her drink. It's Ayahuasca, and we're going to need it. I think I can get us home, but it's going to be a bumpy ride."

"Andrews! Aaaahhhh! I love you!" Mika exclaimed, running over to hug him.

"Excellent! But *how* are we getting out?" Paige asked. She wanted to hug him, too, but refrained and offered a lame, sweaty fist bump instead.

"Well, with some help from Fred. Have you met Fred, Paige? He was here to greet us," Andrews said, smiling back at Mika.

"Yes," Paige said, looking back and forth between them and trying not to let her mistrustfulness overcome her again. "I guess I was greeted, as well. I'm not sure we can trust him, though?"

"Fred doesn't choose sides; he chooses Fred. But he's always genuine about it. And really quite wonderful, once you get to know him," Mika said, stepping away from her half-hug, she was still in with Andrews.

"Yeah, so Fred has shown me how to get to a portal once we escape the ship. From there, it will be challenging. But, the good news is… I have a map," he said covertly, laughing and then presenting a small beverage napkin with odd scratches and delineations across it.

"Oh, great," Paige said sarcastically, looking down at it with disappointment.

"It'll be fine. Probably," he said, smiling at her brilliantly and folding it carefully again. She loved the expressions of his face, the arches of his refined brows, how the fullness of his beard accentuated the exquisiteness of his lips. She smiled back at him and realized, again, how glad she was he was here.

"Yes, Andrews, I'm sure that will get us off the ship. But what about the *actual* map we've been tasked with finding? And the key! The entire imperative of this voyage was to find those and return them to Earth. How can we leave before even trying to get them?"

"Listen, if we get back to Earth, you *know* they're going to follow us there. And they can't stay here much longer. So, I think we have a much better chance of getting that map and key on our home field," Andrews said.

"I agree!" Mika chimed.

Paige reluctantly acquiesced and joined them to gather a few things they thought they might need along the way. Mika and Paige both finished their drink, and they set off down a series of hallways. Andrews seemed quite certain of where he was leading them at first, but the dizzying precision of the white hallways began to make them all feel disoriented.

"Ok, I think we're almost there," Andrews said, leaning against a wall to rest for a moment and take a drink of water.

"That sounds hauntingly familiar. Are you sure? This all looks the same. Where is *there*? And how will we even know when we are *there*?" Paige said, sitting cross-legged after sliding down the wall and taking a drink herself.

Mika started humming a familiar song and started snickering.

Paige rolled her eyes, unamused, but just then they all heard a clicking noise down the hallway. Moving quickly, they all stood close against the wall, huddled together and staring down the hall, listening intently. A moment passed, and still only their breathing could be heard.

Mika started humming 311's *Come Original* again while Paige and Andrews both shushed her.

"What are you doing, Mika? Be quiet!"

"Sorry, I thought we needed a theme song. I mean, c'mon—we're about to be space-time travellers. We need to have a theme song. I feel that's important, you know."

"My god, Mika… quiet!" Paige hissed, looking back down the hall again. Her chest was pressing into Detective

Andrew's back, and her hand was on his arm. She could feel his chest expand, and within it, she found a space unimaginable, a space she thought she might actually fit into. The nearly imperceptible noise of his breathing made her press more tightly against him; she wanted to feel the movement of his body, the vibrations of his essence.

"Andrews!" a voice from behind them called out, startling them all. They turned quickly and saw Ilse, standing there, hands on her hips. "Andrews, you missed it! I said left, left, right, left, right, right, left, right, right, then left. Not right again."

"Yes ma'am, I am sorry," he said, giving her a look that oozed with sarcasm, before laughing.

"Mom! You scared the shit out of us!" Paige said, somewhat loudly.

"Keep your voices down. Jesus! You *all* are terrible at escaping. Now c'mon," she turned and rounded the corner quickly before slipping into a doorway. Inside, a small dark hallway lined with shelves led to a door that was lit from behind, as the light from the outside seeped into the darkened room. They all gathered into the small space, and Ilse hushed them.

"Behind this door, you will follow the light through the grey space to find a portal back to earth. You cannot go back the way you came, not only because it is collapsing, but because Sunka will be watching it. She's not looking for you, but rather a closely guarded map of the ancient paths and portals—rediscovered decades ago by Maxwell in Peru. But he has never respected the ancient ways or the wisdom that outlined how to properly use the maps. He *borrowed* it from the Peruvian archives, claiming it was stolen by archeological art thieves. But he only uses it for his own gain, to bargain for what he wants. Now I've managed to *borrow* it from him and I am entrusting you three with it, knowing that you understand the great power it holds."

She dramatically presented the woven scroll, a contented smile across her face, and passed it gently to Andrews. He cradled it in his hands with the tenderness of a new father, awed at the wonder of it.

"Mom! This is amazing. But, surely its absence will be felt soon! They'll be after us now!"

"Calm yourself, Paige. For decades, I could only catch glimpses of it. But from those glimpses, I started plotting my own map and piecing together the ancient paths. Six years ago, my hand-selected team started exploring various verified routes. It takes tremendous dedication to understanding the ancient ways and a true adventurer's spirit to trailblaze these portals—not only to and from the new colony, but across the space and time of our galaxy. That being said, it is still a bit of a wilderness to us, isn't it, Mr. Andrews?"

"Yes, ma'am," he said professionally, but smiling at her affectionately.

"Ladies, you are privileged to have not only the most renowned trailblazer, but the most handsome, as well," Ilse said, pinching his cheek playfully.

"I'm sorry, Andrews, now you're a space-time traveller? You said you worked for my mother, but you certainly forgot to mention this!" Paige said.

"With. He works with me, not for me. And he's one of the best," she said, winking at him. "Now, the last thing you need to know about—*the key*. You two were each given a gift when you were born: a well-crafted, antique, golden-hewn kaleidoscope. Do you both still have them?"

Both Mika and Paige reached into their jumpsuits and pulled out the small ornaments.

"Excellent! These kaleidoscopes *are* the key," Ilse continued. "I wasn't certain until recently, but now I know these were expertly crafted by ancient alchemists for the cosmic wayfarers. They will activate in the portals with the map to light your journey and keep you on the path. Very, very few of them still exist, and we have not yet been able to successfully recreate them. Andrews has one, as do I and a few others. You both are the guardians of the last two known to exist *and* their secret, the secret of what the key truly is. Many, including your father, are unaware of what the keys are and what they do. Guard them and their secrets fiercely."

"So *that's* why he asked me to bring mine to the SFS camp," Paige said smugly, relinquishing the last hope that he had asked her for sentimental reasons.

"Did he ask you both to bring them?" Ilse asked, now concerned.

Paige and Mika both nodded.

"He already suspects it then, doesn't he?" Paige asked, her stomach sinking.

"It would seem so. All the more reason for you to get out of here as soon as possible," she replied.

Andrews nodded in agreement and hugged her, "I'll keep this safe. Thank you for everything. I'm sure we'll see you soon."

"Yes, of course," Ilse replied before reaching to hug Mika. Andrews opened the door, and a bright light flooded the room. He looked back, then shut the door behind him.

"My dear, we shall have to meet and chat soon. There are so many wonderful conversations I need to have with you now," Ilse said, smiling and then kissing both her cheeks. Mika walked through the door and shut it behind her.

"Paige, my love," Ilse hugged her close, pressing tightly against her. "Paige, you can trust them. I do. And I know why you have to do this. *Never let your fate control you.* That's why I'm helping you. But don't be so naive as to believe that you are not being watched," she leaned in closer, "and it's safe to assume you are being *allowed* to leave."

"I think it's worth giving me the chance to think about it for myself," Paige said, pressing her chin forward insolently.

"Yes, well, the journey itself is important for you. And I understand that. So go. Explore! See the world more clearly. Understand time and space as never before. It really is incredible, and I had no right to rob you of that. But Paige, you need to understand—Earth, or rather how humanity exists on Earth—that fate is sealed, my dear. We can't save them all. We just can't," Ilse hugged her tightly again, tears welling in her eyes. She cupped Paige's face in her hands and whispered in a shaky voice, "I need you to accept this so we can move on. So you can fulfill your brilliant destiny without any of the restrictions of our Earth world. Come! And help us create a new world! A *better* world!"

Tears streamed freely down Paige's face, and she felt her defiance soften as her mother hugged her one more time. Paige stepped back and wiped her nose, finding it much more boogery than she had anticipated.

"I love you, Mom," Paige said, full-on ugly crying now. "But you're right, something tells me I need to do this. Thank you. Thank you for letting me go."

Ilse kissed her once more, carefully avoiding the snot. Paige wiped her face, turned, and walked through the door and into the light, which was blinding. She held up her arm against the brightness, trying to see where she was going.

"Paige," she heard Mika whisper. "Paige! Over here."

She turned to follow their voices, and as she walked to the side, she found the light less direct and less blinding. She could see Mika and Andrews waving at her through the fog.

"This way," Andrews said, waving them into the dense darkness that lay just beyond the periphery of the light. They walked quietly and cautiously through the greyness for some time.

"You know, Paige," Mika said, breaking the silence. "When I teach my undergraduate-level Shakespeare class, after spending most of the semester delving into my favourite selections and having them write about their favourites, I explore Elizabeth Winkler's assertion that Shakespeare was a woman. I encourage them to investigate their own cognitive dissonance, why they might be feeling resistance to the idea, and what the push-back from the wider academic community really points to. There's no right or wrong answer I look for, just a thoughtful examination."

Andrews nodded, mumbled a polite "umhmm," and continued walking.

Paige smiled at her, "Ok, I see what you did there." She laughed lightly, but she was tired of hearing the quotes, tired of walking, tired of the constant company. They continued on in silence until, finally, they stopped to rest.

"How long do you think we've been walking for?" Mika asked, sitting down cross-legged and pulling a granola bar out of her pocket.

"It's hard to say," Paige said. "Time feels very distorted here. But based on the calculations of my physical condition, how my muscles are reacting to the prolonged activity in relation to the assumed density of the atmosphere, combined with the antiquity of my joints, which—honestly, how come they never thought to improve that? Anyway, if I had to guess, I'd say it's been too fucking long, and I hope we get there soon."

"Oh, my! Well, I feel so privileged to finally be meeting the *real* Doc," Mika said, laughing. "*To mingle friendship far is to mingle bloods.*"

"So, now you're calling me *Doc*, too?" Paige said, rolling her eyes. "By the way, if we were to have a theme song, I'd like to submit a request: 'Choice Is Yours', by *Stick Figure*."

"So sorry to interrupt your imperative conversation, here, but we've got some important stuff to talk about," Andrews said.

"Excuse me, sir! This is imperative. Thank you," Mika said sassily. "Yes, Paige, I accept and shall consider your request! Now, Andrews, you may continue."

"Anyway," he continued, seemingly annoyed. "When we get to the gateway, hopefully soon, we will literally be travelling through rickety, old space-time portals. Getting off track, even a little bit, could significantly alter where we end up in space and time. We are aiming to get close to where we were. Since Sunka is guarding the wormhole in Utah, and the next closest from there—Chaco Canyon—is too remote, I say we aim for Cahokia—the ancient City of the Sun. Now located in East St. Louis."

He looked at them and smiled.

"East St. Louis is our *best* option?" Mika snarked.

"Yes," he continued. "But Cahokia is the city of Sunka's birth, and we will not evade her watchful eye for long. Nor her ire that we used the sacred portals of Cahokia. That is, if we can make it there. I've not travelled those pathways yet."

"I thought you were the best at this?" Paige asked.

"Well, now, that's what your *mother* said. I do know my way through certain paths, but like I said, sometimes it gets bumpy, and we might get off track. Plus, the Cahokia portals have been abandoned for centuries and may be… a bit dusty, shall we say. So, you need to be prepared for that." He looked at them with solemn seriousness. "*IF* we get separated in space, the easiest portals to find are at UNESCO World Heritage sites. If you get lost along the timeline, that would mean you're probably still in the American West. To orient yourself, remember you have Cahokia to the east, Poverty Point directly south of there on the Mississippi River, and Chaco Canyon in the remote southwest. But, getting lost in both space *and* time, you'll likely find yourself drifting anywhere across North or South America. So try to stay close to me."

Paige smiled at him and wondered how close would be *weird* close. She affectionately watched him as he reached into the lapel of his suit, pulled out the map and unrolled it.

"I know this doesn't make much sense to you guys, because you haven't travelled through space and time yet, so it's hard to conceptualize. But let's see if this helps."

He then pulled out his own kaleidoscope and set it in the center of the map. Nothing happened.

"Hmmm, ok. Maybe it activates when in the portals? Anyway, all the more reason that you both need to try to memorize this. It *will* eventually make sense," Andrews said, waving his hand over the ancient scroll.

"I've seen parts of this before, during my research! It didn't make sense then. And it doesn't make sense now…"

"Maybe we have to be within the Earth portals for them to work? Mika, just try imagining it as a multi-dimensional map reduced to two dimensions," Paige stated conceitedly.

Mika glanced at her sideways, feeling confused and dismissed. The three sat silently snacking, each trying to memorize the map, but were lost in their own thoughts.

"And then what?" Paige queried aloud, breaking the silence. "What happens once we get to St. Louis? Or Cahokia? They'll be after us, right? Sunka will notice us and draw attention almost immediately. What do we do then? How long can we keep running for?"

"That's a good point. When or where can we go that they can't find us right away?" Mika asked.

"What if," Paige started, but hesitated at the words she was about to unleash. "What if we *did* travel to a different space and time. How difficult do you estimate the navigation would be, Andrews? You know the ways best, what do you think?"

"Well, I suppose we could. There are trace residual markers when we hop, but they're difficult to follow without a tracker. Even a good tracker might lose the trail, though, if we put enough time between us and them."

"How about East St. Louis, circa 1387 CE, prior to the summer solstice?"

"Well, that's not exactly how it works. We don't know how to hop to precise dates yet. It's complicated. But why *that* location and time frame, Paige?" Andrews asked, narrowing his eyes as he looked at her.

"Hear me out. Maybe my father had the right idea in the beginning, before all the creepy DNA mixing and mingling, the lies and manipulation, the new colony—all of which definitely has a very gross eugenics quality to it. What I *am* suggesting is that maybe he was on to something *before* that? What if we could alter a moment in history that would change everything? That might save our species and our planet."

"No! Absolutely not, Paige," Andrews practically shouted. "It is strictly forbidden. I can't even believe you would suggest this! You are much too smart for this kind of thinking! You know that the consequences could be massive and irreparable. It's out of the question."

"Would Cahokia 1300-ish CE be enough distance for them to lose our tracks, though, Detective?" Mika asked. "To be honest, I'm not even sure we'd have the ability to alter events once we get there. I learned from the onboard computer system that our jumpsuits are designed not only to protect us while here and travelling the ways, but to completely mask our presence in any space and time outside of our own. We would be merely observers. But I gotta tell you guys," she said, pausing and looking at both of them with an excited smile. "I would love to *just observe* Cahokia, the City of the Sun, in all its grandeur and glory! What do you guys think? T*o unpathed waters, undreamed shores*!"

Mingling Bloods

Coming Soon! Part II: Undreamed Shores

After entering the portal with Andrews and Mika, Paige finds herself separated from them in time and space. Will her friends be able to find her? Can Paige come to terms with what she's discovered about her parents? About Mika and herself? Or will she accept her fate in the new colony? Maybe she'll finally find the courage to reveal her feelings to Andrews? Stay tuned for Part II!